THE SOMETIME SISTER

KATHERINE NICHOLS

Black Rose Writing | Texas

First printing

This is a work of fiction. Names, characters, businesses, places, events, and incidents are either the products of the author's imagination or used in a fictitious manner. Any resemblance to actual persons, living or dead, or actual events is purely coincidental.

ISBN: 978-1-68433-690-6
PUBLISHED BY BLACK ROSE WRITING
www.blackrosewriting.com

Printed in the United States of America
Suggested Retail Price (SRP) $18.95

The Sometime Sister is printed in Book Antiqua

*As a planet-friendly publisher, Black Rose Writing does its best to eliminate unnecessary waste to reduce paper usage and energy costs, while never compromising the reading experience. As a result, the final word count vs. page count may not meet common expectations.

Dedication

To my husband and our children, Laura, Kate, and Nick. Without them, I would never have understood family and forgiveness.

THE
SOMETIME
SISTER

CHAPTER 1

When my sister Stella and I were speaking, we joked about our mother's "absolutely must be dealt with immediately emergencies." These disasters, as she called them, included a neighbor who had been stealing her copies of *Southern Living,* a careless bank teller, and a rude grocery boy. Whether it was two in the afternoon or in the morning, she had to address the latest injustice as soon as it crossed her mind.

"Just silence it, Gracie," Stella would urge after I'd been up half the night talking Mom off the ledge. But both she and my mother knew I was not the turn-off-the-phone type.

When it rang at 5:00 am on December second, I didn't bother to check caller ID. Before I had the chance to ask if she had any idea what time it was, she began crying.

"Grace, oh God, Grace. Your sister never got on the plane. She promised she was coming home, but she never got on the plane."

"Mom, please. Slow down. You know Stella. I'm sure she changed her mind and forgot to tell you."

She had believed her younger daughter was coming home for the past three years, ever since she and her husband, Ben Wilcott, had to leave the country. He fled to avoid the imminent likelihood of serious jail time resulting from involvement in a suburban drug ring. And she went with him. They settled in Montañita, a city in Ecuador well-known among expatriates fleeing the US in search of a spot with beautiful beaches and a generous extradition policy. Thanks to his illegal activities, he had enough cash to finance a lengthy stay. But Mom had never accepted that her baby had gone willingly. She insisted he had forced her to go and was holding her hostage. Any minute Stella would break free and return. I didn't share her belief.

"Not this time." She blew her nose. "Stella was terrified. She said she couldn't take it any longer and would be on the next plane in time for Christmas. She booked a flight but didn't get on it. Her cell goes straight to voicemail. I must have left a dozen messages. Please, Grace. Please believe me. She was telling the truth. You know Ben. Don't tell me you aren't afraid he did something terrible to her."

My mother had a point. I did know Ben better than anyone else because we'd been two weeks from our wedding day when he ran away with my little sister.

·   ·   ·   ·   ·

After trying for at least thirty minutes to convince Mom we should wait before giving in to panic, I agreed to come to her house for further discussion. I refused her demand to jump out of bed and meet her before sunrise, insisting ten would be soon enough.

I hoped I might squeeze in another hour or two of sleep. Instead, I lay there worrying about my sister.

Many of my memories of life before Stella were like catching fireflies on warm summer nights. If you planned it just right, you could scoop them into a Mason jar before they blinked off and disappeared.

Their golden flashes illuminated the memory of my grandmother sitting beside me, reading about a boy who thought he could fly. She dissolved, leaving only the harsh staccato voices of my parents. They faded away, and my cousin Lesroy popped into view, spinning round and round until he collapsed into a giggling heap on the kitchen floor.

Some nights I caught so many fireflies my jar sent a magic stream of light across the backyard. But I hated seeing those desperate little bugs careening against each other in a fear I could almost smell, so I unscrewed the lid, gasping for air myself as they tumbled toward freedom.

Stella's entrance a few months after my fifth birthday shoved those memories aside. Lonely in the way of an only child with warring parents, I prayed for a little sister for years. My grandmother was the one person who always took me seriously, the one who kept all my secrets. When I told her of my sister-wish, she laughed.

"Honey, you better be careful what you wish for. You just might get it."

When Stella arrived, looking like a tiny rosebud in her pink blanket, I danced with joy. I made it my mission to protect and serve her. Her will was my will. And from the beginning, she was more than comfortable in her role as princess. For her, the crown wasn't the least bit heavy.

She grew into a confident beauty. With her heart-shaped face, wispy blonde hair, and turquoise eyes, she was aware of the effect she had on people and wielded her power with total composure. Other than typical adolescent meltdowns, I could only recall one time when she hadn't been in complete control of her emotions.

Over three years had passed since that afternoon, but the memory still made my stomach lurch. Ben and I had a meeting that evening to finalize details about our reception. My last client canceled, so I decided to drop by his place and surprise him. We'd been so busy with work and the planning, we hadn't had much alone time, and he'd become a little distant. I attributed his moodiness to wedding jitters.

Rather than knock to announce my presence, I used my key to enter the expensive downtown condo where we would live until we found the perfect house. One of the area's most popular decorators furnished the place, but it was too masculine and impersonal for my taste.

I dropped my purse on the heavy mahogany table in the foyer and called for Ben. He didn't respond. Music drifted from the bedroom. The door was ajar, but I tapped on it, stepped inside, and heard water running.

Ben complained I lacked spontaneity and a spirit of adventure in bed. He wanted me to initiate sex more, to be more passionate. I checked my watch and discovered we had almost two hours before our meeting. Plenty of time to be spontaneous.

I slipped my sweater over my head and wriggled out of my pants, humming along to a Taylor Swift song in the background. A glance in the full-length mirror revealed my mismatched underwear, but he wasn't going to see them, so who cared? I unhooked my bra and tossed it onto the bed, then stepped out of my panties.

The bathroom door was closed but knocking politely didn't fit with the take-charge image I planned to project, so I turned the knob and entered the steamy room. A thick sheet of fog covered the rain-glass custom shower, but I could see the silhouette of my fiancé under the water spray.

I tiptoed closer and saw him standing with his head tilted, shampoo cascading in frothy rivulets over his shoulders. I placed my hand on the tile wall and was about to commit when I noticed something was off. In addition to the sudsy trails now making their way to the small of his back, two hands clutched his well-toned ass. For a moment, I remained immobile, unable to process the scene in front of me. Then I glimpsed strands of smooth blonde hair and a pair of tan arms. I called her name. She peeked out from behind him, her face distorted by the steady stream of water.

Stumbling back, I caught myself on the edge of the gigantic bowl-shaped tub. I felt as if I should apologize for putting us all in such an awkward situation. After racing from the room, I grabbed my pants and hopped on one foot while pulling them up. I maneuvered my sweater over my head and snatched my undergarments from the bed just as Ben came barreling through the door with a towel wrapped around him.

"Grace! Wait. It's not what it looks like."

I didn't bother to ask what else it could be. In an instant I had become a cliche: a woman scorned. The added indignity of having my own sister betray me contributed a touch of originality to the humiliation.

CHAPTER 2

I don't know how, but I got home without taking out an innocent bystander and found Lesroy waiting for me. Stella had called to tell him I was upset and requested he check on me. I never asked my cousin if he'd known about Stella and Ben.

And now? Well, now it was obvious my distraught mother expected me to set aside my painful memories and join her in finding out why my sister hadn't been on that plane. It was clear I wouldn't be going back to sleep, so I flung off my grandmother's quilt and dragged myself to the shower.

The hot water cleared my mind enough that I realized before leaving for Mom's, I needed to do my own research. First, I double-checked with the airlines to see if what she had told me about Stella's supposed homecoming was accurate. It was true she had booked her seat and had failed to show.

Next, I logged onto Facebook and found my sister's page. As angry as I'd been at her, I never got around to unfriending her. Silly, I know, but I couldn't make myself click on that most final of social media options. I blocked her posts before she left the country but never cut the online cord.

As usual, her shining face stunned me. I tried to shut out the images from that devastating day and its aftermath. But her choice of profile picture made it difficult. It was a photo of us taken at my engagement party.

In typical Stella fashion, her long wavy hair shimmered with blonde highlights and cascaded over her bare, bronzed shoulders. The only jewelry she wore was the locket Gran gave her on her sixteenth birthday. It was identical to mine. The gold ovals had an antique finish engraved with our initials. Inside were pictures of the two of us. One was of me with Stella on my lap when I'm about ten and she's five. In the other, we're a few years older and standing in an embrace, heads turned to beam at the camera.

Gran would stare at them and say, "You girls are so beautiful, you make my heart hurt."

In most of Stella's pictures, her face glowed with her wide-lipped smile, one custom designed for anyone lucky enough to be caught in its path. But in her profile picture, it's her eyes that made it hard to turn away. They were the same startling color of the Aegean Sea where Ben and I had planned to spend our honeymoon.

I'm barely five feet five, but I seemed to tower over her. My light brown curls, elaborately fluffed and sprayed, were an unfortunate styling choice influenced by my mother, who insisted I do something different with myself.

"It's your engagement party, Grace. You can't wear your hair like that, all straight and ordinary." So instead of ordinary, I looked like a show poodle.

Stella and I inherited high cheekbones and straight noses from our grandmother. On my sister, the overall impression was soft, inviting. On me, it was stern, even though I smiled almost as brightly as she did. But there was a tightness around my eyes—eyes the same silvery gray as Gran's—as I glanced beyond the photographer to where Ben stood with an expression of wonder on his face. His mouth was open, and his gaze screamed of desire. Only he wasn't looking at me. He was staring at my sister.

Immediately after the photographer took the photo, Ben grabbed my hand and led me to the dance floor, making it easy to tell myself I was imagining things.

I shook my head and focused on her list of friends. The number was staggering, over fifteen hundred. Everywhere I looked were pictures of Stella, many with Ben staring at her adoringly. But no one posts candid shots of an unadoring lover. And there's no time to snap a photo just as someone has his hands around your neck or to catch that special moment when you're shoved down a flight of stairs.

I knew firsthand he could turn ugly when angry. He had never directed his fury at me, but I'd seen him slam a tennis racket onto the ground and stomp it over and over. I was there when he threw a chair through the glass door after learning his boss had passed him over for a promotion at the law firm.

So, when Mom told me he was knocking Stella around and asked me to talk her into leaving him, I had no doubt he was hurting her. I just didn't care. Or worse, deep down in my blackened heart, I enjoyed it. If she'd left my future husband alone, she wouldn't be getting her hair yanked or her face slapped.

It was much later I realized if she hadn't stolen Ben, I might have been the one lying on the floor, dazed and wondering what I'd done wrong.

I told Mom if my sister wanted help, she could call me. But she never did. And I never called her.

Shiny faces sped by as I scrolled through until I found her: Alisha Beaumont, our former neighbor and Stella's best friend from high school. Only now she was Alisha Beaumont Simmons. Her profile said she graduated from the University of Georgia a year after Stella dropped out. She lived in Atlanta with a husband and a fluffy white Persian cat.

If anyone knew what was going on with my sister, it would be Alisha. I found her phone number online. Before dialing, I checked the time and was shocked. It felt like days since my conversation with Mom but was only a little after seven. Too early to call someone from the past but not too early to reach out to Lesroy.

He answered on the first ring. "Grace, thank God. I just got off the phone with your mother. I'm grabbing some coffee and heading right over."

He and I experienced a rough patch after Stella and Ben left town. When I refused to talk to her, she called our cousin. Like most people, he'd never been able to say no to my sister, so when she begged him to intervene with me on her behalf, he did. Devastated by his betrayal, I avoided him. If I hated her, he was supposed to hate her. I didn't cut him off, but I was cool toward him for months. He wouldn't accept my cold shoulder, though. He kept showing up at my door with wine and chocolate and old movies until I took him back.

Gran passed her love of the classics to us. She was crazy about dead or aging starlets. She named Aunt Rita after Rita Hayworth, Mom after Marilyn Monroe. My mother inherited her obsession and named me Grace Kelly Burnette. As for my sister, Mom had been more direct. Her very name meant *of the stars*. But our grandmother insisted she needed a proper name, so she became Stella Vivien Burnette.

The doorbell rang a few minutes past eight, and I heard the deadbolt click.

"Yoo-hoo! Are you decent?" Lesroy called as I stood to greet him. "Doesn't matter. I'm coming in anyway."

My cousin was a year older but always seemed younger. He was an elf-like child with bright blue eyes and curly hair that his dad insisted on mowing into a buzz cut so his son wouldn't be a "sissy."

Lesroy was so much a part of my life I can't remember being without him. He never walked into a room; he twirled or tap-danced or spun into it. Together we designed elaborate castles constructed of discarded items we gathered throughout the neighborhood. A dilapidated dresser with a broken mirror became the Evil Queen's prophetic looking glass. A rickety ladder led to Rapunzel's tower. We collected smooth stones from the creek behind my house and turned them into an army of trolls who guarded us when we took impromptu naps on blankets piled inside our palace.

Today, at just under five-ten, Lesroy wasn't a big man, but he was no longer the airy creature from our youth. My cousin discovered gymnastics in his early teens and was good enough to go to the University of Georgia on an athletic scholarship. He considered training for the Olympics but loved to party and spending all that time in the gym didn't fit his schedule.

"I brought you a vanilla latte with extra whipped cream, plus two so-fresh-they're-still-warm Krispy Kremes." He put the bag on the table. "Wait. Where's the beast from Hell?"

"You are such a baby. Scarlett O'Hara is not a beast. She's just misunderstood. Don't worry; she doesn't get up this early."

Lesroy was referring to a seventy-five-pound Doberman who once belonged to Stella and Ben. When he and I were together, he droned on and on about how much he wanted a real guard dog, one who would scare the shit out of intruders. His obsessive desire for canine security should have set off an alarm, but it never occurred to me he had anything needing high-level protection.

About a month before the happy couple left for Ecuador, they sealed their love with Scarlett. I assumed her name was a continuation of the *Gone with the Wind* theme Mom started with Stella *Vivien* Burnette.

Ben hadn't done his homework before selecting the Doberman. Yes, the breed has an imposing presence, and they can be ferocious, but only if someone they love is threatened. So, when the lovebirds ran off to Ecuador, Scarlett didn't make the cut. Like me, she got left behind.

They abandoned her on my doorstep with a note from Stella: *We can't take her with us. She's a wonderful dog, and you're the only one I know she'll love.*

But Scarlett O'Hara didn't love me. She tolerated me.

"You know that monster despises me." He reached out to hug me. We clung to each other for a few seconds before I stepped away.

"It's not personal. She hates most men. They remind her of Ben. So, what did my mother tell you?"

He shook his head. "I'm guessing the same thing she told you. Stella was supposed to come home but never got on the plane. Aunt Marilyn thought she might have called me, but she hadn't. We haven't talked since Easter."

Mom insisted Stella had changed, that she'd had what Lesroy described as a conversion last March. She said she was planning her escape and repeated the same tale to Lesroy. Both had bought the story. Then, like now, she never showed.

"I haven't seen Aunt Marilyn this upset since Gran's funeral." Two years ago, our grandmother had a stroke. She lingered a few months before letting go.

Stella didn't make it home for the service.

"I know you never stopped being pissed at her, but I have a bad feeling about this. I mean, she bought a plane ticket."

"And I'm sure she just changed her mind and is lounging around some expensive spa enjoying some Stella-time. I told Mom I'd check it out. I found Alisha's phone number. If she were going to confide in anyone, it would be Alisha."

He wrinkled his nose. "God, I hate that bitch."

Alisha and her family moved into the house next door when my sister was twelve. Alisha didn't just like Stella; she worshiped her. She saved her a seat on the bus, lavished her with compliments, and laughed at all her jokes. Her ass-kissing didn't stop there. She laid it on thick with me and my mother. But there was one person she did not seek to impress, and that was Lesroy.

Stella was crazy about our cousin. And he was devoted to her. After she and Alisha met, things changed. When that little snit was around, there were whispers and giggles and finger-pointing behind his back.

I should have called Stella out on the hateful behavior. But I couldn't stand the thought of hurting her feelings. I let her hurt my cousin instead.

Although I know he noticed, he never said a word. He turned to his longtime love of Arthurian legends and transformed his childhood wonder into a series of graphic novels featuring knights without armor and damsels without distress.

His drawings were beautifully detailed, and his storylines blended medieval charm with contemporary challenges. Stella and I were the models for his two leading ladies. His renditions of us were remarkably accurate. My sister loved to watch him draw and plastered her room with his sketches.

A few weeks after she and Alisha started hanging out, the pictures disappeared and were replaced by posters of boy bands. When I asked her about them, she shrugged and said it was no big deal. Once again, I should have spoken up, but it was easier to blame Alisha than to question my sister's character. Lesroy never commented on their absence. He continued with his artwork, but he stopped sharing it with us.

"I hate her, too. But I think it's worth a call."

"I'm not talking to the nasty little witch, but you're right. You know, she visited Stella once, about a year after they ran off. Stella said it was awkward, like they'd grown apart."

I didn't know. "I can't imagine her experiencing any kind of growth."

He sighed before taking another bite of donut. "Have you ever thought she did you a favor? Never mind. Honey, you need to let it go."

"Maybe. But not today."

We agreed I would contact Alisha, and he would go through Stella's letters to my mother, searching for clues into her disappearance. Then I told him Mom wanted to talk to me and asked if he would come along.

"It's so much easier dealing with her when you're there," I pleaded.

He put his arm around my shoulder and pulled me into a hug. "Then I'll be there. See you at ten."

I locked the door behind him and leaned against it. For the first time since my mother's phone call, I believed my sister might be in serious trouble.

"Stella Star, what have you done?"

CHAPTER 3

Stella Star was the name Lesroy gave her the day she came home from the hospital. As soon as we heard the car pull into the driveway, he started jumping up and down and shouting, "They're here! They're here!"

"For God's sake, boy," my father said through clenched teeth. "We just got her to stop screaming. If you wake her up, I'm going to —"

"It's okay, Jack." Mom sat on the sofa and settled the tiny bundle on her lap. "She's already awake and looks pretty happy. I think she likes you all."

It was true. I slid beside her, and Lesroy perched on the back of the couch, leaning as close to the baby as possible. She gazed at us with that unfocused focus only newborns have.

"She is the most beautiful thing I've ever seen," Lesroy said. "I'm going to call her Stella Star because she is the most beautiful, beautiful, shining star in the entire universe." My cousin had a gift for hyperbole. But she was lovely with her enormous aquamarine eyes and heart-shaped face. The name suited her.

A soft whine brought me back from thoughts of Stella before her star had tarnished. I met the reproachful stare of Scarlett O'Hara, who sat regal and imposing, ears raised in elegant little points. Ben might be a jackass, but his taste in dogs was impeccable. Like her namesake, Scarlett was a beauty. Black with well-defined reddish-orange markings on her majestic face, the animal was a head-turner. She was also neurotic. Loud noises freaked her out, and she hated to be awakened before eight. It was 7:45.

"Easy, Miss Scarlett." I offered my hand in peace, but she wasn't buying it. Her whine morphed into a low-throated growl. "Okay, okay. I'm getting your leash. Just don't—"

But it was too late. She hurled herself forward and pinned me to the wall. Eye-level with the beautiful creature, I braced myself. She thrust her muzzle into my hair, sniffing frantically. I read the hairline offers a canine vantage point for inhaling an owner's scent—that and the crotch, another of her favorite spots. Trapped in a mad Doberman ritual, the best I could do was wait it out. In a few seconds, she stopped her wild snorting. She dropped to the floor, sighing as she placed her head on her paws. I had been scent-tested and had failed.

"Sorry, sweet girl." I knelt beside the dejected animal. "I'm not her. I'm the other sister." She let me scratch her ears but kept her face turned away. "What do you say we go for a quick walk and forget about her?"

After our walk, I showered and proofread an article I was pitching for a local magazine. After being in advertising over five years, I took the plunge into freelance writing and editing. Requests from former agency clients paid the bills, and Lesroy's graphic design company sent business my way. I picked up work from several area publications. The latest was my piece on the death of romance in the digital age. I was trying a new spin on the topic by comparing love letters my grandfather had written to my grandmother and teenage text messages. I wondered if Ben had written love letters to Stella or had sent her pictures of his penis.

A little after nine, I called Alisha. She picked up, and I identified myself.

There was a long pause. "Grace Burnette. Well, this is a surprise. How long has it been? Three, four years? Wait, don't tell me. It was at your..." Her voice trailed off.

"That's right, Alisha. It was at the engagement party."

"I'm sorry, Grace. Stella was my best friend, but I was as shocked as anyone when she ran off."

I wanted to tell her she was only one of many who claimed to be my sister's best friend, but snarkiness wouldn't help my cause. "I'm calling about Stella. Have you heard from her?"

Another pause. "She and I haven't spoken for over a year, not since I went to see her. Is something wrong?"

"We're not sure. That's why I'm calling." I gave her an abbreviated account of the situation and asked if we could get together. She hesitated before agreeing to squeeze me in between her morning yoga class and an afternoon waxing session. I promised I wouldn't take up too much of her valuable time. The irony appeared to be lost on her.

I flipped the TV on to the local news. Scarlett snorted at the sound and shook her head until her ears rattled. She rose from the fancy orthopedic dog bed Stella had sent her last Christmas and strode out of the room. She hated the news.

The story of the day was the approaching storm: thunder, lightning, heavy wind and rain, possibly snow and ice if the temperature fell. Icy weather in the South is always challenging, but it was the prospect of a thunderstorm that got my attention. Lightning terrified Stella and me. Mom said we inherited it from Gran, who took to her bed at the first rumble of thunder.

Sometimes we joined her. We covered up with quilts and sandwiched Gran between us. She told stories of growing up in the country and meeting our grandfather at a church social. He'd been very handsome and extremely determined to get her attention. At first, she thought he was stuck on himself, but after time, she realized he was the love of her life. Stella and I would sigh and snuggle deeper under the covers.

Years later, whenever I got ready to go out on a date, Stella would sit on the bed and watch me apply my makeup and curl my hair. Before I'd leave, she would ask if I thought this one would be the love of my life. "Just like Grandpa was Gran's true and only love."

When I brought Ben home the first time, she took me aside and whispered, "This is it, isn't it? He's the one and only true love."

Later, I wondered if she meant mine or hers. But it didn't matter because by then I'd realized love like Gran's played better as a story than it did in real life. Maybe it was because times were simpler. Or could it be because my grandfather didn't live long enough to disappoint her?

CHAPTER 4

On the drive to my mother's house, I pictured what life might have been like for Stella and Ben. After they got together, I thought about it all the time. I imagined them in bed, entangled with sheets and each other. I saw them sitting on the couch under a big furry blanket trying to watch TV but getting distracted by passion and at fancy parties, their eyes meeting over glasses of wine, the connection so strong they barely made it home before falling into each other's arms. It was like having a rotting tooth you couldn't stop biting down on.

I had all these images about Stella's life with Ben, but I never considered what my life with him would have been like. I fell into our relationship because he was so charming and good looking, but I hadn't really known him. And he hadn't been interested in discovering the real Grace. Stella might have known him better all along because they were so much alike.

Traffic moved nicely, and I reached Mom's three-bedroom, two bath ranch fifteen minutes early. Mike Pemberton's black Cadillac was in the drive. A retired Army captain, he had been my mother's boyfriend for over fourteen years. He asked her to marry him on at least three occasions. But she never accepted. Apparently, my dad provided all the marital bliss she could handle in one lifetime.

On the curb behind Lesroy's red Mini Cooper was an unfamiliar dark blue SUV. The tinted windows hid the interior, and I assumed the car was empty. The engine started as I passed in front of the vehicle. Startled, I performed an awkward half-jump, half-stumble maneuver before stepping into the front yard.

The driver lowered the passenger-side window and leaned over the seat. With the sun casting a shadow across him, it was difficult to make out his features.

"Sorry if I scared you. Are you okay?" His voice was velvety smooth and deep.

"I just didn't see you sitting there, that's all. But I'm fine, thanks." I strained my eyes to see inside. His dark hair blended with the interior, but dappled sunlight revealed a wide smile and a flash of white teeth.

"Sorry. Next time I'll be more careful." He shut the window and pulled away.

Before I could speculate on what *next time* meant, Lesroy greeted me from the front porch.

"Thank God you're here. Aunt Marilyn is a mess. Mike's been trying to calm her down ever since Ben called."

I stopped in the doorway. "What do you mean *ever since Ben called*? Nobody told me Ben called."

"Don't pop a blood vessel. He called about an hour ago. Your mom must have left him a dozen messages. He finally got back to her."

Mike appeared in the entry hall. At six feet four, he took up most of the space.

"Gracie girl, good to see you!" He surrounded me in his special aura of cigar smoke and Old Spice. I don't like either fragrance, but on him it wasn't bad. "Your mom's in the den. I got her settled down a little. That son of a bitch got to her."

Lesroy and I followed him to where she lay on the faded leather couch with a washcloth over her face. She was so quiet I couldn't tell if she was aware we were there.

"Just resting my eyes." She sat up, cloth in hand, and patted the space beside her. "Sit down for a minute, honey." She tried to smile, but her lips quivered, and she abandoned the effort.

"I'm going to get us something to drink," Mike announced. "And Marilyn, you need to eat. No argument." He touched her shoulder. "Be right back."

Lesroy volunteered to help, leaving me alone with Mom.

"I guess they told you Ben called. I shouldn't have wasted my time talking to that sleazy little bastard. What a fool I was to believe there was a chance he'd tell me the truth. I said I'd been trying to get in touch with Stella, but there must be something wrong with her phone. Then I asked to speak to her, like I didn't suspect anything. He had the nerve to act as if he was worried about her, too."

Mom dabbed at her eyes before continuing. "The asshole said he'd been out with some business associates on one of their yachts the day before and had stayed overnight. When he came home, Stella and her sailboat were missing. He told me he wasn't worried at first because she liked to take the boat out by herself early in the day."

Her voice broke, but she kept on with the story. "When she didn't show last night, he started calling around. No one had seen her. He notified the authorities, but there was a big storm, and they couldn't start looking for her until this morning. He said he'd been out with friends searching for her himself, and that's why he didn't call me back."

Mike returned and set a tray of cheese and crackers on the coffee table. Lesroy brought a pitcher of sweet tea and poured a glass for my mother. She set it on the end table without taking a sip. The men crowded together on the love seat.

"Your mom's sure Ben's lying, but his story sounds possible." Mike cut a sliver of cheese, stuck it between two crackers, and handed it to her. "Eat, baby." She nibbled it and held the remaining bit in her palm.

"Grace knows why it's not possible," she said. "Don't you?"

I did know. My sister would never have taken a chance like that. If she'd been by herself, she would have stayed within eyesight of the shore and, at the first hint of rough weather, would have headed in.

I explained Stella's fear of thunder and lightning to Mike. My mother sobbed in the background.

"Just because he's a liar doesn't mean something bad happened." I put my hand on her back. She shook her head and kept crying.

"Come on, baby. Let's get you to bed. We'll figure something out while you rest a little." Mike guided her to the bedroom.

While he was settling her in, Lesroy whispered to me. "Grace, I think Aunt Marilyn is right. I read through Stella's letters. She never said anything specific, like *I'm afraid Ben's going to kill me* or anything, but she didn't sound like Stella. In her last letter she said something about a big change in her life. Something's not right."

"So, Grace," Mike said as he walked back into the room. "I'll book a flight to Ecuador as soon as possible."

I wanted nothing more than to believe Mike was the one to find Stella and end the nightmare. But sending him to Montañita wouldn't be the most effective way to uncover what had happened to my sister.

"I appreciate the offer, but this is something I have to do. No one knows her better than I do," I said. And, although it was true, that wasn't the only reason I had to go. The need to see my sister, to talk to her, to hold her was so strong my arms ached. Whether Stella was in trouble or just being her usual charmingly inconsiderate self, I was the one who could discover the truth.

"Then I'll go with you," Mike suggested. He sat where my mother had been and patted my knee. "Your Aunt Rita can come stay with your mom."

"She needs you, Mike. I love Rita, but there's no way she could keep Mom from going off the deep end."

"Grace is right," Lesroy chimed in. "My mom is a basket case. She'd have Aunt Marilyn climbing the walls. Mike's right, too." He took a deep breath. "My passport's hardly been used, and work is slow this time of year, so I'll go with you."

"That's sweet," I said, "but you recall what happened the last time you got on a plane, don't you?"

My cousin was as terrified of flying as Stella was of storms, maybe even more so. A few years ago, he and his latest boyfriend set off for a vacation in Costa Rica. Lesroy refused to admit to his companion how much flying frightened him. Instead, he swiped a bottle of his mother's anxiety medication and downed several before take-off.

Once the plane was airborne, he polished off an unknown quantity of alcohol. He never told me what happened between the departure from Atlanta and the layover in Houston—I'm not sure he could remember—but my cousin did not make his connection. He returned to Atlanta alone on the bus and never heard from the boyfriend again.

"I thought we agreed never to discuss that incident." He glared at me. "Besides, I'm better now."

I hated myself for bringing up the traumatic event, yet I couldn't risk an airborne crisis slowing me down.

"I'm sure you are, and it means a lot you'd get on a plane for me. But you know how Ben is about you." My ex-fiancé detested Lesroy, and I suspected the feeling was mutual. "If it's just me, I think he'll open up more."

By the time I left to go see Alisha, we had formed a plan. Mike would handle the travel arrangements and talk to an old Army buddy of his who lived in Ecuador. Lesroy would make the ultimate sacrifice and keep Scarlett O'Hara.

And I would go find my sister.

CHAPTER 5

I was in Alisha's trendy Atlanta neighborhood by a little after eleven. The houses were at least thirty years old. Most had undergone extensive and expensive renovations. The Simmons' house was no exception.

The pale green brick structure sat on a corner lot. Its front steps were a darker shade, as if they'd been rebuilt. The façade looked lovely from a distance, but up close you could see repaired cracks and bolstered saggy spots. Serious potholes marked the steep driveway, suggesting Alisha and her husband had run out of steam or money before they'd finished the upgrades. I parked at the curb and trudged past sculptured shrubbery, followed the stone path, and rang the bell.

"Grace, come in," Alisha, in yoga gear, greeted me. She was thinner than I remembered and very tan, with a ponytail so tight it tugged the corners of her eyes upward.

I stepped into an elaborate foyer in front of a wide, curving staircase. Like an Artic explorer plunging through the icy tundra, I was blinded by light reflecting off the snow. The whiteness of it all threatened to smother me: thick, off-white carpet; smooth, creamy-white walls; ivory-white sofa.

"Wow." The sound of my voice echoed down the hallway.

"Isn't it amazing?" Alisha squealed. "We just had everything redone." She glanced at my feet. "Would you mind taking off your shoes?"

I slipped out of my flats, wishing I'd had that pedicure I so desperately needed, but Alisha didn't seem to notice. She ushered me through the formal living area to a cavernous family room, more beige than white—or did everything appear dimmer in the aftermath of an attack of snow-blindness? She pointed to the center of a three-piece sectional.

"Can I get you something to drink? Iced tea or Coke? There's Diet and Zero Sugar."

"I'm fine, thanks." I sat next to a fluffy pillow that exploded into a fat white cat who hissed as it shot off the sofa.

"Sassy, you naughty kitty! You're not supposed to get on the furniture." She brushed off the seat beside me and took a pink leather book from the ottoman. "Everything's digital now, but I still like to keep albums. I guess I'm an old-fashioned girl."

More like a modern narcissist, I thought, but smiled and nodded.

"This is from the last time I saw Stella."

She scooted closer and balanced the album between our knees. My sister stared out at me, clad in a tiny orange bikini, hair flying wild around her perfect face.

"She's as beautiful as ever, isn't she?" Alisha spoke in a whisper, touching Stella's face with her fingertips. "This was on Ben's boat. Greg wanted to go to Montañita with me, but he couldn't get away and insisted I go without him. He knows how much I loved, I mean love, Stella. He is absolutely the most considerate husband."

She had captioned each picture with the date, location, and occasion. She documented the day on the boat with pictures of Stella sunbathing, Ben drinking beer behind the helm, and Alisha and Stella lounging on the top deck. The next few pages were set on the beach, but the theme was the same. There were no photographs of Ben and Stella together until I got to the middle of the album. It was a party at their home. He had his arm around her waist, his face turned to hers. She was leaning away, facing the camera. Her gold locket glowed against her tawny skin. Her smile was unnaturally stiff, as if forced.

There were more shots of Stella and Alisha at the same party. One included a dark-haired man with intense eyes and a thick, muscular build. Standing between the two women, he was about a foot taller than my sister and looked at least ten years older. He had draped his arm over her shoulder and tipped his head toward hers. Her smile seemed genuine and relaxed.

"That's Adelmo Balsuto. See, I wrote his name here." She pointed to the caption: *Adelmo with us at the party in my honor.* "He's one of Ben's business associates. Very handsome and super-rich, but he gave me the creeps. Always lurking. Ben totally sucked up to him. But Stella, well, you can never tell if she really likes someone or if she's just being Stella."

"You're right. I couldn't tell she wanted the man I planned to marry." I knew how bitter that sounded, but I couldn't help it. How many times had I excused my sister's behavior because it was Stella just being Stella? All the times she'd been late or failed to show because something better came along or the projects she started and never finished or the people she finished with.

Alisha's face turned a vivid shade of pink, providing a splash of color in the otherwise colorless room.

"I doubt if you care and I don't blame you, but she seemed pretty miserable. She and Ben hardly spoke to each other, and he was jumpy and weird." She picked a long strand of cat hair off the pillow beside her. Then she lowered her voice and asked, "You don't think Ben would hurt her, do you?"

"What makes you say that? Did you see something?"

I thought of the times I'd had a peek behind the curtain at what Ben looked like when he lost his temper. My stomach roiled. If I hadn't ignored those little warning signs that the man I loved might have a dark, ugly side, I would have never agreed to marry him. And if I hadn't wanted him, would Stella have found him as appealing? Somehow, I didn't think so.

"No, no. I never even saw him touch her unless they were posing for pictures. It was little things like the way she jumped when he came up behind her or laughed too loud at his jokes. Sometimes it's hard to tell what goes on between a couple when no one else is around."

She paused and ran her fingers through her perfect ponytail. It struck me her marriage might not be so perfect.

"It's hard for me to put my finger on it. She just wasn't her old self. You remember how popular she was."

She looked at me as if she expected a response. "Yes, I remember."

"Well, now she doesn't have any real friends. I felt sorry for her and offered to stay longer. But she said she was fine, and I should go home to Greg. I'm certain there was something she wasn't telling me. I tried to get in touch with her for weeks after I got home, but she never returned my calls."

She looked at her watch and leaped to her feet. "Oh, my God! It's almost one! I'm sorry, Grace, but I can't be late for this appointment. Svetlana is the absolute best. Almost painless. Why don't you take the album? When you bring it back, I'll give you the grand tour."

She hurried me through the Arctic tundra and held the door open for me as I slipped back into my shoes. "I shouldn't have said anything about Ben. He would never hurt Stella. Right?"

"I don't know what Ben might do. But I guess I'm going to find out."

CHAPTER 6

That night I dreamed of Stella. We were in the house we shared with Gran after my parents divorced. My sister and I were playing in the small backyard. She was hanging upside down from a tree branch. The day was so brilliant, I had to shield my eyes. Dark clouds appeared out of nowhere, and rain pelted down. Thunder rumbled in the background. I tried to call out to her, to insist she come down. The words stuck in my throat. I wanted to run to her, but a slash of blinding light cut across the sky, rendering me immobile. My sister smiled up at me from her topsy-turvy angle just before another flash of lightning split the air. The branch electrified with the fiery blast, and Stella was gone.

When I bolted up in bed, a cold wet nose pressed against my cheek. I was eye to eye with the Doberman.

"I'm sorry, Miss Scarlett. I didn't mean to wake you." I rubbed her smooth snout. She put her paws on the bed and scooted herself up with her hind legs. She stepped over me, lay down, and placed her foreleg over my hip, her muzzle on my shoulder. I've never been much of a spooner. But this was the first time Scarlett had approached me in such an intimate way. I accepted her gesture as the gift it was and fell asleep to her gentle snoring.

. . . . .

When I woke, my cell was buzzing. I rolled onto the space where Scarlett had been and answered it. It was my client and friend Carla

Frazier, owner of a boutique lingerie shop that catered to women who, like Carla herself, were more than well endowed. Like Lesroy, she had refused to give up on me. She used her status to lure me to lunches and dinners that had nothing to do with business.

"Hey, Carla. What's up?"

"Most likely my cholesterol." She laughed. "But it sounds like you *weren't* up. I can call later."

I assured her I was wide awake, and we spent the next ten minutes discussing details for her Christmas ad campaign. Since work had always been a positive distraction for me, I promised to revise the spots and send them to her before the weekend.

All I wanted to do was crawl back into bed, but that would only give me time to think about Stella. So, I pulled on yesterday's jeans and sweatshirt and stumbled to the kitchen. Scarlett stood by the door.

"Didn't mean to keep you waiting, Your Majesty." I stepped aside to let her pass into the small fenced-in backyard.

Then I made coffee and took a few sips before a sharp bark alerted me the dog wanted in. Together we wandered to the den. She climbed into her bed, circled three times before plopping down with her back to me. I sat on the sofa with my laptop, trying to come up with an ad that would convince buyers we had created a light, lacy concoction of frills with the protection of full body armor.

Turned out it was no easy task. "Not your grandma's bra" was nostalgic but evoked images of bosoms that had lost their war with gravity. "Throw away your bullet-proof vests, ladies," while reassuring, seemed antagonistic. I settled on "Sensual support."

I stood to stretch, and Scarlett rose to give me her *where the hell's my breakfast* face. When I checked the time, I couldn't blame her.

"I bet you're starving, sweet girl."

After filling her dish, I washed my hands and poured cereal. A few bites in, I lost interest. How could I sit safe in my kitchen eating cereal when Stella might be—no, I would not go there.

If Scarlett worried about her missing mistress, it hadn't affected her appetite. She wolfed down her food and was licking the bowl when I removed her leash from its hook. She sat at attention. Quivering as I attached it, she scrambled toward the front door.

Sunlight spewed over us, hinting today would be one of those mild December days that make you happy to live in the South. We headed down the street, Scarlett lunging while I scurried to keep up. After a few blocks, she slowed to a brisk trot, stopping to sniff at the spot where some phantom night creature had lingered. The trot became a saunter as she examined random sticks and scraggly patches of half-frozen monkey grass.

Now that my survival didn't depend on trying to stay on my feet, I was able to think. But not about Stella. No, I would make myself concentrate on subjects unrelated to my sister. I revisited the copy for Carla's spot, then thought of the last time I'd seen my friend.

I stopped by to check out her new holiday collection. Her hot pink Lexus with its custom license plate BB4ALL was parked in front of the store. The vivid colors of her vehicle correlated with her special line of brassieres for cancer survivors. Her specialty plates represented her philosophy of beautiful breasts for all.

A wintery window display featured a white-tinsel Christmas tree decorated with bras and panties tied into bows. I winced at the bitter contrast of the festive cheer and memories of the starkness of our past few Christmases without Stella.

Carla greeted me with an embrace, then stepped back and stared at me. "So, how are you doing? Remember, I'm a human bullshit detector."

I plastered on my brightest smile. "Much better, more like myself," I lied, unsure what my pre-betrayal self had been.

"Honey, you're never going to be your old self again. The good news is you can be someone better, but only if you want to."

Her remark had irritated me. I wanted to be a better person, to let go of my rage. Who the hell wouldn't?

Today, heading back home with a much calmer Doberman, Carla's words took on new meaning. She was right when she said I'd never be my pre-betrayal self. But it wasn't Stella's behavior that made her assessment accurate. It was because without her, I didn't know who I was supposed to be. I had been a loving older sister devoted to my charming, albeit egotistical, sibling. I had spent so much time excusing and adoring Stella.

Now, the possibility I might lose her forever terrified me. Who would I be without her? Not Stella's older sister. Not one of two daughters. Just me.

I couldn't be sure if it was the dropping temperature or the thought of what that sister-less life might be, but I began shivering so violently I had to hold Scarlett's leash with both hands.

CHAPTER 7

Once home, I slipped into a bra from Carla's not-so-well-endowed collection. She insisted on giving it to me as a thank you for a great quarter. I had to admit it enhanced my attributes, but at over one hundred dollars a pop, I'd have to stick with Target's line.

Dressed in clean jeans and a sweatshirt, I turned to check myself out in the mirror. As expected, my too-thin, hollow-eyed-face stared back at me, but I wasn't alone. Eleven-year-old Stella stood beside me, wearing one of my push-up bras and frowning.

"Grace, when do you think my boobs will come in?" she asked as if they were a reluctant crop of tomatoes.

I weighed my answer, not mentioning my concern that as petite as she was, I suspected she might not receive a bountiful pair. Instead, I assured her she would start developing any day. But I underestimated the generosity of the breast fairy. Like everything else in Stella's life, she was abundantly gifted. She accepted the largess with her usual composure and set about using her new assets to her best ability. At fourteen, she mastered the art of exposing just the right amount of cleavage to captivate her prey without seeming slutty.

I blinked, and she disappeared. But she wasn't done with me as I discovered when I leaned in to apply my mascara and saw not my face, but Stella's.

My sister and I never bore a strong physical resemblance to one another. Her brilliant blue eyes were in sharp contrast to my gray ones, and her blonde hair gave her a glamorous demeanor I would never have. But there had always been a sisterly sameness in our expressions, especially when we were immersed in sadness or lost in thought. Today the similarity was so striking it was as if I could touch the woman in the mirror and, in doing so, I might bring my sister home.

If I were being honest, though, I wasn't sure I wanted her back. Her betrayal with Ben had undone me. For over three months I lost interest in the day-to-day operations of life. I had trouble falling asleep and could barely drag myself out of bed in the mornings. I forgot about life's little niceties, such as maintaining personal hygiene or eating regular meals.

Everyone tip-toed around the issue. Even Mom refrained from mentioning I exuded an aura of refugee from a war-torn country. Finally, Lesroy confronted me.

"Grace, I hate to be the one to tell you, but you look like something the cat wouldn't even drag in. Your eyes are vacant, like the lights are off and nobody's home. And what's worse, Cousin, is you stink."

I don't know if it was his version of tough love or if I had exhausted my capacity for self-pity, but from that point on, I stopped letting myself go. I returned to a regular regimen of bathing and shampooing and eating, but I never regained my sense of me. For over a year after they left, I thought about my sister or Ben or both daily. A song would play on the radio, and I would remember dancing to it with Ben. I'd pick up the phone to tell Stella something funny and realize I had deleted her number. There was no escape from my humiliation.

People promised me the pain would ease as time passed, and while it didn't get much better, it became less intense. Instead of struggling under the crushing weight of my sorrow every day, I experienced lighter moments when I was depressed, not devastated. Lesroy suggested I see a therapist, but I refused to let go of my misery because it was all I had left of my previous life, all that remained of my relationship with Stella.

Still, I was making progress. Or so I told myself, but who was I kidding? In a few days I would drop everything to travel to a country where I didn't even speak the language in search of a sister I would be better off without. Once again, I had gotten sucked back into my sister's drama.

But this would be different. This time I wouldn't return to being the adoring older sister. I would confront her and demand she grow up and accept responsibility for the pain she caused. Then I might forgive her and let go of my sibling loneliness.

I spent the next hour returning client emails and proofing a guest blog post for a fellow copywriter on how to develop a freelance business. Then I fixed lunch and ate it while watching the local news.

The weather forecast continued with dire predictions of the winter storm on the horizon. Outside, the sun cast its brittle light, making it hard to take the meteorologists seriously. But Atlantans have been fooled before and ended up being stuck overnight on freeways and in Waffle Houses. If I hurried, I could make a run to the store and avoid the hordes of people rushing the shelves for emergency supplies.

I gave Scarlett a treat and promised to be back soon, certain she had no concept of time. Since I suspected she was still waiting for Stella to come take her home, I was glad she didn't.

. . . . .

It seemed everyone else had the same idea as I had, and my quick trip became a marathon instead of a sprint. On the way to my car, a frigid gust of damp wind pummeled me.

In the warmth of my kitchen, I put away my purchases: milk, eggs, coffee, bread, toilet paper, and wine. Then I rummaged through the pantry until I found the chocolate syrup.

"I'm thinking about a little hot chocolate for me and, for you, one of those delicious chew-bones," I said to Scarlett. At the mention of bones, she wagged her tail in approval.

After we finished drinking and chewing, we crawled into bed. I hadn't understood how draining having a missing sister could be.

I awoke to the phone ringing. It was Mike, most likely calling with my flight plan.

"I was just getting ready to pack," I improvised. "It won't take me long."

"There's no hurry, Grace. They found Stella."

CHAPTER 8

I sat on the bed tracing the floral pattern on my comforter, hoping Mike would call back and tell me he'd misunderstood what the officials had told him. Yes, some girl's body had been found battered and bruised on the beach. But it wasn't Stella. Yes, it was her sailboat capsized a few miles from the coastline, but she hadn't been thrown from it. She'd been picked up by a passing fisherman and would soon be posting news about her adventure on Facebook.

Both as a child and an adult, I'd never been a big crier. When I fell off my bike and broke my arm, I howled on the way to the hospital but never shed a tear. After discovering my fiancé was gone, I remained dry-eyed as I raged and smashed his favorite mug. I ripped his face from every picture I had. Every now and then, I woke to find my pillowcase damp, but in my waking hours I remained stoic.

I always considered my inability to release my pain in a stream of tears more of a blessing than a curse. But not today. From the moment Mike had delivered his terrible news, my unshed tears became a cruel sneeze that teased then disappeared, leaving me desperate for relief. The pressure threatened to explode and tear me apart. Still, I couldn't cry.

I put off going to my mother's, knowing it would make the horror real. Her face would be etched with grief, and none of us would ever be the same.

Aunt Rita had parked her old Buick in the drive. I pulled in behind her but couldn't make myself step out of the car.

My grandmother told me that Mom's younger sister had been beautiful before she married Lesroy's daddy, but to me she had always been washed out, like the faded pictures in our old family album. Her eyes were a pale grayish blue, her hair a dull brown. For special occasions, she dyed it a coppery shade of red that made my eyes hurt. She was thin—too thin, both my mother and grandmother agreed— and rarely spoke above a whisper unless she and Uncle Roy rolled into one of their screaming matches. Then she shrieked to high heaven.

When I was a kid, we saw Rita almost every day. Sometimes she and Lesroy stayed with us at Gran's for weeks while Roy was on a bender. My mother would beg my aunt to leave him for good, but Rita always returned to my uncle.

I had a hazy memory of a violent phase before Stella was born. The only reason I remember it at all is because Roy kept showing up at the front door drunk as a skunk, cursing and crying.

Over six feet tall and beefy with a big barrel chest, my uncle favored wife-beater T-shirts that exposed thick patches of curly black hair. On his right forearm he had a tattoo of a grinning chimpanzee. After a few beers, he'd flex his bicep and make the monkey dance. That stupid dancing chimp never failed to get a laugh from my daddy, but Lesroy and I hated it. It looked ready to take a bite out of you if you got too close.

When Roy was in a good mood, he would catch one of us up in his arms, fling us high in the air, and whirl around and around until the blood pounded in our heads. Then he hurled us onto the nearest piece of furniture and laughed if we fell off. Luckily, he was seldom in a good mood, and my grandmother kept him out of the house when he was in a bad one.

I realized early Gran was the only person Roy feared. When I asked Mom about it, she laughed and said I'd have to take it up with my grandmother. Years later, I found out Gran had once broken a broom on Roy's head. He'd come over to drag Rita home after an explosive episode that left my aunt with a black eye. Gran came up behind him and cracked him on the side of the head hard enough to addle him and break the broom. She continued to whack him across the face with the stick end until he ran bleeding from the house. My cousin insisted he'd been there when it happened, but my mother said he'd only been about six months old, and there was no way he could remember.

Although he was handy with his fists, physical violence wasn't Uncle Roy's strongest suit. He specialized in a kind of emotional cruelty we children could feel if not understand. One summer night we were sitting on the front porch with neighbors. Well into the second six-pack, one of them asked Roy where he'd gotten the name for his only son. Was it his full name? A family name? Lesroy stood by his daddy at the time, looking at his shoes.

"Hell, no!" Roy bellowed, grabbing his son and rubbing his knuckles over the boy's newly shaved head. "The first time I saw this little squirt I knew he'd never measure up to the Dupree men. I mean, look at him." He grabbed my cousin's shoulder and squeezed. "No way he was gonna be a Roy, Jr., but he might be able to carry a lesser name." Roy slapped his son on the back and cackled. "So, I named him Lesroy! Get it? Less Roy."

I was only five at the time and didn't get it. But Lesroy did. Maybe not the joke, but definitely the meanness. After that, it got real quiet for a minute. Then my grandmother spoke.

"Well, I think the world could do with a little less Roy, myself. Less of good old Roy and more ice cream. What do you kids think?"

The three of us put the mystery of adult cruelty behind us, went inside, and ate ice cream until our stomachs hurt.

．　　　．　　　．　　　．　　　．

Like my own daddy, who abandoned us shortly after Stella's first birthday, Uncle Roy was no longer in the picture.

"Voila!" Lesroy would say and mimic waving a magic wand. "Gone, just like that."

I asked him once if he was glad his daddy was gone. I knew I didn't miss mine much.

"Not really," he replied. "I mean, we can't be sure he's not coming back."

But Uncle Roy didn't come back. A year later they found his truck with him in it at the bottom of a small lake about ten miles from our home. I remember Aunt Rita had "a spell," as Gran called it. Now I suppose it would be termed a nervous breakdown. It made me happy because Lesroy got to stay with us for almost two months while his mother was recovering.

My aunt was never quite the same after they released her. The biggest difference was the way she acted around Gran and Mom, like she was afraid of them. And she stopped visiting. Oh, she would come for holidays and birthdays, but she didn't stay long.

The sound of a dog barking down the street brought me back to the present. I sighed, realizing I couldn't stall forever, and stepped from the car. Lesroy opened the door before I knocked. He grabbed me and held on tight. "It's going to be okay, Grace," he said before releasing me.

Behind him, Aunt Rita leaned against the stair rail. She was smaller than I remembered. Her poofy red hair overwhelmed her thin pale face. Rita's mascara trailed down her cheeks, cracking her face like a porcelain doll dropped one too many times. When she saw me, she began to cry in deep, shuddering gulps. She collapsed onto the bottom step with her head on her knees. Lesroy sat and put his arm around his mother. I knew I should join them, but I couldn't remember why they were so upset.

I was standing there staring at them when Mike appeared. "Let me get your coat, Gracie." He helped me out of my jacket and guided me to the den.

My mother wasn't the sad, broken woman from the day before. Today, she was a mad lady straight from a Greek tragedy. Medusa-style strands of hair snaked around face, bobbing when she strode toward me. Instead of offering me comfort, she grabbed me by the shoulders and leaned in close enough for me to detect the faint odor of vodka.

"Your baby sister is dead, Grace. Murdered by that sick son of a bitch she married. You know that, right?" She didn't give me a chance to respond. "Well, he won't get away with it. He's going to pay. We're going to make him pay. Aren't we, Grace?"

She stared at me with fierce eyes, and when I didn't fill the terrible silence, she shook my shoulders, not hard, but with purpose. She spoke like a drunk determined to appear sober, but she wasn't drunk. "You are going to help me make him pay."

The rest of the evening was a blur for me. Rita talked Mom into taking a Xanax and lying down. Mike contacted the minister of the church he and my mother attended sporadically to discuss funeral arrangements. Everything was in the air since Stella's body hadn't been released yet. And, of course, there was Ben. Although he'd never been charged in connection with the drug ring's operations, he'd represented most of the members at one time or another and was suspected of concealing information. That meant attending a stateside funeral would be a bad idea, assuming he let us bring Stella home.

Mike's friend in Ecuador promised to check in with the authorities to see how they were classifying Stella's death. He warned us not to get our hopes up. There were enough unsolved murders to tax the somewhat limited police force already. They would not be eager to send men to investigate the tragic, but most likely accidental death of a rich American.

Lesroy and I sat on the sofa watching people we didn't know or remember stop by with casseroles, cakes, and pies. The kitchen counter was stacked two deep, and the freezer was packed.

"Are you okay?" Lesroy asked for the third time.

"I'm fine." I'd been trying to think of something I could do, something to make things better. Only things weren't going to get better. My sister was dead, my ex-fiancé was holding her body hostage, and my mother was acting like a character in *The Godfather*.

Mike came from the bedroom and sat beside me. "Your mother's finally out. Rita's sitting with her." He ran his hand across his buzz cut. "I've never seen her like this. She's determined to fly to Ecuador and confront Ben. Demand he give us your sister's body to bring home. And if the police don't charge him with something, God knows what she might do."

"Well, we don't have to worry about Aunt Marilyn going because she doesn't have a passport," Lesroy said. "She talked about getting one to visit Stella but had trouble finding her birth certificate and said to hell with it."

I didn't know Mom had considered visiting Stella. I had accepted the fact that our mother favored my little sister, but I thought she'd been on my side when Stella stole Ben. Yes, she wanted me to forgive, but she had to understand I would never forget.

The muffled hum in the room reminded me of summers spent at the community pool with Stella. We pushed ourselves to the bottom to see who could hold her breath the longest. Even though she was smaller, Stella usually won. She was at home in the water, like a sleek little otter. Although I wasn't much bigger, I was plagued by a heaviness, terrified that at any minute I might be pulled under by an unseen force. Now, instead of childlike fear, memories of my sister dragged me down like concrete blocks.

I wondered if Stella heard a murmur before she died, like when you're a kid trying to fall asleep while the adults keep talking in the next room. You want to let go and drift into another state of consciousness, but you want to stay connected, too. Had my sister struggled to stay attached, to hold on to the sound until the very last moment?

My phone vibrated from inside my pants pocket. "Unknown caller." Normally, I would have ignored it, but I felt compelled to answer. I excused myself and walked to the spare bedroom.

It was Ben.

"Grace! It's so good to hear your voice. God, it's been so long, and it's been…" He gurgled. "It's been so awful. I mean, it's been bad for such a long time, but now with Stella gone. I just don't know."

Know what, I thought. Whether you're going to get away with murdering my sister? Because at that moment, I knew he'd done it. Somehow, he was responsible for Stella's death.

"What do you want?"

"Want? I don't want anything, Babe, except to say how sorry I am about Stella and everything." His words slurred together. "I was so stupid. It should have been me and you. If only —"

"Stop. If you're really sorry, you'll help us find out what happened. And help us bring her home."

There was a long pause. "Sure, Grace. I'll help, but it has to be you. You have to come to me."

I started to tell him to go straight to hell because I knew what he wanted. He wanted to play. He'd always loved games: cards, videos, relationships. The higher the stakes, the better. To him, Stella's death was just another game. With Ben the risk was the best part, almost better than winning. But he always expected to win. Could using his arrogance against him be the key to finding out what had happened to Stella?

I agreed to go to him. I told myself it was only to get my sister back and achieve closure for our family. But when I heard Ben's voice, there had been something, not the same intense desire I'd had when we were together. Something darker, possibly the opposite of desire.

CHAPTER 9

I expected a fight when I relayed my conversation with Ben and announced my decision to go to Ecuador alone. But my mother surprised me.

"Grace is right. Ben knows how the rest of the family feels about him." She took my hand and held it to her lips. "If anyone can reason with him, it's you." She gave Mike a look I couldn't quite interpret, and he shrugged his massive shoulders.

Mike insisted on setting up my travel plans, and I headed for home, troubled at the ease with which my mother was sending me off on a potentially dangerous mission. Settling the cosmic score for Stella was more important to her than preserving the safety of her remaining daughter. Even in death, Stella remained the favorite sister.

I didn't get home until after midnight. Either I had annoyed her by leaving her alone so long, or she sensed Stella's death and was depressed, but I had to coax her into a walk. The temperature had dropped, and the wind had risen, carrying with it the promise of snow. My neighbor's Christmas lights blinked manically from the small, leafless hardwood in his front yard. The decorations were wrapped tightly around the base of the tree, strangling it with seasonal joy. Scarlett and I were both shivering when we returned home.

Once inside, I undid the dog's leash and scratched the sweet spot behind her ear, causing her left leg to jerk wildly. "Sorry, Miss Scarlett, but it looks like our arrangement will be permanent." She shook herself, gave me a mournful look, and strolled into the kitchen.

I changed into flannel pajamas. Exhausted, but wide awake, I opened the bottom dresser drawer. Under fancy, silk underwear I most likely would never wear, I found it. The family photo album Gran had given me a few weeks before she died. Her name, Emmaline Burns Hathaway, was on the first page in her own beautiful, flowing handwriting. She'd kept this album separate from the others, her favorite, she said, and it was right that I have it.

"I know you don't want to think about the past right now, my love, but someday you will," Gran said.

Pictures of my grandparents' wedding day filled the first two pages. Seeming uncomfortable in what must have been their best church clothes, both stared directly at the camera, unsmiling, almost stern. Gran's shoulder-length hair was dark and wavy, like one of the glamorous starlets she loved so much. With her startling, silver-gray eyes and high cheekbones, she wasn't exactly beautiful. She was like someone you see every day for months, maybe years, and don't think much about. Then one day she looks up at you from some ordinary task, like hemming a dress or washing dishes, and she takes your breath away. Was that what happened with my grandfather? Or had the slender, fair-haired young man in the picture taken one look at her and known she was the one?

"Seriously?" I asked myself out loud. "You still believe that love-of-your-life crap?"

The next few pictures were candid shots, several catching my grandparents in mid-laughter. In the last photo my grandfather carried his bride over the threshold of the tiny apartment they lived in above his parents' home. Their happiness was almost tangible.

My grandmother devoted the second section of the album to pictures of my mother and aunt when they were very young. A few featured Mom during her brief stint as an only child. In one, Gran held an infant bundled up in a blanket above the caption: *Home from the hospital*. Another showed her as a grinning toddler stuffing handfuls of cake in her mouth: *First birthday*. A series of other firsts were documented: steps, Christmas, tooth.

Then her solitary reign ended with the birth of Aunt Rita. In most of the following pictures of them, my mother glared at her baby sister.

I didn't think it was possible for a small child to register such intense hostility, but it was clear Mom wanted no part of her sibling.

When I turned the page, I became disoriented. Instead of a continuation of the sisters' childhoods, Gran skipped ahead to me and Stella.

I checked the pages to make sure they weren't stuck together, but they appeared to be in their original, intended order. While pictorial evidence suggested my mother had not welcomed the younger child, my photos with and without Stella told an entirely different story. Before my sister arrived, I was consistently unsmiling. Not frowning in frustration or pouting in protest, just neutral. After Stella showed up, I was a different kid, as if a light switched on for me.

"Okay, Gran," I thought. "You made your point."

I thumbed through the next few pages of sibling glee. Toward the end of the album, Gran included pictures with Lesroy in them. Most shots of my cousin were blurry since he couldn't stand still for more than a few seconds at a time. It made me smile to see the three of us together before we lost our glow of innocence.

There was only one picture on the last page. For a moment I was nine years old again, cowering under the covers with Stella during one of the worst storms of my childhood. We were in Gran's bed, but she wasn't there. Stella whimpered and I shushed her. We had to be very quiet. I don't know why, but it had been terribly important.

The photo was a shot of the giant oak tree at the edge of our front yard. Several branches were as thick as full-grown trees. The largest one, the one we climbed to watch cars drive by, was breaking away from the base of the tree. Blackened and twisted, it dangled precariously over the graveled drive.

The force of the lightning bolt as it struck the tree penetrated through the ground below our bedroom. The acrid smell of smoke clung to my nostrils. My grandmother and mother whispered from behind the bedroom door. This combination of the fury of the natural world and the secrets of grown-ups filled me with a terror only a nine-year-old could know.

I slammed the album shut, shoved it under my bed, and turned off the lights, determined to get some sleep. But questions kept flying through my mind. Why had Gran included that scorched tree along with all those happy family memories? Had she expected me to understand? Maybe, if I could just recall some little detail, the whole story would come flooding back. The more I tried to quell my thoughts, the more restless I became.

Then I remembered the sleeping pills in my medicine cabinet. Right after Ben dumped me, I'd gone for at least three days on less than four hours of sleep a night. My mother was worried, and, as a retired nurse, she insisted she was fully competent to prescribe her own medication for me. They worked so well I slept through a midnight refrigerator raid that left me covered in cheese spread and cookie dough. But tonight, I was too exhausted to care. I swallowed one of the tiny tablets and packed the bottle in my travel bag in case I had trouble sleeping in a strange place.

The savage expression on my mother's face when she spoke of how we would make Ben pay was my last conscious image before the pills took effect.

CHAPTER 10

A sound like BB's pelleting my window brought me out of my pill-induced stupor. It took several seconds to place the noise. Ice.

Transplanted Northerners make fun of Southerners in the snow. Some of their scorn is deserved. Yes, we panicked at the first flake. And we flooded grocery and liquor stores. But we knew behind every snowfall lay the possibility of an ice storm. If you were caught out when the roads became frozen sheets of glass, it didn't matter how adept you were at driving in bad weather; you could be stuck on the roads for hours.

I had enough supplies to outlast at least a three-day storm and would be fine unless the power went out. Then I remembered I was supposed to be heading to Ecuador on the next flight. If the airport closed, that might not be for quite a while.

Outside my window, about six inches of dazzling white snow blanketed the ground. Ice glazed trees and bushes. Scarlett balked at going out back, so I put on old boots and threw my coat over my pajamas before dragging her through the front door. She snorted indignantly before attending to her business and scurrying back in.

I'd just shrugged out of the coat when my phone rang. It was Lesroy.

"Grace, have you looked outside?" He didn't wait for an answer. "It is a beautiful mess everywhere. The streets aren't bad yet, though. Vincent has four-wheel drive, and he's happy to come get you and the beast. Come party out the storm with us."

Vincent and Lesroy had been living together for almost a year in a bungalow-styled home in the trendy Virginia Highlands area. A big, burly contractor who specialized in renovating older homes wasn't who I would have pictured Lesroy with, but I'd never seen my cousin so happy. I enjoyed hanging out with them, but people have been known to get stranded for days during Atlanta ice storms, and I wasn't sure I could handle that much fun.

I assured him the dog and I would be fine.

"You're a real buzz-kill, Grace. Besides, you shouldn't be alone right now. Please stay with us."

"I appreciate the offer, Cousin, but I don't mind being by myself. And I need to be ready for the first flight whenever that is."

"That could be days." Lesroy sighed.

He was right. The ice melted a little during the day and highway crews cleared major streets, but everything refroze overnight, creating havoc for early morning commuters and shutting down the airport. My driveway remained a solid sheet of ice, making a simple trip to the mailbox a treacherous journey. But the power held. I spent my spare time looking up information about Ecuador and trying not to think about my sister's last days.

Other than it being the jumping-off point for the Galapagos Islands, I knew very little about the country. I read in the papers how Edward Snowden, the former National Security contractor accused of treason for revealing state secrets, had taken sanctuary in Ecuador's London embassy. This was interesting considering the country's record on government transparency. It was fine for the other guys, but their own government reserved the right to censor anything or anyone it didn't like.

Navigating a country that provided a haven for someone like Ben, while strong-arming its own people could be tricky. I was glad I had Mike's friend to help.

On the third day the temperature stayed above freezing, and it looked as if we were through the worst of it. With the backlog of passengers who needed rescheduling, however, it was another day before Mike could book a flight for me.

"You're set to leave on the first flight out tomorrow morning. I've put some contact information together for you from my buddy in Guayaquil. I'd bring it over myself, but I don't like leaving your mother alone, so a friend of mine is going to drop it off tonight."

"That's not necessary. I can pick it up."

"Absolutely not. Your mom would never forgive me if you had an accident on the way."

Mike was from the generation where men take care of all sorts of irritating little details for women, and a part of me liked it.

"His name's Justin McElroy. His dad and I were in the same unit in the service. Justin joined the Marines Special Forces, a real hotshot, but a nice guy. He'll be there a little after seven. Your mom's resting, but I know she'd want me to tell you she loves you."

I would have suspected Mom of trying to set me up with this Justin guy, but she was too devastated for matchmaking. I checked in with Lesroy about taking care of Scarlett and dragged out my suitcase.

CHAPTER 11

At 7:05, the doorbell rang. Scarlett walked alongside me, and we looked out the paneled window by the entrance. The man on my front porch wore a heavy leather jacket with the collar turned up and a black knit cap pulled low over his forehead. He was obviously Mike's friend, but I asked for identification before I opened the door to let him know I was security savvy.

"You must be Grace Burnette," he said, pulling off his woolen hat and extending a gloved hand to me. "I'm Justin McElroy, your mom's and Mike's friend." There was no mistaking that voice. It was the man from the dark SUV.

"Uh, right. Grace. That's me," I stammered, wishing I'd at least put on a little mascara or lipstick. The man at my door was more imposing than conventionally handsome. He was tall, not as tall as Mike but close, with wide, muscular shoulders. His black hair was short and wavy with a few threads of white woven in near his temples, and his eyes were a deep, dark blue. A slightly crooked nose and scruffy-looking five o'clock-shadow gave him that bad-boy edge most women would find hard to resist. But it was his mouth that held my attention—full, smooth lips, and incredibly white teeth.

He removed his gloves, and we shook hands. His touch was warm, and I held on a beat longer than usual. Scarlett growled as I slipped my hand from his firm grip.

"Do you mind if I come in?"

I nodded and stepped aside. He wiped his feet on the welcome mat and crossed the threshold, holding his hand out to the dog.

"Careful," I warned. "She's not fond of strangers, and she hates men. Easy, Scarlett." I waited for the Doberman to bare her teeth. Instead, she sniffed his ankles and nuzzled against him, wagging her tail.

"Nice place," he said, moving toward my combination library and sitting area. Scarlett followed him.

"Mind if we sit? Mike wanted me to go over some stuff with you before tomorrow." He took off his jacket, sat on the love seat, and put a thick folder on the coffee table. I took a seat across from him. Scarlett, the little traitor, pranced over to him and plopped down at his feet.

"Mr. McElroy, I appreciate your taking the time to stop by, and I know you must have more important places to be. I can go over this material on my own. I love Mike, but he is very protective and doesn't understand that I'm used to traveling alone." I sounded a little snippy, but I was being bulldozed by two alpha males. My guest didn't appear offended or impressed by my attitude.

"Mike said you'd say something like that. But it's not so much about the traveling as it is about the type of people you'll be dealing with when you get there."

"I can assure you, I'm perfectly capable of handling Ben Wilcott. And Mike's Army buddy can help me with the coroner or police or whatever."

"Mike's friend is the one who suggested you might need more help." He opened the folder and placed several eight by ten pictures on the table.

In the first, Stella was laughing up at the same dark-haired man from Alisha's album. She stood with her hair tossed over one shoulder, the way she did when she was in the process of captivating a potential suitor. On the other side, her husband stared intently over her head at the same man. The next featured only the two men, each with his eyes locked on the other. The final shot had been taken from a distance. Ben and three men whose faces were out of focus stood on his fancy speed boat.

"I don't get it. What do these pictures have to do with me?"

"Your sister's husband is involved with some pretty shady characters." He pointed to the dark-haired man. "That's Adelmo Balsuto."

I didn't see any reason to tell him I already knew who he was.

"He's one of the wealthiest men in Ecuador. His family were originally cacao farmers. When the oil boom hit in the late sixties, they got richer. They put most of their money in Miami, so when Ecuadorian banks crashed, the Balsutos came out better than most of their countrymen. The rumor is Adelmo has expanded the family business to include exportation of cocaine." He returned the photographs to his envelope.

"I still don't see what any of that has to do with me getting Ben to let me bring Stella home."

"It may not," he admitted. "But word is your brother-in-law crossed Balsuto. It's possible your sister's death had something to do with it. If that's the case, Wilcott's not going to want any more attention from the authorities."

"But Ben's the one who wanted me to come to Ecuador."

"That's why Mike wants me to go with you."

"Mike wants what?" I jumped to my feet, causing Scarlett to scramble to hers and stand between me and our visitor. "I'm absolutely not taking a babysitter with me." My mother's willingness to send me into harm's way made sense. She never planned for me to go on my own. This insight should have made me feel better, but it didn't.

"Easy, now," McElroy said, looking up at me. "I know you don't need a babysitter. I'm just—"

"I don't care what you are. Just leave the contact information and take this other stuff with you when you go." I motioned toward the envelope with the pictures.

"Miss Burnette, it's important you understand why I have to go with you."

"Okay, but make it quick. I'm not done packing." I perched on the edge of the chair.

"Mike wants me to go with you because he thinks it's dangerous. But your mother had another request, one she made when Mike left the room, one she made me promise not to tell anyone. But you need to know." He leaned forward. "Grace, your mother hired me to kill Ben Wilcott."

CHAPTER 12

My mother's hitman didn't stay long enough for me to recover from the shock of his announcement. He put on his coat and walked out the door, without giving me the chance to ask for more details.

We watched him drive away. Then Scarlett turned, gave me a reproachful gaze, and ambled to the back of the house.

I stayed at the window, wondering who the hell Justin McElroy was. He didn't send out murderer vibes, but had I ever met a killer? And if he was planning to kill my ex, did I care? If Ben had something to do with Stella's death, he deserved to pay for it. He should be arrested and extradited to the US where his money wouldn't save him from justice. From what I discovered about the Ecuadorian government, I doubted they would be too cooperative. He had always been good at reading people and was smart enough to connect with authorities who weren't averse to accepting bribes.

While I didn't find the concept of murdering Ben disturbing, my mother's role in the transaction concerned me. I wasn't worried about her getting caught. As a member of the Marines Special Forces, Mike's friend would be more than competent. He would know how to execute a man and get away with it.

What I couldn't wrap my head around was the idea my mother had hired him to commit murder. If it had been my grandmother, I wouldn't have been surprised. Except she wouldn't have hired it out. Stella's betrayal had been difficult for her, but she reconciled her conflicting loyalties by blaming everything on Ben. She would have killed him herself.

Still, I couldn't picture Mom committing or assisting in an act of real violence. Not that she wasn't tough. She divorced before it was commonplace. With emotional help from Gran, she supported two daughters on her own. As a nurse on a psychiatric ward, she had once tackled and held down a two-hundred-pound man who convinced himself he could fly and was climbing out the window to prove it. But hiring someone to kill Ben was beyond her.

I wanted nothing more than to talk to Stella. My frustration led me to recall a conversation we had a few months before I popped in on her in the shower with my fiancé.

She asked me if I remembered the last time our uncle had been at our house. At first, I hadn't, so she prompted me.

"Aunt Rita rushed in crazy-eyed and banged up with Lesroy in her arms. Roy followed them in that beat-up old truck of his."

How had I forgotten that night? Stella and I had just come inside with a jar full of fireflies. We had our usual argument: I wanted to let them go right away; she wanted to keep them to light up our room. I agreed to wait a little while before releasing them. We were on our way to place them on the dresser when the commotion started.

A car door slammed, and our aunt burst in, screaming bloody murder. Seconds later, Roy's truck crashed into the curb, and he dashed in behind them. Gran, in her old flannel nightgown, stood in front of Rita and Lesroy while our mother stopped him.

I cowered in her shadow and shivered at how easy it would be for him to brush her aside like a cobweb. Only he didn't even try. Instead, he backed out, arms held out in surrender. He tripped on the threshold, and Mom shoved him the rest of the way. I had forgotten how she faced down a man almost twice her size until Stella reminded me. It hadn't been her commanding presence. It had been Grandpa's shotgun, pointed at my uncle's chest.

After he stormed off, we put Lesroy on the sofa. His eye was swollen shut, and he wasn't moving. Gran sent us to her room, and I heard her calling an ambulance. Rita and Mom rode with our cousin to the hospital.

"And Gran stayed home," Stella added. "But she didn't come to bed. It was just you and me. I was crying, and you held me and kept saying everything would be fine. Then the storm came."

If I could forget a night like that, how many other memories were bobbing below the surface of my subconscious? And why were they so elusive? I had no immediate answer, but I realized one very important thing: there was more to my mother than I'd thought. It no longer seemed impossible she would do whatever it took to avenge my sister's death.

Several times I stopped packing and threw everything on the bed. If I stayed put, maybe McElroy wouldn't bother going. But I didn't believe that.

About three o'clock, I gave up on sleep. I dressed and logged onto Google, where I searched for *Justin McElroy, Atlanta Special Forces Marines*. There were lots of McElroys on Facebook and Linked In, but none were mine. I landed on an obituary for Army Major Joseph Allen McElroy from Lawrenceville, Georgia. Surviving family members included his son, Captain Justin McElroy, Marine Corps, Special Operations.

I ran another search on Special Operations and discovered the training program was among the toughest in the Corps. Prospective Special Ops candidates learned about everything from foreign weapons to emergency medical assistance and internal defense. I understood why Mike thought I'd be safer traveling with McElroy. But what would he think if he knew my mother had arranged her own special ops?

I had to establish rules about how the trip would go. First, all discussions with Mike's friend and the authorities would include me. Second, I would be the one dealing with Ben. And third—or should this have been the first—there would be no killing.

When I shut down my laptop, the dog leaped off the sofa.

"What's with you and this Justin McElroy character, Miss Scarlett?" At the sound of her name, she came to attention. "Are you attracted to dangerous men? Or do you sense something I don't?" She continued to stare at me. "Whatever. Let's get you walked and fed, so you'll be ready for Lesroy."

. . . . .

McElroy pulled into my drive at exactly 5:00 a.m. Scarlett barked once, and I promised to be back before Christmas. She yawned and went back to sleep.

I trudged out the door, dragging my bags behind me. He bounded up the steps and made a move to take my luggage.

"Thank you, Mr. McElroy, but I've got it."

"Okay, *Miss* Burnette." He grinned and walked toward the SUV. The wheels on my suitcase snagged on the stone walkway. He maintained a neutral expression as I yanked it free, then opened the back of the vehicle and waited as I struggled to sling it in. After two unsuccessful attempts, he took it from me, and, with one hand, tossed it by his duffel.

The average December temperatures in Montañita were in the high seventies, so I packed light enough to get everything into one carry-on with the overflow stuffed into my computer case. Next to his, however, my luggage looked excessive.

He held the car door open for me. I wanted to shut it and reopen it on my own to emphasize my independence. Instead, I opted for a dignified ascent. Unfortunately, my jeans were too tight, and I was too short to carry it off. I ended up using the overhead hand grip to hoist myself, more forcefully than I intended, onto the seat. The straps of my passport holder got tangled with the buttons of my coat. While I tried to extricate myself, my unwanted traveling companion waited. I broke free and snapped myself in.

We drove in silence for several minutes while I rehearsed my three-point speech about not murdering Ben.

"I'm not sure what Mom and Mike told you about this trip, but all I want to do is find out what happened to my sister and..." My throat constricted, and I had to swallow hard before continuing. "And bring her body home."

"Of course." He kept his eyes on the road.

"And about that other, uh, thing, the one my mother wanted you to do."

"You mean the agreement about how to handle the situation if we find out your sister's death wasn't an accident?"

"I just want you to understand I can't be part of anything like, well, like that."

He glanced at me with a raised eyebrow. "What is *that*, Miss Burnette?"

"You know perfectly well I'm talking about what you discussed with my mother."

"We talked about a lot of different issues, including you. You need to narrow it down." In profile, Justin McElroy's full lips contrasted with his chiseled jaw.

"You talked about me?" I felt myself flushing. "Wait, never mind. What I'm trying to say is I don't want you to…" I lowered my voice. "I don't want you to kill Ben. I mean, that is absolutely unacceptable."

"Unacceptable," he echoed. "Sorry, but I'm not at liberty to discuss this issue with you, Miss Burnette. That arrangement is between me and your mother. I shouldn't have mentioned it. Client confidentiality and all. I can assure you, however, that I won't put you in any compromising position. Any more concerns?"

"I'm serious, Mr. McElroy. Or should I say Captain McElroy?"

"Checking me out, Grace? I mean Miss Burnette." He flashed ivory teeth at me.

"Just doing my homework. Anyway, I want to be sure you understand that if I think you're about to do something violent, I'll do whatever it takes to stop you."

"Thanks for the warning," he said as he pulled into international parking. "How about we finish outlining your terms after we get through security?"

We took the shuttle and were at our gate forty-five minutes before our 7:00 am boarding. Mike insisted on buying my ticket and had sprung for first class, not my usual method of traveling. An hour layover in Miami meant it would be at least eight hours before we reached our destination; first class definitely made for an easier trip.

There had been little opportunity to continue the conversation with my companion in the shuttle or the waiting area, neither of which were the best places to discuss delicate subjects. Settled in the plush leather seat beside him before take-off didn't seem to be a good place to bring up an alternate course of action to assassination either. When it was safe to turn on my laptop, I continued reading about Montañita.

I learned the trendy spot was more than a destination for back-packing surfer types. Besides a high gringo population, people from all over South America called it home. Unlike the rest of the country where the authorities enforced rigid drug laws, the beach town was more relaxed. Filled with liberal tourists and active nightlife, it was the perfect place for Ben and Stella.

Before I read further, the pilot announced we were approaching Miami. I made it a point not to look at my seatmate during the short flight, but it was impossible to ignore him while attempting to get my carry-on from the overhead without injuring fellow passengers.

He reached past me, lifted the suitcase over my head, and dropped it in front of me. I struggled with balancing my computer case on the larger bag but got them both down the aisle by myself.

"We have time to grab some coffee; I hate that crap they serve on the plane." McElroy spoke in the friendly way you would to someone you were vacationing with rather than the way you'd talk to the person you were going with on what promised to be the worst trip of a lifetime.

"I'm good, thank you." I walked past him and took a seat near the gate. While waiting, I answered a few business emails and checked a text message from Lesroy.

"I hear Mike sent a Marine hunk to protect you. Bet you love that. LOL. Not a bad idea, though. Miss Scarlet hasn't ripped out my throat yet, but I plan to sleep with one eye open. Love you."

I included a few hearts and smiley faces as a reply.

"Boyfriend?" McElroy eased into the seat beside me.

I shook my head. "Cousin." If I knew my mother, she would have alerted my companion I didn't have a boyfriend. But if murder was her priority, stressing my availability might have slipped her mind.

He held out a Starbuck's cup. "I wasn't sure what you like, but the barista assured me everybody loves a latte macchiato, whatever the hell that is."

Seeing no reason to let the sugary beverage go to waste, I took it and thanked him. He smiled, sipped his coffee, and picked up a newspaper.

I finished my drink the same time first class began boarding. Despite the jolt from my latte, I was feeling the results of a sleepless night and planned on napping during the rest of the flight. I had just settled into a comfortable position when McElroy handed me a package.

"Your mother wanted you to have these. My instructions were to give them to you before we landed. They're from your sister."

Inside were three stacks bound with rubber bands, all three tied together with twine. On top, there was one envelope labeled "Read this first" scrawled in my mother's familiar handwriting. I hesitated before opening it.

Grace, before you get mad, I understand why you don't want to talk to your sister. What she did was terrible, maybe unforgivable. But she is your sister, and family is everything. Stella wanted to explain herself, but she knew you wouldn't want to hear it. So, she sent these to me. She made me promise not to read them, to hold on to them until I thought you were ready. It was hard, but I kept my promise, Grace. But now, ready or not, you can't wait any longer. Love you.

Mom grouped and labeled the letters chronologically. Three stacks, one for each year I refused to talk to Stella.

Beside me, McElroy appeared engrossed in his paper. My hands were shaking as I opened letter number one.

Dear Grace,
I feel funny writing a letter most likely no one will ever read. I mean, I hope you read it someday, but I understand if you don't. So, I'll pretend "Dear Grace" is "Dear Diary." That way I can tell you secrets I would never tell an

actual person. Remember when you said that to me, Grace? When you gave me my first diary? I bet you don't, but I do.

It was my eighth birthday. Mom gave me a Madame Alexander doll with red hair and freckles. I loved that doll, but the diary was my favorite gift. It was light blue covered in tiny hummingbirds and had a little lock and key. You said I should use it to record my private thoughts and should keep it hidden from Mom. And that's what I did.

I wrote about how I wanted to grow up to be just like you, Grace. Smart, beautiful, funny, and kind. And every time I fell short of being like you, I confessed it in my diary. Like the time I took ten dollars from Gran's wallet and spent it on cheap perfume I could never stand to wear. Or the time I stole the poem you wrote about the ocean and used it to win first prize in the fifth-grade writing contest. I couldn't tell anybody I'd won. I pretended I was sick the day they gave out the writing awards. When my teacher gave me the certificate later, I buried it in the backyard.

Even if you'd found out about the poem, though, you would have thought it was some kind of mistake. Because to you, I was the perfect little sister, the one Mom and Gran told me you prayed for over and over. When I looked at you, Grace, it was like you were this magic mirror. No matter how ugly or flawed I was, in your eyes I was Stella Star. Until you met Ben. Then I disappeared.

It sounds like I'm blaming you for what happened, but I'm not. You kept on being you — smart, beautiful, funny and kind. And it wasn't about jealousy, me wanting what you had. It's just you looked at Ben the way you used to look at me. It was as if his face blocked my image from that magic mirror, and I had to see the real me. I'd be lying if I said it wasn't exhilarating to give up trying to be the Stella you thought I was. I did whatever made me feel good, took whatever I wanted. But like that cheap perfume, once I got what I wanted, the smell of it sickened me.

I wish I could take it all back and be the girl in the magic mirror.
Stella

I folded letter number one and put it in its envelope. I couldn't tell if it was Stella being Stella or if my sister had changed. Either way, it wasn't just my hands that were shaking now. My entire body convulsed with the weight of my sorrow. I hadn't cried when she and

Ben eloped because I still had her. And, despite my denials, I held onto the hope that someday she would come home, that we'd be sisters again.

McElroy must have felt me trembling. He set his paper aside and turned toward me. "Are you okay?"

I heard a high-pitched wail somewhere in the distance, getting closer and closer. It was several long seconds before I realized the keening sound came from me. He shoved up the armrest separating us, slipped one arm around my waist, and pulled me to his chest. I dissolved into wracking sobs.

"Can I get her something?" I heard the anxious voice of the flight attendant but didn't look up.

"Some water, please." He patted me on the back. "Just let it out; you'll feel better."

I don't know how long my full-fledged crying jag engulfed me, but the pain from loss of hope subsided, and I gasped for air. I saw the worried face of the young attendant. A serious-looking man in a light blue shirt and wrinkled khaki slacks stood beside her. Where the crew member regarded me with a look of cautious compassion, he gazed at me as if he thought I might set off an explosive device after my recovery from a raging attack of hysteria.

The attendant handed me a bottle of water. When I tried to thank her, I began crying again, quieter this time, until the hiccups started. McElroy opened it and helped me take a sip. He reached into his pocket and produced a handkerchief.

"Blow," he commanded. I did.

"Is there anything else you need?" the flight attendant asked.

"It's Brenda, right?" He turned on the charm. "I think we could both use something a little stronger than water. I'll have a Scotch rocks, and for the lady here." He paused and looked at me.

"Vodka tonic with lemon, please." I hadn't realized how much I wanted a drink.

The man in the khaki pants was still standing by our seats. "Do you have yourself under control, Little Lady?" he asked.

Something about his tone sent a shot of white-hot fury up my back. "I appreciate your concern," I began. "And I do believe this little lady is just about all settled down. Of course, if I start thinking about my dead sister and how the man I used to think I was in love murdered her and how my mother is home losing her mind about it, it's possible, just possible, mind you, that this little lady might lose her shit again."

Mr. Khaki Pants took a few steps back.

"No danger here, Air Marshall." McElroy said. "It is Air Marshall, isn't it, sir?"

"Just a concerned passenger." He sidled away.

"Was he really an Air Marshall?" I asked.

"Can't be sure, but I'd take odds on it." He smiled. "So, is this little lady all settled down?"

"I'm sorry about that. It hit me so fast and so hard."

"You don't have to be sorry, Grace. Oops, I mean Miss Burnette."

"Grace is fine. Miss Burnette is a little formal for someone who just got snot all over your shirt."

"No big deal. I have other shirts."

Brenda returned with our order, and he eased back in his seat.

"My dad passed a few years ago," he said. "It's not the same as a sister, but I understand how sudden the reality crashes down on you. And you haven't had time to grieve. Why don't you get some rest?"

"Excuse me." A sparrow-like woman with short blonde hair leaned across the aisle. Fine lines dusted her skin, but her eyes were a clear, bright blue. I judged she was in her early sixties at the most, but her outfit—a pink silk sweater set and a long strand of creamy, white pearls—suggested she came from an even earlier generation when people dressed up, rather than down, for air travel. "I couldn't help overhearing, dear. I know a little about losing loved ones."

I braced myself. After Gran died, people came to me and shared stories of death and destruction. I suspected they thought it was somehow a comfort. But it was more an initiation into a club you never wanted to join. And they wanted to teach you the secret handshake.

Instead of over-sharing, however, she motioned to Justin. "This will help."

He held out his hand, and she dropped three small, pale-yellow tablets into his palm.

"It's Xanax, dear. I always keep some handy for when I fly. Sometimes, I take them when I'm not flying."

Before I could thank her, she returned to her magazine.

He gave me the pills, and I stuck them in with my vitamins and Ambien. For now, the vodka was doing the trick, but I might need them later.

When I woke, the pilot was announcing our approach to Guayaquil.

"You were out. I almost held a mirror up to you a few times to check for signs of life. Then you started snoring, and I knew you were good."

I ran my fingers through my hair and wiped the sleep from my eyes. Justin grinned and tapped the corner of his mouth. I touched my own lips and discovered what I hoped was only a small amount of drool.

"I must look like hell," I said and excused myself to go to the restroom.

In the harsh lightning, I saw the damage was worse than I expected, but I attempted a quick clean up, dabbing at smudged mascara, applying lipstick, and brushing out tangles. The result was less than satisfactory, but it wasn't as if I were going to a party. It was more as if I was preparing for a wake.

CHAPTER 13

The pilot announced our descent to Guayaquil and informed us it was the largest city in Ecuador. From the air we could see an array of brilliant greens and blues. He explained that the Guayas River ribboned through the dense foliage. The pearl of Ecuadorian commerce, it often changed course twice a day. From what I had read about the area and its manic history, this fickle body of water was the perfect symbol for the country Ben considered safe. Not so much for Stella, though.

From the window I saw an array of colorful rooftops stacked into the hillside. At first, the city grid was carelessly defined. Streets started and stopped with no apparent plan. Buildings were scattered like children's blocks. The nearer we got to the airport, the more order was restored. Our landing was a moderate white-knuckler for me, as we bumped and bounced to a halt. Justin continued reading his magazine until the plane came to a full stop.

I was stiff and sluggish waiting in the customs line. A website I visited warned of dishonest agents rifling through bags to steal loose valuables, but I saw no evidence of anything suspicious. The interior was modern with an organized and efficient system in place. The personnel were polite and friendly. Several mounted plaques proclaimed Guayaquil's airport the best in South America.

Once they checked our passports, we headed for ground transportation, where Mike's friend waited to drive us to the hotel. Before I could ask Justin how we would recognize him, a bronzed man in an orange and green shirt covered with parrots, knee-length denim shorts, and an Atlanta Braves cap approached.

"Grace Burnette," he said. "Mike sent me your picture." He held up his cellphone with a photo of my mother and me at her last birthday party on the screen. "I'm Harry, Harry Davenport. Welcome to Guayaquil." He tipped his hat, revealing short salt and pepper hair. His smile unleashed multiple creases around his eyes and mouth. "And you must be Justin McElroy. I've heard good things about you." The men shook hands.

"Here, let me take that." He picked up my bags, and I didn't protest. Almost ten hours of traveling weakens a woman's need to assert her independence.

While my mother's boyfriend had the build of a former college football player, tall with wide muscular shoulders and long legs, Harry Davenport was more of a wrestler. I guessed him to be around five-nine with thick arms and thighs. Like Mike, his stance suggested he'd been in the military.

Justin looked our escort up and down before following him to the parking area. He put his hand on the small of my back in either an unexpected gesture of affection or a proprietary statement. We passed a winding pond filled with fat goldfish and surrounded by palm trees, the only exotic touch in an otherwise typical airport setting. A steady drizzle emphasized rather than relieved the heat. Harry set our bags on the curb and instructed us to wait while he brought the car.

Minutes later he appeared in a black Ford Bronco. He hopped from the driver's seat and escorted me to the passenger side. Justin loaded our luggage and sat behind me.

"Mike's got you booked at the Wyndham," Harry explained as he pulled out of the lot. "You'll have an incredible view of the river from the Malecon, the city's Riverwalk."

The farther we drove from the airport, the less modern the city became. Small dwellings with roofs and doors painted in tropical colors were sprinkled in next to newer multi-storied buildings. Little chapels shaped like ice cream sundaes interrupted commercial areas with an occasional full-fledged cathedral asserting itself in the middle of the block.

He continued his narrative. "Guayaquil doesn't have much in the line of tourist attractions. And the local bigwigs are fighting the reputation of being Ecuador's most dangerous city. They beefed up security at the Riverwalk and around your hotel, but I'd still be careful. And avoid those yellow taxis. They aren't always the real deal. Passengers get kidnapped, robbed and beaten and worse."

I shivered at the duality of the place.

"Here we are," he announced as he turned into the Wyndham lot, situated across from tenement dwellings painted in vivid oranges, reds, blues, and yellows. As we neared the boxy units, they became less vibrant. Peeled paint and cracked foundations, so close to the casual elegance of our building, were disorienting. A lighthouse with a swirled blue tower, topped by a golden dome, overlooked the apartments. Next to it, the Ecuadorian flag waved high above the cluttered chaos of the city. The hotel curved outward toward the river, away from the hillside homes. The arrangement was a subtle reminder that proximity means little in a world of haves and have-nots.

Harry parked in the check-in area and we walked into the lobby. Soft gray carpeting and furniture were surrounded by multi-paned windows, which offered spectacular views of the river, now sheeted in mist. A tree decorated in gold and silver with rows of twinkling lights sat beside a Nativity scene, reminding me Christmas was less than three weeks away. Only a week and a day since someone had murdered Stella, but it seemed a lifetime ago.

Before, whenever anyone asked if I had any siblings, I would shake my head and smile. "No brothers, but I have this incredible sister." Now, what would I say? The simple answer "no" wasn't right. Wouldn't that negate Stella's existence and somehow lessen my own? But "yes" didn't work either. I'd entered the ambiguous world of loss.

I had become the main character in a fairy tale gone horribly wrong. Once upon a time, I had a sister, but an evil force ripped her from me.

I turned my back to the glittering tree and the Virgin Mary's luminous face.

"Earth to Grace. You were a million miles away," Justin said. "Why don't you check out your room and freshen up. We can meet in the bar in an hour, get some dinner, and talk about what to do tomorrow."

Images of steaming water and luxurious soap and shampoo were so enticing I barely noticed the conspiratorial looks exchanged between the two men. I suspected Mike had talked to them and they were making plans without me. It made sense for them to be in charge but giving up power gave me a helpless feeling.

When Ben and I were together, I'd given him permission to make important decisions for me. After he left, it took a long time for me to regain confidence in my judgment, to retake control. I never wanted to lose it again.

An attentive young man in a loose-fitting cotton shirt bearing the Wyndham emblem helped me with my bags. I worried on the way up about how much to tip him. To single-handedly dispel the myth that women are bad tippers, I give more than necessary. Lesroy said it's because I'm an insecure feminist. My ex cautioned against the habit, especially if I was staying more than a day or so since it set an unrealistic tone.

I pulled a ten-dollar bill from my bag and watched the boy's smile grow wider. Screw you, Ben.

My room was bright and clean. The blue carpet matched the trim of the thick white comforter on a king-size bed covered with six enormous pillows. A large flat-screen TV was mounted above the dark wooden dresser. The bath had a shower tub and lots of expensive-looking lotions and shampoos. In the next twenty minutes, I used them all.

I slipped on a pair of black jeans and a long-sleeved white T-shirt. Thanks to Lesroy's insistence, my layered haircut was both stylish and easy to manage. Requiring a minimum of fluffing and drying, it framed my face with strands of caramel highlights my stylist promised would emphasize my high cheekbones and make my silver-gray eyes pop. After a little mascara, I'm not sure if pop was the right word, but I looked better than when we'd landed. And I accomplished it all in less than forty-five minutes.

With time to spare, I considered Stella's letters, lying on the dresser. After my mid-air breakdown, I knew to be more cautious about how to approach them.

I distanced myself from the pain by telling myself *These aren't from your dead sister. No. They're clues to a mystery you have to solve. No reason to get emotional.*

I opened the envelope marked "Letter two." She wrote it in May, a few months after they left the States.

Dear Grace,

It's early morning — no, not Stella-early like you and mom used to say — but early early, just after sunrise. I see a lot of sunrises from my bedroom window. Today I wanted to watch it from the balcony, but I didn't want to wake Ben. Now that he doesn't work every day, he hates mornings. Should I not mention him? It's hard not to because so far, I haven't made any new friends, and he's the only one around to talk to, except for Eva, our housekeeper, but I don't think she likes me. And I keep thinking by the time you read this, he'll only be a bad memory for you. I guess that means I will be, too.

Anyway. What I meant to say is that when I woke up and saw the ocean, I wanted to take a picture and send it to you because I know how much you love the beach. But you wouldn't look at it, so I stayed in bed. I thought about the nights we stayed awake talking in our room at Gran's. Mom yelled at us to get quiet, but Gran never raised her voice. She came in and whispered it was time to go to sleep so something good could happen in the morning. I always tried to wake up before you, so I'd be sure to beat you to whatever good thing was waiting. That's what I did today. I didn't stand outside on the balcony and breathe in the sunrise and let the salty air wash over me, I lay waiting for that something good to happen.

Still waiting.

I folded the letter into its envelope and placed it back in the packet. I pictured Stella miserable and alone and dismissed our grandmother's optimism.

CHAPTER 14

Justin and Harry were at a table near the entrance to the bar, drinks in front of them. Harry stood, pulled out a chair for me, and said, "You look livelier."

Justin signaled the server. When I asked her about the beer selection, she recommended a pale ale brewed in Montañita. It was the country's first and only beachside brewery, and they had just started shipping to Guayaquil.

"I wouldn't have taken you for a beer drinker," Justin said as our server delivered my order and poured it into a cold mug.

"There's a lot you don't know about me." I guessed there wasn't that much since Mom had most likely provided a full bio on Grace Burnette.

"I'm sure there is," Justin replied and lifted his drink. "Here's to finding out more."

"Sounds good to me," Harry chimed in and we clinked our glasses.

The golden ale went down easily, malty with a fruity aftertaste. I stared into my drink as the bubbles drifted upward. Ben had been a pseudo-wine-connoisseur, throwing around terms like rustic, oaky, and vegetal. He'd insist I try this or that Merlot or Pinot when all I wanted was a Bud Light.

"Harry and I've been discussing the best way to approach the situation. Why don't you fill her in?"

Harry finished chewing a pretzel and washed it down with a sip of his drink. "Most people get their ideas about autopsies and criminal investigations from TV and movies. The truth is even in the States, it's not an exact science."

He caught the eye of our server. "In Ecuador it's even less so."

I fought the bile rising in the back of my throat, painfully aware of where this was going. This time, I ordered a vodka tonic.

"Are you saying they refused to do an autopsy on Stella?"

"It's more complicated than that, Grace," Harry continued. "A few years ago, Guayaquil's police force—hell, the entire country—came under scrutiny because of the high murder rate. It was only slightly higher than the US's, but it wasn't doing the tourist industry any good. Guayaquil doesn't offer much in that department anyway. But it is the jumping off point for the Galapagos, and the bigwigs were afraid people would hesitate to come to one of the most violent cities in a violent country."

My drink came, and I downed about a third of it. Justin pushed the bowl of pretzels toward me, but I ignored them.

"The government pledged to lower the murder rate, and, according to their data, it's working. They cleaned up local police departments—better training, more funding. The emphasis was on getting people to work with the authorities to prevent murders. That meant the pressure was on the cops to perform. One way to cut down on the killings is to under report them. Nobody's been keeping track of accidental deaths."

"Are you saying they ruled Stella's death an accident?"

"That's right, accidental drowning."

"But I thought Mike said something about her body being..." I couldn't put the description of a broken Stella into words.

Justin spoke. "They explained her condition as trauma from the wreckage of the boat. They aren't planning to investigate."

"We could find a doctor in the states and ask for a second opinion, right?" That Ben might get away with staging my sister's death as an accident filled me with anger strong enough to pull me from despair.

"We'll try, Grace," Harry said. "But don't get your hopes too high. The only one who can request anything regarding the case is Ben. I set up a meeting with a friend at the consulate's office to see if he'll help us."

I stood, rushed toward the restroom, and made it just in time to throw up into a gold inlaid toilet. I sank to my knees for another round of vomiting followed by dry heaves that wracked through my body. When I emptied the contents of my stomach, I remembered I hadn't eaten anything since lunch on the plane, at least eight hours ago. After what I hoped was my last bout of heaving, I realized someone was holding my hair back.

"All done?" Justin asked.

I struggled to my feet, avoiding eye contact with the man who had just seen me hugging a toilet. Sure, it was a sleek marble toilet, but it was still a toilet, and I'd been clinging to it with my head only inches from the water. He guided me to the seashell-shaped sink complete with elaborate gold-plated faucet. For an awful second, I feared I would throw up again, this time all over the sparkling fixtures, but the feeling passed. He handed me a wad of wet paper towels, and I held it against my throat.

Before I could thank him, the restroom door flew open and three giggling women burst in. They were dressed for clubbing—sheer peek-a-boo blouses, visible bras in shades of black and red, short tube skirts, and frighteningly high heels.

"Sorry, ladies." Justin blushed and turned to me. "If you're okay, I'll wait for you outside." He was out the door before I could reply.

The women assumed positions at the mirror, applying and adjusting make-up while I made sure my face and dress were clean before rejoining the men at our table.

"Are you all right, Grace?" Harry asked.

I was still shaky, but it was the genuine sincerity of his tone that almost brought me to tears. Dealing with people locked in grief is tricky. If you ignore the pain, it's as if you don't care. But if you acknowledge it, you risk unleashing the beast. I breathed in deeply, then said the worst had passed.

Justin suggested I needed to eat and rest. I questioned the wisdom of eating but agreed to order something later. He insisted on escorting me to my room before he and Harry went to dinner.

My stomach lurched with the sudden motion of the elevator, and I stumbled as dizziness overcame me. He wrapped his arm around my waist as we walked down the hallway. After prying the key from my shaking hands, he opened the door. Once inside, he led me to the bed and eased me onto the mound of pillows. While I tried to get the room to stop spinning, he brought a cool, wet cloth and put it on my forehead. Then he ordered toast and ginger ale.

The same happy bellboy who carried my bags delivered the food. I noticed what I took as a look of disappointment when Justin tipped him. Even in my sorry state, a twinge of triumph at striking a blow in defense of female tippers lightened my mood.

I assured him I felt better and promised to eat, but he sat on the end of the bed and refused to leave until I finished my toast. Then we made plans to meet downstairs for breakfast at eight when Harry would take us to talk with his friend.

"Remember, Grace," he cautioned on his way out. "If Ben fights it, there may be nothing we can do."

CHAPTER 15

When my alarm sounded, I had no idea where I was. Sunk deep into the thick bedding, a sudden attack of claustrophobia came over me. I threw off the comforter, gasping for air. Thanks to thick shades, the room was still dark. Lying there, I was momentarily disconnected from reality. I wanted to remain like that, unaware of where I was and why I was here. But my emptiness and sorrow returned along with the realization my sister was dead.

I dragged myself to the shower and stood under the spray, waiting for the cold water to turn warm. The exotic gel held no interest for me, and I skipped the luxury shampoo. I finger-combed my damp hair, applied a little make-up, and slipped on jeans, a short-sleeved pink sweater, and beige sneakers.

Even though I made it to the restaurant ten minutes before eight, both Harry and Justin were already seated at a table complete with a pitcher of pale rose-colored juice.

Harry wore what I would come to think of as his uniform: another bright, floral shirt with a clean pair of jean shorts. Justin was dressed in a light blue polo and khaki pants. They stood when I approached.

"You look like you had a good night's rest." Harry winked at me and turned to Justin. "Doesn't she look great?"

"Yes, she does." He smiled.

A vaguely familiar sensation of warmth started somewhere low in my stomach and traveled upward until I could feel the flush spread from my chest to my neck to my cheeks.

"I bet you're starving," Harry said. "They've got excellent food here. Empanadas, humitas, belon de verde."

"I don't know about Grace," Justin said. "But I trust you to order for us."

I hadn't expected to be hungry, but I was. I assured Harry I trusted him. When our waiter Emilio arrived, he and Harry carried on a lively discussion in Spanish. Emilio nodded in approval and walked to the kitchen. We drank our juice and talked about the weather. The rain had stopped and shouldn't return until evening.

Emilio returned with an enormous tray of delicacies.

"Those are empanadas. And the little dumplings are belon de verde, made from fried plantains and stuffed with sausage. The cake-shaped ones are humitas, crunchy cornmeal mixed with onion, eggs, and cheese," Harry explained.

Harry waited while I selected an empanada. The contrasting flavor of cheese, onions, and sweet plantains was delicious. The three of us demolished most of the pastry tray, and Emilio appeared with a huge fruit platter loaded with familiar favorites: papayas, passion fruit, and kiwis. It also included exotic delights, like Ecuadorian blackberries, larger and tarter than the ones back home, and egg-shaped granadillas, small pinkish-orange fruit with a delicate flavor similar to strawberries.

By the time Emilio checked back in, only a few lonely berries remained. He and Harry had another brief exchange in Spanish before he nodded and disappeared.

"Most of the good Ecuadorian coffee gets exported, so the locals end up drinking instant," Harry explained. "Tastes like shit. Excuse my French. I wanted to make sure the hotel has Cubinato or Little Cuba, typical Ecuadorian irony."

The brew was dark and strong. They drank theirs straight, but I opted for almost as much milk as coffee and two teaspoons of sugar. Harry glanced at his watch, then requested the check.

"We're only about fifteen minutes from the Palace. With so many more people on the road, you never know how long it's going to take. And if there's an accident, forget about it. The cops are likely to leave the car, haul both drivers away to jail, and sort out blame later. It can be hours before they wrap up a simple fender-bender."

He insisted on picking up breakfast. Then we headed to the Bronco. Once we were buckled in and on the way, he explained how he'd met Luis Cordoza.

"I was consulting with a security company, and they sent me to work with the Ecuadorian government."

He turned onto a four-lane highway lined with palm trees.

"Luis was working with the government?" Justin asked.

"Hardly." He laughed. "He was an attorney representing one of the indigenous groups protesting mining development. Scrappy little fellow. The government reps were thugs, but he managed to score some major points for his clients. The president was impressed and pissed off at the same time. He set him up with an office in Guayquil's city hall, El Palacio Municipal. He thought if Luis was on the payroll, he could control him." Harry smiled. "But he's not the kind of guy other people control."

I could tell how much Harry liked Cordoza, but I was confused. "I don't quite understand how your friend can help us."

He swerved to avoid being hit by one of the city's big red buses. "Ecuador is a complicated country. There's a big divide between those at the top and bottom and not a lot of trust in the system. Reminds you of home, doesn't it? Anyway, communication among all the different factions can be tricky. We need him to guide us through the process."

He spent the next few minutes explaining that his friend would be able to cut through the red tape involved in our request for Stella's body. Cordoza would also know how to determine who had the most to gain if there was a cover-up in the investigation of my sister's death.

"But remember, Grace," Harry said. "Luis may not have all the answers."

Even if he did, I thought, what detail about how she died could bring her back?

No one spoke as we drove alongside the river for the next few miles. I watched the fishermen standing on small flat canoes the same way their families had done for centuries. Double-decker eco-touring boats, filled with the environmentally conscious, floated past. A sleek motorboat flitted in and out, leaving everyone else bobbing in its wake, much like Stella's death had left me.

Harry was right about the traffic. The fifteen-minute drive had already stretched to thirty.

Justin asked him what kind of fishing was good in Ecuador, and the two launched into an incomprehensible conversation about bait and optimal times and rods and God only knew what else.

Just about the time I was contemplating jumping from the slow-moving car and covering the remaining distance on foot, Harry pointed to an enormous statue of two men shaking hands.

"That's Hemiciclo de la Rotunda, Simón Bolívar and San Martin, great South American Liberators. That means we're almost there."

The monument towered in front of the river. A row of slender columns topped with flags was flanked on each side by sturdier ones. Together they formed a semi-circle around the gigantic figures.

"This is as good a place as any," Harry said, pulling into a small parking lot. Stepping out of the air-conditioned car felt like slamming into a hot, damp wall. Justin joined me, and two young boys approached. Their size made them appear younger from a distance, but as they got closer, I guessed the taller one to be around twelve or thirteen. The smaller one couldn't have been much more than nine or ten. Their coppery skin shimmered in the morning heat.

The older boy greeted Harry in Spanish, and they began what I assumed was a negotiation over parking fees.

Justin pointed to a stately alabaster building ahead of us. "That's the Municipal Palace."

Lovely Hellenic columns graced the front of the structure; an arched passage divided it into separate sections.

"It's something, isn't it?" Harry asked, after reaching a satisfactory agreement with the boys.

"It is incredible," I agreed.

The air cooled as we passed beneath a tunnel covered with an iron and glass dome. Crystals gleamed in the filtered sunlight, and shafts of light played through the thick-paned panels. I felt as if I were floating in an underground stream and stopped to regain my equilibrium.

We entered through the side. I read security getting into the building was tight, so I brought only my passport, a credit card, and a little cash tucked into my pants pockets. Two men in black and white uniforms stood inside. One of them checked my documents and commented to his partner. All I could make out was the word "American." I couldn't tell if he was smiling or sneering when he said it. When I told him I didn't have a bag, he gave me a skeptical look, then motioned me to the body-wanding area, where I breezed through without setting off a single alarm.

Except for the signs written in Spanish, the inside was much like local government buildings at home: the glare of fluorescent lights reflecting on shiny tile floors, the echo of heels down endless corridors. It seemed bureaucracy created an ambiance of its own, regardless of nationality. An attractive young woman greeted us from behind a desk in the middle of the entry. Harry explained we were a few minutes early for our appointment. She requested we wait in the reception area while she contacted Señor Cordoza.

Harry and I sat on a stiff-backed love seat while Justin paced. He stopped to glance at his watch once, then continued walking briskly back and forth. It was the first time I'd seen him looking anxious, and that feeling of hopelessness returned, stronger than before.

"Hey," Harry said, taking my hand and squeezing it. "It's going to be okay."

I was pretty sure we both knew it wouldn't be, but I smiled and nodded.

After about ten minutes, a gentleman in a pin-striped suit approached us. Like many of the Ecuadorian men I'd seen, Luis Cordoza was slightly built and only a few inches taller than me. His shiny black hair was combed neatly to the side. Wire-rimmed glasses sat high on the bridge of his nose and magnified his dark eyes, lending a serious expression to his slender square-jawed face.

Harry held out his hand, but Cordoza grabbed his arm and pulled him in for a man-hug. "It's been a long time."

Harry endured the close contact for a few seconds, before pulling away to introduce us.

"Always a pleasure to meet friends of Harry Davenport. I am sorry to have kept you waiting. Let's go somewhere we may talk privately."

We followed our host down a narrow hallway. He stopped in front of a door leading to a windowless office. Shelves lined with books left little room to breathe.

"Thank you so much for seeing us, Señor Cordoza," I said as I chose the seat closest to his desk. Harry and Justin took the remaining chairs.

"It is Luis, please." He had a gentle smile that eased my anxiety. "Harry has told me about your situation, and I would like to express my deepest sorrow for your loss. It is especially painful to lose someone so young."

My throat constricted and tears stung my eyes. But I held it together.

"I only received a copy of your sister's file a few minutes before you arrived. I ask for your patience while I look through it."

We watched as he read papers that reduced my sister's life to the circumstances of her death.

When he finished, his smile was gone. "It appears your sister's death was handled as an accident from the beginning. There is no mention of anything other than drowning as the cause. And the police always include photographs in the report. There are none here, only notes about the condition of the victim. The description of the body is troubling."

"The description of the body," I whispered.

Luis stopped and cleared his throat. "Please, forgive my insensitivity." He looked at me before continuing. "Considering the fact that there could have been additional causes for your sister's death, it is unusual there was no request for further investigation. In most cases, that request comes from the closest family member."

The room went quiet, so quiet I could hear the big, round clock over Luis's desk ticking away the seconds. We all knew Ben would have been considered the closest family member. I wanted to set the record straight. To tell Luis and the Ecuadorian authorities that I was the closest. I had known her longer, loved her better. But if I'd really loved her better, she might still be alive.

Justin broke the silence. "Is there any way Grace could make that request as the surviving sister? Ask that they take another look at the, um, at the, uh, case. We have letters showing how close the two of them were. There might even be something incriminating in them about Stella's husband."

He frowned. "Might be? You don't know what is in them?"

"We haven't read all of them yet," I said. "But if we could have a little more time, please."

He shook his head and closed the file. "I am so sorry, Señorita Burnette. Policy prohibits the release of the contents of the official folder, but I am going to make an exception for you."

He pressed a button and asked his secretary to copy the files.

"Unfortunately, there is nothing else I can do. You see, it is too late for further consideration. According to the wishes of her husband, your sister's body was cremated two days ago."

CHAPTER 16

I don't remember leaving the Palace or the ride back to the hotel. A darkness engulfed me, and it wasn't until we were parked at the Wyndham that I broke through it.

"So, I guess that's it. He wins," I said to no one in particular. And then I remembered my mother had accounted for the possibility the system might not deliver justice for Stella. She found her own brand of insurance policy guaranteeing Ben wouldn't get away with murder. And for a long, black moment, I was glad she had.

"I know it looks like he's guilty," Justin responded. "And he probably is to blame. But it's possible he might not have been the one who killed your sister."

I thought of the photos he had spread across my coffee table and the picture of Stella at her party next to the dark-haired man with the intense eyes. "You mean Adelmo Balsuto?" I asked.

He nodded. "If Ben somehow crossed him, it stands to reason a revenge motive is a good possibility. Or maybe Stella's death was a warning."

"He has a point. Balsuto is dangerous," Harry added.

"I guess there's only one thing to do. I have to go straight to Ben and ask what happened to Stella."

"Hold on, Grace." Justin leaned forward in his seat. "That might not be such a great idea. If he killed your sister, we can't be sure he won't hurt you. And if Balsuto had something to do with it, you could be the next lesson he decides to teach Ben. Even if neither of those possibilities exists, what makes you think he would tell you the truth?

He doesn't have much of a track record in that department. And how would you know if he was lying?"

It was true Ben and Stella blindsided me, but I had to admit I hadn't been clueless. How many times had I sensed something was off? Moments when he had said he was golfing with a buddy or getting a drink with the guys, and a tiny alarm had sounded way, way back in the primitive part of my woman brain. But I ignored it, preferring to reside in my own special fairy tale. I had no explanation for why I was so sure I would know if he was telling the truth this time. Hell, I didn't understand it myself. But I was certain if I stared into his eyes and asked if he'd killed my sister, I would know beyond certainty if he was telling the truth.

"I just will." I dismissed Justin and faced Harry. "Besides, he might have a copy of the pictures missing from her file. Can you call and set up a meeting? If I do it, he'll start denying shit over the phone, and we'll lose the chance to catch him by surprise."

He looked at Justin, who shrugged and shook his head in what I took as a gesture of defeat. Or maybe he was secretly okay with me seeing Ben. If I told him I was sure of Ben's guilt, wouldn't that make taking him out easier for Justin? *Taking him out?* My mother's mob boss mentality seemed to be taking root.

Harry agreed to set up the meeting, then hopped out and walked around to open my door. Justin stood by the car, holding the manila envelope Cordoza had provided. I had forgotten about it after leaving the embassy, descending instead into a mental horror show where images of flames engulfed my sister's body.

"If it's okay with you, Grace," Justin began, "I'd like to check this out before, well, uh…"

Harry took my elbow and eased me out of the car. "He's right. There's no need for you to read the report until we vet the information."

Of course, I knew *vet the information* meant screen it to make sure the contents wouldn't throw me into another fit of despair, but I was too tired to protest.

Even though it was past lunchtime, I wasn't hungry. I needed time to process Stella's letters. Harry promised to get in touch with Ben after lunch, and the three of us made plans to meet for dinner.

The windows in my room opened to brilliant sunlight sparkling on the river below. There was no evidence of the sprawling poverty hovering on the hillside. Red umbrellas sheltered diners at the outdoor restaurant. Couples walked hand in hand along the brick walkway or rested on wooden benches under trees that provided the illusion of shade. Well-dressed children in varying shades of neon-colored tennis shoes ran in and out among the adults, climbing on artistic structures of metal and stone.

I sat cross-legged on the bed, opened the packet containing Stella's letters, and removed the third one in the series so carefully cataloged by our mother. I imagined there had been little doubt in her mind I would someday read them and forgive my sister. I suspected she never considered Stella wouldn't be around when I did.

She had written it in early June. There was no mention of Ben or sunrises. She spoke of long walks alone on the shore and tossing stranded starfish back into the ocean the way we'd done as children. She asked me if I remembered our family vacations, knowing full well I would never forget them. We stayed at Seagrove Beach between Destin and Panama City because it was cheaper if you were okay being a few blocks from the water.

In her letter, Stella reminisced about the days Mom would slather us with sunscreen. She reminded me of the way Lesroy always got burned in strange places, like behind his ears and under his armpits, because he was unable to stand still enough for his mother to even out the thick gooey lotion over his wriggly little body. She wrote of the times we spent all day at the beach constructing sand cities, designed to Lesroy's specifications, and roasting marshmallows over the fire Gran built.

She spoke of the bunk beds in the hallway and of Lesroy curling up in a sleeping bag on the floor. And sneaking out after dark to chase crabs and tell ghost stories.

I closed my eyes and for a minute I saw us throwing ourselves into waves bigger than we were. Lesroy would almost always go under, and we'd scream and laugh until the surf tossed him onto the shore where he'd shake himself like a wild little terrier. I wondered if Stella had been recalling happier days or if she had been playing me, knowing the effect these memories would have. Then her letter took a strange turn.

Remember how quiet and still he got when we asked him why Aunt Rita stopped coming? And how he finally broke and told us it must have had something to do with the night his daddy disappeared? He'd heard Gran and our mothers arguing a few weeks after Uncle Roy left. His mother had said there were some things you could never forgive, but Lesroy didn't know what they were and who couldn't be forgiven for them.

I never forgot what he told us, but when I mentioned it to him last year, he acted like he didn't remember it at all. That seemed strange because Lesroy never forgets anything. If you ever read this, you should ask him about those things that can never be forgiven.

The rest of her letter focused on how hard it was to fill the long days, but that she was at least making headway with Eva. The housekeeper had moved from tolerating her to enjoying her company. She hoped they might become real friends.

I wanted to dismiss my sister's words as an attempt to make me feel sorry for her. But I kept seeing the little girl on the beach, sand flying as, desperate to keep up, she ran behind me and Lesroy. I walked to the balcony and stared below. From my vantage point, the people hustling and bustling all seemed to be going to some happy or important place. Or were they, too, trying to keep up with the ones they loved?

I realized I'd spent over thirty minutes on one letter. If I kept letting my emotions get in the way, I would never finish reading through the packets before my meeting with Ben. Even if I distanced myself from the lonely melody threaded throughout my sister's words, it would take hours—hours I might not have, depending on how quickly Harry arranged things.

Time wasn't the only problem. It was as if Stella was speaking to me as I read. She had a lovely voice, clear and strong, warmed with a gentle Southern drawl. For about half a minute, she considered a singing career but never pursued it. The realization I'd never hear her again filled me with a heaviness that threatened to suffocate me. I needed help.

Justin was the logical choice. Through his connection to Mike and his unholy alliance with my mother, he had some insight into my family. My instincts told me he wasn't a cold-blooded killer. But they had also told me Ben would make a good husband, so there was that.

Cold-blooded killer or not, Justin McElroy was my best option for discovering clues hidden in Stella's letters.

I called to explain what I needed, and he showed up in less than ten minutes. His wavy hair was damp from the shower, and he smelled like fresh-cut lemons.

"I really appreciate this. There are so many of them. I'm usually a fast reader and an excellent skimmer, but for some reason I keep getting bogged down." My throat thickened as I ran out of reasons for my inefficiency.

"Not a problem," he said, touching me lightly on the shoulder. He took the envelope marked July and picked up a highlighter I'd placed on the square glass-topped table near the window. "We've got at least three hours before dinner. Both of us will mark anything that looks helpful. Then we'll trade letters."

His plan helped me distance myself from Stella and her loneliness. Her voice faded as I read four remaining ones from June. It seemed she had made friends other than her housekeeper. She mentioned learning to surf and hanging out at several bars.

Despite my increased speed, Justin had already finished August and September when we stopped to review each other's work. I've never been a very precise highlighter. Once I get started, I have trouble stopping. My system in college was complicated and clumsy. I used yellow for what would definitely be on the test, blue for what might be on the test, and green for stuff that would never be on the test but was kind of interesting. The bookstore never gave me any trade-in credit, and my roommate asked to document my biology book as data for a psychology paper she was writing on the connection between sociopathic behavior and OCD in women ages eighteen to twenty-five.

It was no surprise it took Justin almost as long to get through my June highlights as it did for me to read his July, August, and. September.

"Now we need to chart our ideas," he said. "Note cards would be great, but we can fold and tear…."

Before he finished, I pulled a small packet from my bag and put it on the table in front of him.

"You scare me a little, Grace." He took a few index cards and gave me back my letters. "Write down anything about people and places she mentions. Include any social stuff—parties, shopping trips, lunches, and any references to Ben. Add the month and letter number on the bottom."

In less than ten minutes, we covered most of the bed. Eva's stack was the thickest.

"Now we've got a pretty good idea about the beginning of Stella's life in Montañita. Let's work on the rest of her first year. Look for more info on the people and locations we marked and any new names and places. You're better at picking up mood shifts in your sister, so mark those, too. But for God's sake, go easy with the highlighter or we'll never get through them."

I worked on October and November while he took December through March. I breezed through until I hit Halloween, Stella's favorite holiday. My sister loved being scared or pretending to be since she was fearless. She adored the excess of all the candy you could carry and intricate jack-o'-lantern carvings. She even enjoyed scooping pumpkin goo with her hands and squeezing the seeds out for Gran to bake.

But most of all, Stella was crazy for costumes. When we were little, our grandmother would coordinate our outfits with Lesroy. We hit all the popular choices: 101 Dalmatians; Huey, Louie, and Dewey; Dorothy, Toto, and the Wicked Witch (Lesroy's favorite of all). After we were too big to go trick or treating, we threw extravagant parties as an excuse to continue the tradition. The pressure to become more elaborate got old for me, and by my first year in college I was over it. Stella was devastated when she found out I wasn't coming home to celebrate the holiday. Lesroy volunteered to be her costume buddy, but she turned him down. Without me, she said, it wouldn't be the same. So, she became a solo act on Halloween: Cher, Madonna, Marilyn. Stella was the most herself when she was someone else. I wondered if she became me when she was with Ben.

When she discovered Halloween in Montañita was little more than an excuse for heavy drinking, she decided to throw her own party. Her last October letter detailed the plans. She had pumpkins shipped in from the States and got Eva to help her put together a haunted house in the garage. Since people weren't accustomed to dressing up for the occasion, Stella ordered costumes in all shapes and sizes. She chose her absolute favorite, Scarlett O'Hara in the famous green outfit made from curtains. She thought Ben would be super pissed when he saw the bill, but it would be too late by then. I highlighted only one line from her narrative: "But Ben's super pissed most of the time anyway, so no big deal."

I expected a detailed description of the party in Stella's first November letter, but it was surprisingly stark. She said everyone loved her costume, but Ben had refused to don the Rhett Butler outfit she ordered for him. He went with Phantom of the Opera instead. Someone else had been Rhett, and he made a very interesting counterpart to her Scarlett, much better than Ben would have. After that, "Rhett" appeared frequently.

"I've got some Rhett guy showing up in just about every letter from December through March," Justin said when we were ready to compare notes.

I explained how and when he had shown up, and we speculated who he might be. The obvious choice was Adelmo Balsuto, but he insisted we shouldn't jump to that conclusion. He pointed out a place she had frequented, Olon. "It's so much quieter and gentler than Montañita," she wrote. She described houses built on top of cliffs dangerously close to disintegration and spoke of hiking to a waterfall and swimming in the cold, clear water. My sister mentioned hummingbirds hovering like jeweled clouds, creating a shimmering light across the entire sky. She never came out and said Rhett was with her, but there was no way she would have traipsed through the forest alone. Stella was athletic but had never been interested in being one with nature.

"I think we made some real progress." He stood and stretched. His shirt slid up enough to give me a quick view of the bottom third of what appeared to be a very impressive six-pack.

"Me, too. But I won't be able to sleep in the middle of an active investigation." I pointed at the cluttered bedspread.

"It would be a shame to destroy our hard work. Let's see if we can come up with some other place you might spend the night. Strictly in the interest of preserving research." He smiled and wriggled his eyebrows up and down.

I felt a flutter south of my waistline but ignored it. "If we're careful, we should be able to move the bedspread to the floor without messing up the cards."

Justin laughed and took out his cell phone. "I'll take some pictures. Then we can transfer our stacks to the table."

After he snapped a few shots, I busied myself with organizing our work.

"Harry should be in the lobby in about thirty minutes. Meet you there."

I walked with him to the door where he stopped and turned to me.

"And Grace." He leaned close.

I held my breath and looked into his dark blue eyes. He grasped my chin in one hand, and I parted my lips. Then he said, "You've got highlighter on your face."

CHAPTER 17

As usual, the men were already in the lobby when I arrived five minutes early. They were so engrossed in conversation, neither noticed me until I was in front of them.

"You look especially lovely tonight," Harry said, as he pulled out my chair.

"Thanks for noticing." After scrubbing the highlighter off my face, I spent extra time with my make-up and hair.

"You clean up good, but I kind of miss the highlighter," Justin added.

I ignored him and asked Harry if he'd gotten in touch with Ben. I was second-guessing my decision to have him make the initial contact since I was the better choice for gauging Ben's reactions first-hand and in person.

"I left two messages," he answered. "Don't worry. It's only been a few hours."

"Harry's right," Justin said. "Men like Ben always want the last word. And then there's seeing you. No way he'll let you leave the country before you talk to him."

"Relax, Grace. There's a great restaurant about fifteen minutes from here. It started as a curbside grill. Now it's tucked in a nice little neighborhood. More locals than tourists." Harry threaded his arm through mine and ushered me out the shiny chrome and glass doors.

Traffic thinned as we drove farther from the river. The streets narrowed, and harsh modern lighting dissolved into a softer glow from European-style streetlamps. A pastel haze glimmered over sidewalks in front of two-story buildings, painted in pale shades of pink, blue, and green. Intricately patterned wrought iron framed narrow balconies. He parked on a side street, and we walked a short block to the restaurant.

As soon as we entered, a man in a black jacket greeted Harry. They clapped each other's backs and chattered in Spanish while Justin and I looked on. Round tables covered with golden cloths, linen napkins and simple but elegant silverware filled the small dining area. Only the brilliant red and orange flowers in crystal vases hinted of the exotic nature of our locale. Harry's friend seated us by the window.

We ordered wine, then Harry went over the menu, skipping an item I'd never heard of.

"Wait. What's cuy? A local specialty?"

He grinned. "Well, I've never eaten it any other place. Cuy is guinea pig. Tried it once after three or four too many beers. Tastes like chicken."

Mr. Reeces Cup, Lesroy's chocolate and beige pet guinea pig, squealed in the back of my mind. The plump little creature danced in delight whenever we ran up to his cage.

"Okay, then. I'll have the shrimp and coconut sauce."

They each ordered steak cut in thin strips, served over rice and beans. We shared orders of yucca bread, fried in rounded pieces with warm, chewy centers, along with meat and cheese empanadas. Despite the memory of Lesroy's beloved Mr. Reeces, my appetite returned, and I cleaned my plate.

Harry suggested we try aguardiente, a local favorite distilled from sugar cane and fruit juice. "Sounds harmless, but it packs a real punch," he warned.

I took a sip, gasped for air, downed half a glass of bottled water, and coughed uncontrollably. Justin patted me on the back. The choking sensation subsided just as Harry's phone sounded. He looked at caller ID and then at me. "Ben," he said and left the table.

I pushed up from my chair to go with him, but Justin took my hand and shook his head. "It's better if he handles it without you there."

As infuriating as it was, he was right. Ben didn't need to know I was there. And there was a good chance I'd start screaming and yelling obscenities at the sound of his voice. He paid the check, and we waited on the sidewalk. It was after eight and cooler, but the humidity seeped into my hair, frizzing it into a giant puffball.

"Why is it taking so long?" I paced beside him.

Before he replied, Harry came from the side of the building.

"What a jackass. He said you're the only one he'll talk to. I told him you got in late and were exhausted. He wants to see you as soon as possible. We set it up for tomorrow afternoon at his house in Montañita."

"I'm not comfortable with that." Justin faced me and held my shoulders. "He's a complete asshole, and when assholes get desperate, they're unpredictable."

"He won't hurt me," I asserted. "If he did, he'd be the bad guy, and he always has to believe he's a good guy."

They continued to insist on accompanying me. Although their protective attitude was comforting, I resented the implication I was incapable of handling the situation. Whether it came from the need to prove something or from the perverse desire to confront my ex alone, I was determined to go on my own.

After a heated debate, I agreed to let them drop me off and stay as close as possible to the house. Neither was happy until Harry suggested I wear a wire in case I got in trouble. The prospect of being wired up excited me more than I cared to admit.

On our return trip, I remembered the folder. Several times I intended to ask what about my sister's death warranted further investigation. But there had been no suitable moment for such a terrible revelation. With the evening almost over, we couldn't afford to delay.

"I'm guessing you both examined Stella's file. What was in it that made Luis so uncomfortable?"

Justin cleared his throat before explaining there were marks on the body, around the neck specifically. "I don't see how drowning could have caused them."

"Are you saying she was strangled?" It surprised me how easy it was for me to say the words, as if I were talking about someone else's sister.

"We shouldn't jump to conclusions. And without the pictures, there's no way we could prove it."

Normally, I would have demanded to read the report myself, but for once I was willing to accept Justin's word.

When we reached the hotel, Harry dropped us at the front entrance, explaining he had things to do before morning. It was less than a two-hour drive to Montañita, and he wanted to leave me at the villa while he and Justin checked out Ben's house. We would meet at 7:30 for a quick breakfast and an early check-out.

"Are you up for a drink?" he asked after Harry left.

I discovered grief has a dual effect. One minute, getting out of bed was an insurmountable task. The next, you're filled with an erratic energy like tiny bolts of electricity shooting through your body. Ever since Harry confirmed my meeting with Ben, I sizzled with that current.

"I'm not in the mood for another drink. What if we just took a walk?" I hoped to learn if what I observed from my window was happiness or freneticism.

He liked the idea. We crossed through the lobby to the river walkway and strolled in silence. Not a comfortable one like people who've been married for over fifty years enjoy but not awkward either. Streetlights reflected off the black water, sending silver ribbons over the surface. We passed graceful structures of metalwork topped with airy sails. Abstract periscope pieces built into walls along the path blended with statues of famous Ecuadorians. Overhead, slashes of crimson, violet, and emerald flooded the sky, trailed by strains of classical music.

"Come on," Justin said, taking my arm. "I read about this on the plane. It's the Fuente del Agua Danzantes."

The growing crescendo guided us to a crowd gathered by a large fountain where distant flashes streaked through the clouds. Bursts of color rose like the breath of some exotic creature. The pounding of my heart echoed the rhythm.

My knees weakened and I leaned against him. Without speaking, he took my arm and steadied me. We remained close for the rest of the show.

As the lights dimmed to a faint glow, a sense of peace descended, and the crowd grew quiet. We had been a part of something beyond ourselves, something that obliterated thoughts of where I was and why I'd come. But as the final chord faded, and the last firework split the heavens, Stella came to me, her face lit with the wonder of it.

Silent again, we returned to the hotel. In the glass elevator, I searched the night sky for a trace of color but only found a brilliant spray of stars. When we reached our floor, Justin spoke. "I was hoping we might finish going through Stella's letters. I have a bad feeling about sending you to Ben without looking at the rest of them. If you're okay with it, let's read them tonight, unless you'd rather do it by yourself."

I didn't want to do it alone. Seeing her precise handwriting made my heart ache. After two unsuccessful swipes, my key card worked. I stepped inside and gasped. The comforter and blankets lay in a tangled pile on the floor. Blank index cards were scattered everywhere, and drawers had been tossed on the bed. My computer bag was upside down, empty except for the dangling power cord.

"You okay in there?" Justin called from the hallway. When I couldn't find my voice, he rushed in. "Holy shit!"

We stopped and stared at the mess before he took a few tentative steps. He waved me back when I started to follow. "Don't touch anything before we call the cops and hotel security.

I didn't need a bunch of men in uniforms to tell me what the thieves had taken. Other than my laptop, the only things missing were our stack of notes and my sister's letters.

CHAPTER 18

It was after two before the investigation wrapped up. I had been right about the stolen items. The officers were unconcerned about the letters and offered little hope of recovering my laptop. Only the hotel manager was disturbed by the break-in. He insisted his system was the best in South America, and he trusted his staff implicitly. Having seen the living conditions of the people who resided near the property, I imagined it would be easy for a person to bribe one of those employees.

After the authorities left, I sat on the freshly done bed. Justin joined me.

"Are you sure you don't want to take the manager up on that offer to change rooms? It's not like they'll come back. They got what they wanted. But wouldn't you sleep better somewhere else?"

"I am not giving Ben the satisfaction of knowing how freaked out I am."

"You understand, your ex might not have done this, right?"

"How could anyone even know I had the letters? And why would they want them?"

"We can't be sure who Rhett is. Whoever he is, he might not be the only one she was seeing. And I doubt she mailed them herself."

I thought of Eva. Had she betrayed my sister to Ben? Or was she working for someone else who wished Stella harm?

"Either way, I'm not leaving this room." Mostly because I felt as if a leaden chain was twisting around my body, squeezing the air from me.

"Then I'm staying with you," he announced. "No argument. It's not safe for you to be alone."

Too drained to put up a fight, I accepted the offer. And although I hated to admit it, I was glad I wouldn't be alone.

After brushing my teeth and washing my face, I slipped into a T-shirt and a loose-fitting pair of gym shorts. While I was in the bathroom, Justin found an extra pillow and blanket and was lying on the sofa bed looking at his phone.

"Whoever broke in was sharp enough to take our note cards, but I can have the pictures printed and blown up."

"If hadn't been such a baby, I would have gotten through all the letters, and we'd have a better idea why they were stolen."

"Don't beat yourself up. If you rushed through them, you might have missed something. And if we hadn't read them in order, they wouldn't have made sense."

"But now I'll never find out what Stella went through in her last days." Those letters were the only remaining piece of my sister, and they were gone.

"We're not finished, Grace. There are other ways."

Was "other ways" code for beating the information out of Ben? Before I could decide if I wanted to know, he shut off the lights.

"Since we have to be up in a few hours, let's try to get some rest."

Light from the hallway outlined his body as he stood and slipped out of his shirt. The springs squeaked when he sat, and the change in his pockets jingled when he tossed his pants on the floor.

Before I wished him good night, his breathing settled into the rhythm of sleep. I've always marveled at how quickly men fall asleep. I lay staring at the ceiling, thinking about how much had changed. Stella's death created a void that I hadn't had a chance to acknowledge. In a little over a week, I catapulted from my safe world into a strange and dangerous land. Once angry and bitter, I had become burdened with a sorrow I never imagined.

And now I was sharing a room with a man I barely knew but had entrusted with my life.

CHAPTER 19

At 6:30, the hotel alarm jolted me from a disturbing dream about Uncle Roy. All I could recall was Stella standing behind him, her fingers to her lips. The reason for her insistence on silence seemed important but eluded me.

Justin had toothpaste-glued a note to the bathroom mirror.

"I don't think I've ever spent the night with a woman who snores as loud as you. See you at breakfast."

"Ha, ha," I said, before stepping into the shower. I gave my hair the usual fluff and dry and spackled the dark circles under my eyes with extra concealer. I packed most of my things after the police left, so I made it to the lobby at 7:15. The men still beat me.

"Justin told me about the break-in," Harry said. "I believe we should rethink your meeting. If he stole the letters, it means he suspects something. Even with the wire, we might have a problem getting to you."

I was adamant we stick to the plan. So what if Ben took them? He couldn't be sure how much I'd read. And once I got him talking, I was certain he'd be so eager to prove his innocence, I could easily manipulate him. Men with egos his size often let their big mouths get the best of them.

Over breakfast, they continued to point out potential problems with the plan. What if Ben was threatened by my questions? What if he got angry or abusive? Didn't we suspect him of hurting Stella? What made me think he would have a problem harming me?

I brushed off their concerns and told them I had never been afraid of him and would not start now. They weren't happy but agreed we would pick up a rental car for me, and they would follow in the Bronco. Harry came up with a safe word for me to use if things got weird. He suggested I say *vase* if anything spooked me. I laughed at the image of being in the middle of a dangerous situation and coming up with ways to work *vase* into the conversation. I could croon "what a lovely vase" or ask "did you get that vase as a wedding present?" or announce "I'm going to hit you over the head with that vase." Neither of the men thought I was funny.

Harry explained the drive to Montañita was a little less than two-and-a-half hours. But we were traveling during the busy season. Scores of surfers flooded the area, chasing waves often as high as twenty feet. Sun-worshipers and partygoers thronged the beaches.

Despite our expectations of heavy traffic, we made good time getting out of the city and, except for two llamas crossing the curvy road and one donkey watching as we passed, the drive was as familiar as any coastal trip. As soon as I saw the bright blue of the ocean, I opened my window, closed my eyes, and stuck my head out, the way Stella and I used to do on our way to the beach. The wind whipped my hair across my face as I breathed in the salty air.

"Hey, Grace, maybe put that up a little." Justin protested from the backseat. "I'm getting blasted back here."

I shut it partway and ran my fingers through my tangled curls. "So, this is Montañita."

What the travel brochure described as a "vast expanse of golden sand" was vast all right, but more dirty beige than golden. Tiny thatch-topped huts, bright beach umbrellas, restaurants, and bars dotted the landscape. Surfers bobbed in and out of foamy waves, and everywhere young people strolled along the water's edge. Despite the clutter of commerce and humanity, the ocean retained its power. Stretching until the horizon melted into the water, it reminded me of my insignificance.

Harry pulled off the main highway and turned onto a paved two-lane road. It wound upward until we reached a clearing where a sign announced we had arrived at El Parasio. He parked, and we walked down a stone pathway lined with palm trees. A fat iguana blocked our way. He paused for a few seconds, gave us the lizard eye, then sauntered into the thick ground cover.

Management had painted the entryway to the hotel office in dazzling tropical colors, outlined in startling neon green. A thatch-covered roof erupted in gables just over the entrance and seduced guests with the illusion they were walking into a nature-made palace. Pink and green tiles led us to the front desk where a very tan man sat with his feet propped up, reading *Transworld Surf*, the swimsuit edition. His bleached-tipped blonde hair reminded me of the lead singer in one of Stella's favorite boy bands.

He looked at us and flashed a hundred-watt smile. When his eyes met mine, the wattage dimmed, and his gaze flickered. He regained his beach-boy poise so quickly I wondered if I imagined it.

"Greetings, fellow travelers. I'm Preston Allen, but you can call me Prez. You guys must be, like, the Davenport party."

"We aren't just like the Davenport party," Harry said. "We are the Davenport party."

Our greeter seemed puzzled, then connected the dots. "Right, I get it, dude. That's funny."

The sixties-seventies vibe of the lobby suggested we might have slipped into a time warp. The skunky-sweet smell of marijuana completed the aura.

Prez checked us in, handed Justin the room keys, and pointed toward our villa. He added that they set up for happy hour daily from four to six at the Cabana Bar. Although it was only a little after ten, I suspected he had already started his happy hour. Or was every hour happy in Montañita?

Our unit was clean and well-lit, my two main requirements for lodging. The men gave me the room with the queen-size bed and private bath. They took the singles and shared a bathroom. The living area was furnished with a jungle-patterned sofa and plush recliners trimmed in wicker. Since my meeting wasn't until one-thirty, the plan was to let me freshen up while Harry and Justin made a reconnaissance trip to Ben and Stella's house. They would decide the best vantage points, pick up the rental car, then return to base camp to wire me up.

I was disappointed to discover the devise was only a tiny transmitter that I slipped into the lining of my bra, not the dramatic body-taped affairs they wear in the movies. I cheered up, though, when Harry gave me a can of military strength Mace to put in my purse.

While the men were on their surveillance mission, I checked out my wardrobe. I wanted to go with something subdued but sexy. I laid out my outfits and realized I needed someone else's wardrobe. I decided on a short floral skirt and a knit top with a plunging V-neck that, thanks to a painful push-up bra, provided an ample view of cleavage. I added eyeliner and more mascara along with blush and lipstick. Three-inch open-toed power heels perfected an image that said, *You're going to want to touch me, but if you do, I'll shove my shoe up your ass, pointy end first.*

They returned about an hour after me. Justin looked startled when I opened the door. "Jeez, Grace."

"What Mr. Smooth meant to say is you look very nice." Harry took out a digital camera and sat down at the round wicker table in the kitchenette. "I think it would be a good idea for you to check out the house ahead of time."

He showed me a pamphlet he picked up in a real estate office on the way to Ben's. Montañita Estates was a proposed subdivision of luxury homes with a clubhouse, tennis courts, and pool. Next, he took out his camera and scrolled through pictures of vacant lots with incredible views of the ocean and a few construction sites occupied by skeletons of unfinished structures.

The last series began with a shot of an enormous structure of three rectangular two-story, boxlike sections. The gray stucco exterior gave the house an industrial look alleviated somewhat by the sparkling glass-paneled front.

"We couldn't get a good view of the back without drawing too much attention. But there's at least one balcony off the master bedroom." Harry shook his head. "Looks like a giant fish tank, no privacy. Of course, Ben's is the only house for miles, so that's not an issue."

"It also means we won't be able to get as close as we need to," Justin said.

"That makes it even more important for you to be careful," Harry repeated. "I think you should act as if he's nothing more than a grieving husband. Show him a little sympathy to keep him off guard."

"I'm not sure I could convince him I felt sorry for him. If I remember correctly, the last time I saw him I told him to rot in hell." The men exchanged looks. "Don't worry. I'll be careful."

We left before one. Justin would ride with me in the rental car most of the way. When we were within a few minutes of Ben's, I would drop him off, and they would drive to the overlooking hill.

"The turnoff is just ahead," he said.

I edged to the side of the road, and Harry came up behind us.

"I'm serious, Grace," he said before opening the door. "Don't do anything crazy."

I promised once more to be cautious. Then they left me alone with my wire and wits.

I was less than a quarter of a mile from where Stella had spent her last few years and possibly where she died.

The house was more oppressive in person than in Harry's pictures. It sat on an incline separated from the roadside by a concrete and stone wall. Short, thick shrubbery lined the top of it, dividing the native beauty of the area and the man-made obstruction above it. Rather than navigating the steep driveway, I parked on the street and followed the pathway up to the entrance. There was no porch, only an alcove constructed of open beams. The door was camouflaged amid all the glass.

At the entryway, I strained to glimpse what lay beyond. But sunlight on the windows bounced back, leaving the interior dark and lifeless. Instead of a luxury dwelling, I was looking into an elegant prison. For a moment, I felt as if I were Stella trapped in this rectangular cage far from home and family.

I rang the bell and waited for what seemed like forever before a boy who was still in his teens opened the door. His thick, dark hair hung low on his forehead. He pushed it back, and I noticed a small half-moon and three shooting stars tattooed on his slender wrist. He smiled and motioned me into a two-story foyer with an elaborate chandelier of metal cylinders composed of organ pipes. While I marveled at the fixture, he disappeared down a side hall.

Standing alone there, I began to lose my nerve. What made me think I could outwit my ex? I turned to bolt for the door.

"Grace!" Ben called from the winding staircase. "I knew you would come."

CHAPTER 20

Clad in a pink polo and khaki shorts, he descended with outstretched arms. The rubber soles of his Ralph Lauren boat shoes stuck on the marble tile, and he stumbled. He regained his balance and stood in front of me, still in hug-mode.

The changes in Ben were shocking. He had taken great pride in his body, working out daily and running ten miles a week. The result had been impressive: broad shoulders, washboard abs, narrow hips, strong calves and legs. His sun-streaked hair had been thick and smooth, and, with the aid of twice a month two-hundred-dollar haircuts, it retained a casual look suggesting he was a bit of a rebel but still respected the establishment. Ben's dark-brown eyes remained clear even after a night of heavy drinking. With a firm chin and muscular neck, he had exuded the confidence of someone who thinks money can solve all his problems.

The man standing in front of me was not the person I'd found dangerously desirable. Seeing this ruined version, I couldn't fathom why losing him had been so devastating. It was like that moment when you look at a picture from your high school yearbook, the one with your hair in a pile, bangs teased and tufted, and think "What the hell was I thinking!"

This Ben had melted into himself. His shoulders were still broad but stooped. The line of demarcation between his chest and stomach had blurred into a small, but definitive, beer belly. The shorts hung on his butt, not quite low enough to hide scrawny thighs. A network of deep lines etched jaundiced brown eyes, and his once firm jawline had slackened. The hair he'd been so proud of was greasy with the specter of baldness looming over it. Despite his physical decline, he reeked of arrogance.

He ignored my obvious reluctance to touch him and spoke as if we'd shared a warm embrace. "I can't tell you how good it is to see you. Let's go into the den. I'll have Juan bring us drinks. We have a lot of catching up to do."

"It's a little early for me. But we do have things to talk about." I followed him down a hallway that opened into a vast open space. The back wall was all windows with an incredible view of the contrasting blues and greens of ocean and sky. This was the balcony scene my sister, a self-made Rapunzel, had described.

The rest of the room was a study in gray. Smokey gray walls, pale, grayish wooden floors covered with a geometric-print accent rug in shades of gray with touches of yellow. A gigantic leather sectional, complete with dual recliners, the kind Stella had once declared incredibly tacky, was charcoal. The effect was somber and drab.

Ben called for Juan to bring him a gin and tonic straight up.

"Sure you don't want something?"

I shook my head and sank into one of the matching chairs, so gigantic they rendered an average-size person childlike. He sat across from me.

"You're looking great, Grace. You've always been a beautiful woman, but there's something new about you, a kind of glow."

Ben had must have forgotten he'd used that exact "kind of glow" line on me when we first met. At least, he was right about there being something new. Now, the glow was from having seen the light of what a pretentious asshole he was.

"You know why I'm here. We don't have a lot of time, so I'd appreciate it if we could cut through the bullshit and get to the point. I want to find out what happened to Stella." I hadn't meant to be so direct, but sitting near the man who might have killed my sister with him thinking he could charm his way back into my life sickened me.

His eyes narrowed, and he glared at me as if I were a spider he planned to squash. I got a glimpse of what Stella saw every time she angered him. I surveyed the room to see if I could spot a vase and saw only a rectangular cut-glass piece filled with gray pebbles. It would do in a pinch. But the look passed, and I put my safe word on hold.

"I can't imagine how upset you must be, Grace. But I told your mother the same thing I said to the authorities. She got caught in a storm and, uh, you can read the rest from the accident report." He unwrapped the napkin around his drink and dabbed at dry eyes.

I wanted to scream he knew Stella would never go out if there were even a hint of risky weather, but I didn't. Ben was the consummate liar. He'd stick to his story no matter what. I needed to try another approach.

"That's what you say happened, but there's more to it, isn't there? What was going on between the two of you that made her tell Mom she was coming home?"

He stopped mid-sip and curled his lip. The movement was quick and subtle, but I struck a nerve

"I won't deny we had our troubles. Your sister was a passionate woman. But, of course, you know that don't you, Grace?" He paused, clearly looking forward to my reaction, but I kept my cool. He continued, "There are things you're unaware of. Things I've spared you from until now."

I looked over him at the ocean. He shifted in his chair.

"At first, it was great between us. She loved the water and was crazy about the house. We flew in a decorator from Miami and I let the two of them splurge. The guy was a real twinkle-toes. Said we needed a 'modern-rustic' approach, whatever the hell that is. When they finished spending my money on chandeliers and shit, she was happy. Being the most beautiful woman in the room when we entertained thrilled her. She took up surfing, against my wishes, I might add. It was too dangerous, but you know how strong willed she could be."

He downed his drink and called for Juan to bring another. Only a quarter after two and Ben was on his way to getting hammered. I decided this could work to my advantage.

"I've forgotten a lot about my sister," I said. "Please, refresh my memory."

He swirled the gin and tonic before tipping it to his mouth. "Stella always wanted more. The woman was never satisfied. More clothes, more jewelry, bigger parties. The cost of living is low here, Grace, but my finances aren't unlimited." He gave me what I guessed he thought was a pitiful look. I had never known how much he'd inherited from his parents, but I suspected it was a hefty sum. That along with the drug money should have been enough for two lifetimes in Ecuador. Tiny beads of sweat coated his thin upper lip. I was gratified at the knowledge my silence was getting to him.

"Anyway, your sister became very critical of our lifestyle. I was patient. I understood she was homesick. She missed her family and friends. And, frankly, Grace, she was a wreck over her relationship with you."

There it was. Ben was going to shift the blame for Stella's death to me. Still, I kept silent. Now droplets of sweat gathered on his forehead.

"The last year Stella became, for lack of a better word, completely irrational." He gulped the rest of his second gin and tonic.

"That's two words, but, please, continue."

He held up his empty glass. "You know how I hate to drink alone, Grace. I insist you join me."

I sensed a threat in the invitation but needed him to keep drinking.

"Juan," he shouted. "Another round but make the lady's vodka."

The young man brought the drinks so quickly I suspected he made Ben's ahead of time. He served me first. I thanked him, and he responded with a shy smile and the briefest of eye contact. As he was delivering the gin and tonic, Ben knocked his hand and some of the drink sloshed onto the floor.

"Goddammit, boy! Watch what you're doing."

He apologized and scurried from the room. I double-checked the location of the vase before asking Ben to explain what Stella's irrational behavior entailed.

"Well, she would disappear for hours and hours without telling me where she was or when she was coming home. When I asked her about it, she'd give me one of her killer smiles and tell me she was reading at the beach or having lunch with a friend or surfing or some other shit, and lost track of time. Then she accused me of bullying her. She flew into uncontrollable rages. I was a little afraid of her, Grace."

He stood up and opened his arms to the panoramic view of sand and sea.

"She had all this. And still couldn't be happy. I was really worried, so I called a doctor friend of mine, a psychiatrist. He suggested she suffered from a dissociative disorder." He slurred so badly through the diagnosis, I wondered just how much he had to drink before I arrived. "That's when it became clear to me. Stella was a true sociopath. I know it's hard to hear, but it's the only thing that explains her behavior." He stumbled back into his seat.

"A sociopath, huh?" I gulped my vodka and tonic. "Elaborate, please. What about Stella screams sociopath?"

He bobbed his head in an enthusiastic nod. "Everything, Grace. I mean, I never wanted to tell you, but your sister was the one who came on to me. She waited for me in my car after our dates. Scared the shit out of me, sitting there like a statue. Then she was all over me. I resisted for as long as I could. Our relationship meant everything to me. You know that, right?" He gave me his best sad smile.

"Yeah, sure. Everything."

"I knew you'd understand. I told her to lay off. I didn't want to crush her spirit, so I was very gentle. But that girl wouldn't listen. Kept telling me how much better suited we were for each other. I still said no, but then you started planning the wedding. And, well, to be perfectly honest, you got so wrapped up in choosing flowers and dresses and caterers you neglected me."

I remembered those months. Days where I was constantly pulled between Mom and the bossy planner and the rest of my life. Ben never offered to help. That was the bride's responsibility, the price for snagging her man, he said. He also never complained that I was neglecting him.

"I neglected you?" I repeated.

"Right." He nodded. "And Stella, well, she was there. And like the typical sociopath, she showed no guilt, no remorse. Blamed it all on you, Grace. Had me convinced you'd be better off without me, that you didn't need me the way she did. She said all she wanted was to make me happy. She was very convincing."

If he hadn't been so serious, I would have sworn he was being intentionally ironic. But he lacked the depth to appreciate irony. It was obvious he considered himself the wronged party. Then I remembered Stella's words about seeing herself through someone else's eyes. When she thought she lost me, she sought out my one true love—a man who actually was the perfect sociopath. When she looked in his eyes, she became a shallow, manipulative creature with the ability to lie and cheat to get whatever she wanted.

But his mirror was different. It was like the House of Mirrors at the State Fair when Stella was eight and I was thirteen. She begged to go in, but I insisted on saving my ticket for something more exciting. The truth was I hated being trapped, surrounded by images of myself: some real, some distorted. I was terrified of being unable to find the way out, doomed to forever run into multiple versions of myself.

Stella, however, had never been in a house of mirrors and was hell-bent on going even if it meant she had to go alone. When I heard her screaming, the carnival operator refused to let me in until I paid, but I brushed by him and raced to where she lay cowering in front of a monster-like image of herself. I guided her outside where the ticket-taker was muttering threats about calling the police. I ignored him and took her to buy cotton candy.

Later, Stella told me she hadn't been afraid of not being able to find her way out. She'd been frightened by the sight of her own face glowering at her, contorted into a mask of horror. She thought she was the monster in the mirror. It was only when I found her that she realized it was an illusion.

If I'd come to visit her, I could have helped her see this luxurious home was her house of mirrors. And Ben was the monster.

He interrupted my reverie. "It's okay, Grace. You were young and in love. And Stella knew how to get her way." He must have taken my lengthy silence as recognition and remorse over my callous behavior. "It must be true that everything happens for a reason. I hate Stella's gone, but you're here now, and we're together just like old times. Sounds like fate to me."

I dug my nails into my palms to keep from leaping from the chair and scratching Ben's eyes out. Then I took a deep breath in through my nose, out through my mouth. So far, it had been just like old times. Ben told me beautiful lies, and I smiled and listened while he manipulated me into compliance. The difference was I no longer pretended I believed they were true. Now, I would use them to get him to do what I wanted.

"I'm not sure I believe in fate." I shook my head sorrowfully. "But it is familiar, being here with you like this. Only there must be more to Stella's death. Could she have gotten involved with something or someone dangerous? If I could find out the answers to those questions, I might be ready to move on with my life. And who knows what that would mean?" I pressed my arms together and leaned forward for maximum cleavage exposure.

Ben set down his drink—the ultimate compliment—and focused his full attention on my chest. "There's nothing I would like more than to find those answers. Anything, Grace, I'll do anything to help you get past this tragedy and live your life again. Just tell me what to do."

Despite the Lifetime movie delivery, I thought he had convinced himself he had no part in Stella's death. Whereas I compartmentalized emotional issues, he rewrote them. But I had to acknowledge that nagging notion in the back of my mind: Was it possible he hadn't been the one with his hands around my sister's neck?

"Since I didn't get to see her, I've been having trouble believing she's gone. Could you request copies of any photos in the police report?"

He frowned. "Boy, I wish I could help you with that, but I don't believe there were any."

"That's strange. My friend's government contact said they always take photographs."

His arm jerked, and he dumped most of his drink in his lap. "Dammit! Juan, get in here with a goddamn rag and clean up this mess. And bring me another." He stood and shook his hands, sending drops of gin and tonic into the air. The sunlight caught them and turned them into liquid dust motes.

"Why the fuck would you do that?" He hissed at me through clenched teeth. "You're stirring up shit you don't understand. People could get hurt, and you could be one of them." He took a step toward my chair.

I should have shouted *vase* into my bosom, but I hadn't finished.

"Why would you worry about that if you had nothing to do with Stella's death? And why did you have her body cremated so quickly? I know you're hiding something. You might have been able to beat and bully Stella, but you're not dealing with my sister anymore. You're dealing with me."

I had planned on making a dramatic exit, but he made the mistake of grabbing my arm. I tried to break away, but he tightened his grip and leaned in close enough for me to feel the heat of his alcohol-infused breath.

"With you," he snarled, stroking my cheek. "When has that ever been a problem?" He moved his hand to the back of my neck and squeezed hard.

I yanked myself from his grasp, removed the Mace from my purse, and sprayed it full force into his fat face. He fell backward and tumbled onto the floor, screaming and rubbing his eyes. Juan rushed into the room and stared at his boss, who was now writhing on the geometric pattern of the rug. Then the boy looked at me and smiled.

"Por favor, Señorita. May I show you out?"

We hustled down the long hallway, and he opened the door for me. I could hear Ben calling for him.

"Thank you, Juan." I listened to Ben's continued screaming as it grew louder and louder. "You should go see about him. I wouldn't want you to lose your job."

"I will be okay. Not so many people wish to work for Señor Wilcott," he said. "And please," he smiled again. "My name is Eduardo."

CHAPTER 21

Pride and my poor choice of shoes forced me to maintain a brisk walk instead of a full-on sprint as I left the house. Harry pulled up seconds after I reached the car, and Justin leaped from the Bronco before it came to a stop. He met me halfway on the stone pathway.

"What the hell!" he said, grabbing my shoulders. "So much for not doing anything crazy. What happened in there? The last thing we picked up was Ben saying you could get hurt. Then there was this awful, high-pitched screaming."

I gripped each of his forearms and freed myself. "We can talk about this later."

"If that asshole laid a hand on you," he glared and took a step toward the house.

"I'm fine, really. Let's just go."

Ben stopped wailing and, while I doubted he had recovered enough to be a threat, I didn't want to take any chances.

Harry was by the Bronco. "You okay? Scared the hell out of us when we lost your mic."

I slipped my index finger inside my bra and searched for the tiny device. "Shit! It's gone. It must have fallen out somewhere. I'm sorry. I'll reimburse you for it."

"Money's not the issue. Let's just hope nobody finds it. Small as it is, that's not too likely." Then he laughed. "And if that was Ben caterwauling in the background, he won't be in any shape to be looking for much of anything."

I assured them it was my ex's agonized cries trailing me on my way to the car and urged that we leave. Harry took off, and Justin insisted on driving the rental back to the hotel. He gunned the engine, spewing dirt and gravel in our wake as we sped away. He didn't speak until we reached the main road.

"I'm really pissed. You were supposed to play the son of a bitch, not send him over the edge."

"Okay, it was stupid, but all I could think about was Stella stuck in that house with him. How helpless and alone she must have felt, knowing he could do whatever he wanted to and get away with it."

The adrenaline rush I experienced after hurrying down the hill had dissolved, and I began shaking. Recalling his slack-jawed shock when that first blast of Mace hit him made me laugh, a low-pitched chuckle quickly reaching a crescendo of hysterical giggles.

"It's not funny," Justin said.

I couldn't stop laughing.

"Shit!" He slowed the car. "I mean it! There's no telling what he could have done to you."

Tears were streaming down my face. My laughter had turned to chest-rattling sobs.

He stopped on the side of the road and leaned over the gear shift to pull me close.

"It's okay."

Only it wasn't. Yes, I enjoyed seeing Ben rolling on the floor in agony. But I had blown any chance of sweet-talking information out of him and hadn't even remembered to ask him about the stolen letters. Worse still, now he would be very unlikely to release Stella's ashes, especially not to the woman who had not only caused him physical pain but had also humiliated him. I buried my head deeper into Justin's chest.

He kept his arms around me. "Don't beat yourself up. I've known lots of guys like Ben, self-satisfied pricks who aren't happy unless they're in charge. No way would he ever do something that might make him lose the upper hand." He lifted my chin and looked into my eyes. "But we'll get him. I promise."

I couldn't remember the last time I'd been this close to a man. Casual sex had never been easy for me. I'm not good at casual anything. Lesroy says it's because I think too much. Whatever it was, after Ben left, I gave up on relationships.

Looking into Justin's dark blue eyes, then down to his lips, I stopped thinking about the past. I wanted to get even closer. I traced his jawline with my fingertip.

His breathing quickened and his eyelids fluttered, then opened wide; he moaned.

"This is not a good idea."

"It's a terrible idea," I whispered into his ear. "Really, really terrible." I touched the tip of my tongue to the hollow spot at the base of his throat before bringing my mouth to his lips.

If not for the vibration in Justin's pocket, I don't know how long we might have stayed locked together. It was Harry. I could tell from the one-sided conversation he got worried when we weren't behind him anymore. Justin told him we stopped because I felt queasy but was okay now. I surmised he would wait at the bar for another strategy meeting. Then he began giving abbreviated responses, and I gave up trying to follow.

My lips were swollen, and my mouth and chin sported the beginnings of a rash from Justin's beard. I finger-combed my disheveled hair into a semblance of order and dragged out lipstick and powder.

He delivered one last, "Right. Sounds good." Then ended the call. "What's going on?"

He explained Harry planned to ask around about Adelmo Balsuto. My encounter with Ben had made me forget about the mystery man's existence, but the idea of him exhilarated me in a strange way. If he was as powerful as we'd been hearing, he could be a much better source of information. But Harry wasn't confident about the reliability of his sources when it came to getting anything solid on a man like him. He wanted to talk with our stoned hotel concierge. When I asked why, he said they were sure Prez had lots of friends in the surfing community, the type of people who could fill in details about how and with whom Stella had spent her last year.

Once we arrived at our suite, I changed out of my heels and checked my email. I hoped Justin would come with me to talk about what had happened on the way back to the hotel, but he went straight to the bar. There was a message from Mike telling me Mom was "hanging in there."

I debated how much to share regarding my meeting with Ben. Rather than admit my encounter was a disaster, I said Ben had been less than forthcoming, and we were pursuing other avenues. I promised to give details later.

After slipping into jeans and tennis shoes but keeping the V-neck, I headed to happy hour feeling anything but. I didn't regret those moments with Justin but was clueless as to what they meant.

Cheap lights dangled from the fake thatch awning over the bar, reminding me it was only a few weeks before the holiday that had always been a big deal for Stella. Santa Claus and decorations and presents. She was super into the whole thing. Her first Christmas was the last one our family celebrated together before Dad went out for cigarettes and kept on going. Maybe that's why we all worked so hard to give her the magic we lost.

Harry and Justin were the only customers. They had taken a table near the small bar. Prez Allen was seated with them. He wore a multi-colored shirt covered with dancing flamingos, cut-off jeans, and bright orange and purple tennis shoes. The open-air set-up provided a spectacular view of the ocean. Surfers in vibrant greens and yellows and violet swimsuits slashed in and out of the frothy water. Prez sipped draft beer and gazed longingly at them. He seemed startled when Harry stood and pulled out a chair for me.

"Prez has been telling us about the culture here in Montañita," Justin said.

"Not sure I'd call it culture, but it's definitely a cool place." Once again, his brilliant smile faded a little when he looked at me. "You meet people from all over the world here." He drained the last drop from his mug. "I'm having more beer. You guys want one? And what can I get for the lovely señorita?"

"Prez is the bartender, too," Justin explained. "A real Renaissance man."

"It's Fresno, Dude. I'm from Fresno."

"Of course," Harry interceded. He and Justin ordered another round, and Prez suggested I try a locally brewed wheat.

"There's no extra buzz from it, though." He laughed and ducked behind the bar.

"No buzz?" I asked.

"Ecuador used to be famous for their special honey. They got it from bees who flew over the coca fields. People said it had a little extra zing. Must be something to it since the US doesn't import it anymore."

How appropriate that Stella would have landed in a country where wholesome honey had a dark side. Prez returned with our drinks, and I took a cautious sip. The tangy taste of wheat balanced nicely with a sweet tartness. If it was drug laden, I couldn't tell.

Our bartender continued his narrative on the virtues of Montañita. Harry encouraged him with general questions and suggested we share a pitcher.

I drank slowly and noticed my companions did, too. Both kept refilling Prez's glass while the younger man praised his new home for its festive and open qualities. After about an hour, he was slurring his words. That's when Harry got more specific.

"Montañita sounds almost too good to be true. Rumor is things get a little dicey if you land on the wrong side of certain people here. Local gangsters and thugs.

"I'm not sure what you mean." Prez's tone sharpened, and I wondered if he was as drunk as I'd thought.

"When we were in Guayaquil, a friend told me we should be careful here who we offended. He mentioned somebody named Balsuto, Adelmo Balsuto, I think." Harry started to refill Prez's glass, but he covered it with his hand.

"I'm good, thanks," he said and rose from the table. "You guys seem cool and all, so I'm going to help you out. Like I said, everybody's pretty laid-back here, but it's not smart to go around mentioning names and asking questions. Unless you're interested in doing some business." He looked at Justin.

"And if we did want information on, say doing a little exporting?" Justin asked. "Would you be able to connect us with the right people? There'd be a finder's fee for you."

"I can't make any promises, but it's possible I could put you in touch with some guys." He picked up the empty pitcher. "Better get back to the bar."

Harry waited until he was out of earshot before speaking.

"That guy's a piece of work," he said.

"Agreed, and I bet he has at least a working knowledge of the criminal element here in paradise." Justin drained his glass. "I can't speak for you two, but I'm starving. Mr. Chamber of Commerce recommended a place before you joined us, Grace. Best Mexican food in town, he says."

I got up too quickly and stumbled against my chair. Justin noticed and took hold of my elbow to steady me. "I just realized I haven't eaten since breakfast. I might be a little drunk."

"I'll settle the bill, and we can go straight to the restaurant," he said, without releasing me. "I don't see our bartender anywhere."

"I'm sure he'll run a tab. Or maybe the drinks are on good old Prez," Harry offered.

On the way to the car, I glimpsed our bartender, talking on his cell phone behind a scraggly palm tree. He glanced in our direction, then turned away.

The guy might have been flaky, but his restaurant recommendation was solid. We shared orders of fish tacos, burritos, guacamole, and empanadas. Harry and Justin had another pitcher of beer, but I stuck with naranjilla juice, like orange juice back home but more tart.

After we returned to the hotel, the men had coffee at the bar. All I wanted was to take a quick shower and go to bed. The combination of adrenaline let-down from my meeting, the heated encounter with Justin, too much food and alcohol, and general disappointment at what we'd been able to find out about my sister had left me exhausted and depressed.

The pathway was darker now. Scattered lanterns hanging from tree branches cast wavering shadows. I picked up my pace. When we were kids, Lesroy always wanted to play shadow tag. He and Stella would laugh and race all over the backyard trying to overcome what she called our ghosties. But the game creeped me out. Seeing my shadow-self was like watching a part of me shift and dissolve into nothing.

As I inserted my key, I started at the sound of footsteps. Before I could face whoever was approaching, my potential assailant slipped up behind me. I recalled what I learned in the self-defense class Stella and I had taken with Mom, her idea of mother-daughter bonding, and jabbed my elbow into my attacker's rib cage.

"Dude!"

I turned to see Prez fall back, arms wrapped around his chest.

"What the hell are you doing?" I demanded.

He rubbed his injured ribs and gave me an accusing look. "That was like, really hostile. You could have done some serious damage."

"Don't be such a baby. I didn't hit you that hard. Besides, that's what happens when you sneak up on people in the dark. What in God's name do you want anyway?"

He stood there with the same weird expression on his face I'd noticed when he first saw me and later at the bar.

"I said, what do you want? And what's with that stare you keep giving me, like I've got two heads or something?"

He moved toward me. When I stepped back, he extended his hands, palms up. "It's just that one minute you're her spitting image. The next, you're nothing like her at all. Freaks me out."

"Who do mean?" I demanded. Even though I knew, I needed to hear him say it.

"Like her, Stella, your sister. It was your eyes that confused me. Hers were that crazy blue green. And yours are all gray and shimmery. But they're the same shape. And the way you tilt your head when you talk to somebody, giving him that *you're the only one in the world you want to be listening to* vibe." He sighed. "She and I were friends. I'm guessing that's why you're here, to find out what happened to her."

Without realizing what I was doing, I leaned in and grabbed his wrinkled cotton shirt in both fists. "What do you know about my sister?"

"Chill, Grace." He pried my fingers open and freed himself from my grasp. "Sorry, but I don't know much. Stella showed up at the beach about two years ago. One day she came up and asked if I would teach her to surf. I thought she was, uh, coming on to me. It was common knowledge she was married to some rich guy. People said he was a jerk. I was like sure. I mean, she was super-hot. But she just wanted to learn to surf, and she was a natural." He shrugged. "I was cool with that. We hung out a few times a week, depending on the waves. And then she stopped showing up."

"How long ago was that?"

"It's been a little over a year. I tried getting in touch with her, but she wouldn't pick up, and she never called back."

"In a place like this you must have seen her or heard something about her."

"There was talk she was seeing somebody, but no one wanted to say too much about it. This is a small town, and you can get in serious trouble for talking out of school. I liked Stella, though, and she really missed you." He gave me another strange look and shook his head. "So, I made some calls when I realized who you were. If you want, I'll set you up with someone who might help, but she'll only speak to you. And you have to ditch the muscle."

"You mean Harry and Justin?" I wanted to ask how he knew my sister really missed me, but I needed to stay focused. "That won't be easy." Thinking of how upset Justin had been when I'd gone off script with Ben, I thought it would be impossible. "And who is 'she'?"

"It's Eva, Stella's housekeeper. They were pretty tight. She called me after Stella went missing. Wanted to know if I had any word from her. She sounded real worried. Told me Wilcott had flipped out when Stella disappeared, but she didn't buy it. She asked me to get in touch if I learned anything. Then they found her. Don't worry about your buddies. I can take care of that for you. Just be ready tomorrow at ten o'clock."

Prez jumped at the sound of voices. It was Justin and Harry coming down the pathway. "Quick!" He stepped out of the shadows into the villa's entrance. "Get inside and let's keep this between you and me." He turned the key and shoved me through the doorway. "Remember," he whispered. "Be ready at ten."

"What do you mean 'take care of that'?" I asked, but he had already vanished into the night. I eased the door shut and rushed to the bathroom. By the time I got out, the lights were off in the living area and the entire apartment was quiet. I put on my pajamas and sat on the bed, wondering if I should tell Harry and Justin about the proposed meeting with Eva.

I had no doubt they would insist on going with me or on following Prez and me. And while he might not be the sharpest tool in the shed, I suspected he'd spot a tail. But if I let him "take care of it" would I be putting the men in danger? Or would I be walking into it myself? Several times I almost knocked on Justin's door to tell him about my plans, but I didn't trust myself to stick to business.

I would wait until morning to see how he planned on getting rid of my chaperons. If it looked as if they might be in trouble, I'd come clean. If not, what harm could there be talking to the one person Stella could have confided in?

CHAPTER 22

The morning sun streamed through my window. I watched the slow rotation of the ceiling fan and thought of the peaceful flight of the gulls in my dream. A thick blight of sorrow and dread dimmed the sunlight. Would this be the course of every day for the rest of my life? A few moments of emotional amnesia, then hours and hours of painful reality. Before I could fall any deeper into the grief pit, there was a knock on the bedroom door.

"Are you awake?"

It was Justin. I grabbed my robe. "Almost."

"Harry and I need to talk to you. I've got coffee started."

"Sure. Just give me a minute." I needed more time to consider whether to tell them about my late-night visitor, but stalling wouldn't do much good. I put on a pair of jeans I'd only worn once and a fresh T-shirt, sloshed mouthwash, fluffed my hair, and joined the men in the kitchen.

Justin handed me a cup of steaming coffee.

"Hope you slept well." Harry didn't wait for a response. "We've got a situation going on. Luis Cordoza called late last night. There's been a security breach in his office, and he needs my company to get involved. I'd send one of my guys to check it out, but he said it was an extremely sensitive issue. He wants me to take care of it. Says it could be several days. I feel good with Justin handling things here, or I wouldn't consider it. You two can manage without me, can't you? If you want me to stay, say the word."

Luis Cordoza? There was no way Prez had gotten to one of the chief political advisors in the country. Was there? Harry was still waiting for my answer.

"You should go. We'll be fine."

"You're a trooper. Remember, I'm less than three hours away if you need me." He shook Justin's hand and left.

"I hope you meant what you said about us being fine because we will be." Justin began pouring another cup of coffee for himself. "I want to run something by you, too." He gave me a piece of paper with block letters printed on it, reminiscent of a ransom note. "Prez stuck this under the door."

"*McElroy, if you're serious about doing business here, this is your man. Be there at 10:00 am. Come alone.*" He'd written the name Franco with what must have been a local address beside it. On the back was a roughly drawn map.

"I hope this doesn't piss you off, but you need to sit this one out. I'm guessing Franco is a front for Balsuto, and I don't want to spook him."

If Prez's plans included putting Justin in danger, he wouldn't leave an incriminating note. But what if he was too stupid to know better? Should I play it safe and fill Justin in what was going on, or let him go on what would, hopefully, be a harmless wild-goose chase?

He seemed to take my silence as anger. "I promise I'll go over everything he says."

I felt guilty at his desire to please me.

"Besides, you could use some relaxation. Shop a little or go on a nice long walk on the beach."

"A nice, long walk on the beach?" I wanted to tell him what he could do with his long walk. And, seriously, did he think I'd enjoy a shopping trip knowing the man who probably killed my sister was lounging around drinking gin and tonic? Then I realized he had given me the perfect out.

"That sounds lovely," I said, smiling sweetly. "You go on and see what you can find out. I'll just relax.

He tilted his head as if he misheard me.

"Well, then." He took his cup to the counter. "It's after eight and Prez's directions say I'm an hour out. I want to get there early to scout out the area. Are you sure you'll be all right by yourself?"

The genuine concern in his voice gave me another pang of guilt. I remembered the way his lips felt when he kissed me. But I was determined to follow through.

"I'll be fine. I need to take a shower before I head out. Promise to call and let me know you're okay."

"Why wouldn't I be?"

Well, because the whole thing is a set-up, and I'm a terrible person for letting you walk into what might be a really, really dangerous situation. "I'm sure you will, but stay in touch anyway, please."

I darted for the bathroom to avoid more questions. Showering in Montañita was quite the challenge. The water had to be brought in, and the pressure was almost nonexistent. I danced under a lukewarm trickle, trying to lather and rinse. I took my time to make sure Justin had gone before I came out of my room. Lukewarm turned to cold, but I was well-rinsed. I wore the same skirt with a modest short-sleeve blouse. No need to distract Prez with cleavage.

At ten on the dot, he knocked; we were in his Jeep Renegade and on our way in less than five minutes. My escort looked as if he had taken time with his appearance—fresh shave, combed hair, a clean shirt, and pressed shorts. Was he trying to impress me, or was Eva much younger and hotter than I imagined?

We rode to the highway in silence while I planned how to ask about Luis Cordoza and how he'd gotten him to request Harry's presence. I decided on a direct approach.

"So, how did you pull it off, Prez?"

He kept his eyes on the road. "Pull what off?"

"Getting Harry to go back to Guayaquil, that's what. Who do you know at the government office? And who is Franco?"

"I'm not the one who took care of Harry. The plan was for Justin to go alone and have Harry follow another lead. That Cordova fellow really did send for the old dude. And Franco's a buddy of mine. He knows how things work here."

"How do they work here? Can you get away with murder in beautiful Montañita?"

He turned to me with wild eyes. "Be careful what you say, Grace. I mean murder, wow. That's harsh. And I can't tell you anymore. You'll have to wait until we're there."

Prez took a narrow road near the ocean. After about fifteen minutes, I began to worry.

"Where does Eva live?" *Or should I ask how many miles from town do we have to be for you to bury my body? And how foolish had I been not to tell anyone where I was going?*

"She had a change of plans and won't be home until later. We're taking a side trip, a place your sister liked. But don't worry. It's not that far and we'll have plenty of time for both."

When the crazed killer tells you not to worry, you know you're done for. I took out my phone, but who would I call? I could text Mike and tell him Prez Allen was the last person to see me alive. Of course, that would scare the hell out of him. But I needn't have been concerned. There was no cell reception.

"Service is sketchy out here. We're almost there."

I wondered if he and Stella had spent more time together than he indicated. Maybe I had misunderstood his relationship with my sister.

"Did you and Stella go here a lot?"

He ignored my question and posed one of his own. "Have you ever seen a blue-footed booby?" Prez glanced at me and grinned.

"I'm sorry. Did you say blue-footed booby?"

"Funny, right?" He giggled like a middle-school boy. "Booby." He laughed again. "It's not what you think." He paused. "It's a bird."

My lack of response must have seemed an insult to the booby, and he repeated emphatically, "A bird. A seagull with big blue feet. You can't get this close to Los Piqueros Patas Azules without checking out the boobies of Puerto Lopez." He chuckled again.

"Look, Prez. I don't see what looking at some blue-footed birds has to do with finding out the truth about Stella. And is that where we're going? Los Piqueros whatever? How far is it anyway?"

"Chill, Grace. Get in touch with the universe. Trust me, the booby is the way to go." Thankfully, he managed not to crack himself up.

"And don't be so hung up on time. We have all we need." He smiled at me, took a CD from the visor, inserted it, and began singing along with Jerry Garcia and The Dead, "A Friend of the Devil is a Friend of Mine."

I didn't read too much into his choice of music and surrendered to the universe. Splashes of color from lavender, yellow, and red flowers growing wild lined the road. A warm breeze rippled through them, carrying their sweet scent with it.

The farther we got from Montañita, the more deserted the beach became. A few surfers slipped in and out of the waves, and groups of sun worshipers draped themselves over chairs or napped on blankets in the golden-brown sand. Clouds skimmed the ocean, casting reflections that made it impossible to determine where sea and sky separated.

We passed stretches of uninhabited shoreline. It was after eleven, and I was getting close to demanding he take me back to the hotel when a large, wooden sign featuring seagulls with big blue feet announced we were in Piqueros Patas Azules.

"We're here," he said and pulled the car into a gravel parking lot.

The combination bar and restaurant featured open-air seating. Hammocks with views of the ocean were strung between palm trees. Colorful umbrellas over wooden benches offered additional places to sit. About a dozen patrons sat at the tables scattered along the shoreline. One couple, entangled in a hammock, swung lazily back and forth.

"It's the Piqueros Patas Azules, the Blue Booby. They have the freshest seafood in the entire world. And there's a cool museum here. I've never been inside, but the sign looks cool." He hopped from the jeep, came around for me, and made a big show of helping me out of the vehicle. This was the first time he had been so gentlemanly, and it struck me as odd, as if he were trying to impress someone other than me.

When we walked in, the bartender greeted Prez by name. They shared an elaborate handshake before my escort introduced me as Grace from the States. Then he ordered two drafts and carried both to the table closest to the beach, set them down, and pulled out my chair.

He asserted they had the best ceviche in town and insisted I try it. At home I would have avoided raw seafood, no matter how wonderful the citrus sauce marinade was. But he was convincing, so I agreed to give it a shot.

"I'm good with whatever, as long as it's not guinea pig."

When he left to place our order, I strolled back through the bar in search of a restroom. Nautical memorabilia covered the walls. Crinkled, carelessly framed maps seemed in danger of disintegration. A rusted anchor the size of a plump five-year-old child sat in a corner. Besides the bells and compasses scattered throughout the restaurant, a gigantic tortoiseshell hung next to an enormous jawbone identified as belonging to a killer shark.

The restroom was all the way in the back. When I returned, an assortment of food awaited me.

"Just in time," he said. "Dig in."

The tart aroma of citrus and the yeasty smell of freshly baked pastry was a perfect combination.

"They make their empanadas with beer dough," Prez explained between bites. "It's unfreaking believable."

We dug in. Our only conversation was if I wanted another drink. I did and he went to get them.

The tide had gained momentum. Bronzed creatures, predominantly male with a few intrepid females in the mix, paddled out to the invisible line where the waves grew into monstrous forces. These fearless surfers rose from the sea to mount crests with the power to toss them aside as if they were rag dolls. Most rode with admirable prowess. Occasionally, one would disappear under the weight of the water, and I would hold my breath until the ocean spewed him back to the surface.

A tiny blonde woman paddled out, farther and farther from the shore. She rose on her board and hovered like a hummingbird before launching her slight frame up and onto the top of a wave. For a moment, I was certain Stella was alive, flying above the sea with the birds from my dream.

A sudden shadow blocked my view. At first, I thought Prez had returned. But this man was shorter and thicker.

"May I please join you?" He sat and removed his Panama hat. His shoulders were more bent than in the photograph, and he'd grown a full beard. But there was no mistaking those blazing, intense eyes. It was Adelmo Balsuto.

"I do not mean to frighten you, Grace Burnette." He spoke with what Stella and I had called *the late-night DJ introducing a seduction song* voice. He kept those burning eyes fixed on mine.

"You didn't," I lied. "I just wasn't expecting you. I was supposed to meet Eva. What are you doing here?"

He stared at me before answering. "It is strange how much you're like her."

"Listen, I'm with someone and if you don't leave—"

"You are here with Preston Allen. I asked him to bring you here so we could talk."

"What would we have to discuss?"

"Ah, Grace. Stella said you could be strong willed, but you are also clever. I understand you want to uncover what happened to your sister. I will help you with that. Would you be so kind as to come with me?" He extended his hand.

Something about Adelmo Balsuto made his request seem more of a command, gentle but still an order. I never follow orders from men I have just met, but he was different. It could have been because he'd known my sister so well, or because I desperately needed to learn what he knew. Whatever it was, I put my hand in his, and he led me from the safety of the beach to the other side of the bar. We walked to a narrow pathway that slipped behind low-lying dunes. I squealed when a streak of color scurried across my feet and disappeared down a hole in the sand. Two stalks with eyeballs at their ends periscoped up and watched as I hurried past.

Balsuto laughed. "We have disturbed the locals. Red, yellow, blue—beautiful little crustaceans."

We continued several more yards until the pathway narrowed, making it necessary for him to walk ahead of me. We passed a thick plexiglass display with shards of pottery inside it. Among the broken pieces, an intact pot lay on its side.

My mysterious guide stopped and pointed to the container. "That is a funeral urn containing the skull of a former resident," he explained and continued walking.

I looked closer and, indeed, there was what appeared to be a human skull lodged in the container. Shuddering, I hurried to catch up. We came to a small clearing and a long rectangular building. A wooden sign announced we had reached El Museo de las Antiguedos, The Museum of Antiquities, according to my limited knowledge of Spanish.

"Please, Señor Balsuto, why have you brought me here? What does this place have to do with my sister?"

"If you would indulge me." He pushed open the door. The dimly lit room was at least ten degrees cooler. Shafts of sunlight laden with dancing particles of dust illuminated the shelves of ceramic pots and tiny wooden figures.

"Welcome to what remains of the Valdivian culture. A friend of my father is the curator and owner of this modest facility dedicated to preserving a small portion of the history of my people."

He took my hand again, and we walked past the exhibit room through the back exit. I blinked in the punishing light. When my eyes adjusted, an explosion of color greeted me. The contrast between the darkness and the brilliant hues was other worldly. We sat on a stone bench in the middle of the garden.

"Lovely, isn't it? Perhaps a reminder to us that while we think we are the masters of the universe, it is nature that will prevail. Do you smell that? Ecuadorian roses. The most beautiful fragrance in the world."

An aroma of musk and strawberries drifted through the air.

"We came here often. She said it reminded her of home, your grandmother and her flowers."

I hadn't thought of Gran's garden in years. Tea roses, somewhat temperamental and difficult to cultivate, were her favorite. My sister picked the buds to watch them spread open in a vase. But I hated that. I wanted to let them stay outside and blossom in the sun.

"Thinking about home was hard for your sister. She missed you and your mother very much. She would not talk about it, but I guessed you and she had a falling out. I gathered her husband was involved." His upper lip curled. "I could not comprehend how such a man captured someone like Stella. Now I cannot fathom how he could have attracted a woman of your caliber."

"I don't understand it myself. But I didn't come here to talk about me. Do you have information about her or not?"

"I will tell you all I know."

"That would be wonderful, Senor Balsuto."

"Yes, but you must call me Adelmo." He held my hand. "Agreed?"

I nodded, surprised at the flutter I felt at his touch.

"We met at a party Wilcott had for some of our mutual business associates. I intended to make an appearance and leave. But then I saw her, standing on the deck, gazing at the ocean. Her white dress was cut low in the back. Her skin shone with moonlight. When I reached her side, she turned and smiled. But the smile stopped at her eyes, so beautiful like the sea." He sighed and looked toward the water. "It is, how would you say, corny?" Adelmo laughed softly. "Yes, corny. But I was lost."

I started to tell him he wasn't the first man to get lost over Stella; instead, I nodded and waited for him to continue.

"I explained I knew her husband through business connections, and the smile disappeared. She backed off as if to run. I begged her to stay. I thought at first, she would refuse, but, to my surprise, she led me to a secluded spot where we could see the ocean. We spoke for hours before noticing the last of the guests was leaving. Stella told me I must go. She seemed frightened, but I could not leave so soon. I pleaded with her to meet me the following day at a café in the village. She agreed to try but made no promise."

"Please, Adelmo," I interrupted. "I love a romantic fairy tale as much as the next person, but I'm pressed for time. Do you think you could cut to the chase?" He looked puzzled. "Could you skip to the part that pertains to how she died?"

"The story cannot be rushed, dear Grace. I need you to understand our relationship was no cheap dalliance. We had a deep connection from the beginning. I loved your sister very much. But I will try to, as you say, slice to the chase."

He told me there were many parties after that, including Halloween when he had become Rhett to Stella's Scarlett. He knew these elaborate get-togethers were her way of fighting her growing unhappiness in her marriage. At some point they became "intimate," and he discovered welts and bruises on her body. When he questioned her, she denied it was her husband, but Adelmo was no fool.

They saw each other whenever Ben was out of town. He realized what they had was much more than some tawdry affair. Stella admitted her husband was hurting her, and she wanted to leave him and go home. Even though it would have meant losing her, he vowed to help. About that time Ben became suspicious. She insisted she was being followed, so they took a break. They stayed in touch through letters delivered by Eva until Ben intercepted one and fired her. The next day he received another note telling him they were finished.

"But I did not believe her. I knew she loved me as much as I loved her. Something had frightened her. She feared Ben was desperate, that she might not be the only one he would hurt. That he might go after someone she loved. He had made threats in the past. And he knows many dangerous people, both here and in the States."

"You think he threatened me or my mother?"

"She never said so directly, but I am most certain he did."

The possibility Stella had stayed with Ben to protect our family had never occurred to me. But according to her calls to Mom, she was coming home. Either she hadn't been that worried about his threats, or something more powerful had moved her. If I could discover which one it was, I might be closer to finding out how she ended up dead on the beach.

"Before she died, Stella booked a flight to the States. Why would she do that if she was afraid Ben would hurt us?"

He looked away before answering. "I had not seen her for over five months. I tried to reach her, but it was as if she had disappeared. She meant everything to me, but I cannot say what was in her heart. That we will never understand."

We sat in the garden watching the iridescent blur of a dozen or more tiny hummingbirds as they fluttered above the fragrant blossoms. The creatures filled the air with their jeweled colors—jade, emerald, amethyst, ruby. A soft chirping melody accompanied their frantic movements, and the low buzz of their wings in motion was a hypnotic backbeat. Their flickering dance reminded me of the fireflies we chased as children.

Before we left the garden, I turned to my sister's lover. His heavily lashed eyes were downcast, giving him the look of a much younger man despite his thick, gray-streaked beard. Adelmo's interlaced fingers dangled in front of him. I imagined them on Stella's body and trembled.

"I should return you now, I suppose." Once again, he reached for my hand. I hesitated, fearful he might feel me trembling and read my mind. But the moment passed. His touch brought nothing but sadness for our mutual loss.

On our walk to the beach, I told him about Stella's stolen letters and my laptop and how much I wanted them back. He promised to check in with his contacts in Guayaquil but offered scant hope.

"I'm sure the thief was after your computer and grabbed the letters without thought. Most likely he disposed of them as soon as he discovered they were of no value."

When we reached the beachside table, Prez was waiting for us. The men exchanged greetings and excused themselves to talk while I sat gazing at the sea. I was surprised to see how low the sun had sunk. It was after three, later than I thought. A lone booby approached me with a hopeful look.

"Sorry, little guy, but I'm not supposed to feed you." He flipped his tail feathers before waddling off, leaving me to wonder if Stella had seen the same bird. I watched him join a larger group of birds. Seeing that he wasn't alone on such a beautiful afternoon brought me a glimmer of happiness.

I flinched when Adelmo touched my shoulder.

"I didn't mean to startle you. I can stay no longer, but I promise to let you know what I discover." He gave me a card with his contact information. "Please go now with Prez to see Eva. But be very careful about discussing your sister with anyone else. And stay away from Wilcott. Also, do not believe everything you hear while you are with us in Montañita. It is a place of lies and deception." He raised my hand to his lips and kissed my palm, lingering before releasing it. "But there is one truth you may count on, Grace Burnette. I will find out why our Stella did not come home to her family, and I will set things right."

His eyes no longer blazed with intensity. Instead, they were cold. Cold enough to make me shiver in the warm sunlight.

CHAPTER 23

Prez and I stayed until Adelmo disappeared inside the restaurant. Then we proceeded to the jeep, where he explained Eva's was on the way back to the hotel.

My companion wasn't his chatty self, leaving me to wonder what they had discussed while I had been conversing with the booby.

As we cruised along, I replayed my conversation with Adelmo. Other than confirming he and Stella were lovers, the only surprise was Stella's five-month absence. I couldn't understand why they had spent the time apart. But why would he lie? Had he given me a clue when he warned me not to believe all I heard in Montañita?

Prez proved true to his word, and in about ten minutes we turned onto a one-lane gravel road that dead-ended in a clearing. Chickens scratched around the front yard of the square house set on cement blocks. When we pulled up, they scattered. A few roosted on the thatched roof, clucking angrily as we passed. A bear-like creature charged from underneath the steps.

As he closed in on us, I backed up and bumped into Prez, who seemed unconcerned about the beast.

"Hey, there Bruno, my man." He held out his arms, and the dog leaped into them.

"Bruno!" Someone called from the doorway. "No, no! Perro malo!"

"No problemo, Señora Eva." He pushed him aside. "It's okay. You're a big baby. Aren't you, boy?" Bruno ambled alongside us as we proceeded on the smooth dirt path.

A woman with skin the color of creamed coffee stepped out. She was shorter than me, maybe five three or four. Her long, dark hair, parted in the middle, accentuated her slender face. Gold-rimmed glasses gave her a scholarly demeanor. She wore a simple peasant blouse and a bright red and yellow, ankle-length skirt.

"Buenos dias," she said. "This must be Grace." She held out her hand, and I took it. "I am Eva. So pleased to meet Stella's beautiful sister." Smiling, she led us to her doorway. Prez stopped at the bottom of the steps.

"I'll wait out here, so you can have some privacy."

The air in the front room was cool and almond-scented. Floral curtains were closed, and it was several seconds before my eyes adjusted. When they did, the first thing I saw was an intricately patterned tapestry, separating the room into two spaces. Interwoven shades of blue and green reminded me of the ocean view from Stella's home. Eva drew back the drapes, and sunlight dappled the thick white rug that covered much of the floor. Two delicately carved wooden chairs with leather seats sat on either side of a matching table.

"Please." She motioned toward a chair. "Sit. I will bring limonada." She glided through the tapestry opening with Bruno at her heels, leaving me alone in the simple, but spotless home. A crucifix held the position of honor above the small fireplace, and family pictures adorned whitewashed walls. There were several spots where it looked as if she had removed photographs. Perhaps she, too, had lost someone she loved, and the sight of his or her smiling face had been too much to bear.

She returned with a tray, two glasses of lemonade, and a plate of snow-powdered cookies.

"Polvorones." She pointed to the platter. "We make them at Christmas with ground almonds and sweet milk. Please, eat." She sat beside me with Bruno at her feet.

Despite my heavy lunch, the sweets smelled too good to pass on. "Thank you." I bit into one and moaned as it melted on my tongue. "Oh, my God. This is the best cookie I've ever tasted."

She smiled. "They were also a favorite of your sister. She would eat them straight from the oven, covering her mouth and chin with the powder of the sugar."

Stella always had a sweet tooth. When we were little, Gran banished her from the kitchen because she ate the cookies as fast as we baked them. I dropped my half-eaten cookie onto my plate, not realizing I was staring at it until Eva spoke.

"I cannot think how you must miss her."

My throat closed, and I erupted into a coughing fit. She suggested a sip of lemonade.

"I've missed her for so very long. But I always thought there would be plenty of time to fix things, to stop missing her. I can't accept I'll never see her again. That's why I came. I have to find out what happened, why she's gone."

She ran her fingers through Bruno's fur. "I'm afraid there is very little I can do to help. I was not with her these last months. Señor Wilcott set fire to me."

I sat up straighter, then remembered what Adelmo had said about Ben letting Eva go. "He fired you?"

"Yes. Not such a problem, not working for him. But I hated to leave her alone with that hijo de puta."

My Spanish was rusty, but I recognized puta.

"I'm sorry to say, but your sister's husband is an evil man."

"Don't be sorry. I couldn't agree with you more. Do you believe he is responsible for her death?"

"I cannot say. I know he was rough with her, but I never saw it myself. Sometimes she had terrible marks on her arms and legs. Once, even on her neck. But she refused to admit it was him."

Ben would have been too clever to let anyone see him abuse Stella. But there was no other explanation. Still, it was a stretch between knocking her around and killing her in cold blood.

"She told me things were not so pleasant between you. She did not explain why, only that she had done something terrible and was afraid you could never forgive her. She wanted to make things right. I urged her to return to her home."

I wiped my eyes. "You said Ben let you go. Did he give you a reason?"

Before she could answer, Bruno jumped to his feet and began growling. An engine roared and tires ground on gravel. She rushed to the front of the house.

"Are you expecting someone?"

"Mierda! It is that ass-hat police captain, a friend of Señor Wilcott."

I laughed. Ass-hat had been Stella's "go-to" insult. Her high school biology teacher for failing her, her boss for insisting she be on time, a policeman for ticketing her—all ass-hats.

"We cannot talk in front of this person."

"Don't worry. I've got this." I walked to the porch where I saw a uniformed man leaning on Prez's window. Prez was gesturing wildly. I hoped he'd left his stash at home. Leaving Eva and Bruno standing in the doorway, I moved toward them.

"Can I help you, officer?"

He turned to me, his enormous belly threatening to burst out of his shirt. "I am looking for Señorita Grace Burnette." Echoes of five-year-old Stella in the grocery store announcing the woman behind us in the checkout line was *the fattest lady she'd ever seen* came to mind. "You found her," I said.

"Señorita Burnette, I am Officer Ricardo Ramirez, and I have an order to detain you on charges of assault." He handed me the paper and unclipped a pair of handcuffs from his belt. "I would ask that you come peacefully."

At some point, Prez slipped out of the car. He stepped between me and the police officer and took the document from my shaking hands.

After a quick glance, he spoke in rapid Spanish. Ramirez shook his head and spat out several sentences while pointing at me. I checked to see if Eva was watching, but she and Bruno had disappeared behind the front door. I hoped I hadn't brought trouble to the one person who seemed to have cared for my sister without wanting anything in return. The men continued to argue. The officer threw up his hands and stomped to his car.

"What the hell is going on?" I demanded. "Am I under arrest?"

"Not exactly," Prez answered. "It's more complicated here than in the US, especially with tourists. The warrant requires you to go to police headquarters, so he can make a formal charge. He was going to take you in himself, but I explained how that might not look so good for him to be seen dragging in a helpless American woman who just lost her sister. I got him to agree to let me drive you to the station." He took my elbow and began leading me to the jeep.

"Wait a minute!" I stopped. "You mean you're taking me to jail?" I pictured being locked up with scantily clad hookers.

"Don't worry. I'll make some calls. The worst that happens is you sit in a detaining cell for an hour, maybe less. We've got to get out of here before Ramirez changes his mind and takes you in himself. Trust me; you do not want to ride in the back of that squad car."

We followed the police car for several miles before Prez got a signal. Once again, he spoke in Spanish. He hung up and dialed another number before I could question him. The second call lasted over ten minutes.

"Okay," he said after disconnecting. "We've got a plan. A lawyer friend of mine will be waiting for us. You let him do all the talking. I mean all of it. Don't admit to anything. If they ask questions, play dumb."

I leaned my head against the window frame and closed my eyes. Only a few days ago, I'd been safe inside my tidy life, far away from this strange place. I had a job I liked and my sister's dog, who tolerated me. I wouldn't say I was happy, but I wasn't a felon. Now here I was, thousands of miles from home on my way to jail.

After about twenty minutes, we pulled into a gravel lot near a whitewashed building with a triangular roof and POLICIA written on the awning. There were only three other vehicles. Ramirez got out and waited by his car.

"You will walk in with me, Señorita." The officer grasped my upper arm and guided me inside. Prez followed, and a slender, white-haired man greeted him.

"My good friend, Preston Allen!" They shook hands and patted each other on the back while I stood by the unmanned reception desk. Ramirez barked out something unintelligible and stomped away. Prez introduced me to Charles Douglas, attorney at law. With his silver hair and thick, matching mustache, he looked like a TV star in a courtroom drama. He assured me there would be no problem, and I was not to worry. Then his cell rang. He excused himself to answer it.

"I'm heading out now," Prez said, patting me on the back. "You're in expert hands. Nobody here knows about that jury tampering thing in the States."

"But I thought you were staying." I inhaled a deep cleansing breath before the rest of Prez's statement registered. I lowered my voice. "Wait, did you say jury tampering? Wouldn't they disbar him for that?"

"Relax. As far as anybody here's concerned, he's still a full-fledged attorney." He shifted his weight from one foot to the other. "I'm not so popular with the local police, though. Me being here isn't much of a bonus for you. But don't worry. McElroy's on his way to post bail." He scurried out just as Ramirez reappeared accompanied by an older officer with a much calmer demeanor.

The men spoke to my lawyer as if I wasn't there. Ramirez shouted and shook his fist in my direction. I pretended to study the wanted posters on the bulletin board while watching out of the corner of my eye. The second policeman put his hand on Ramirez's back and whispered to him. Mumbling to himself, Ramirez strode away. After another few minutes of chatting, the others approached me.

"We have come to what I like to call a gentleman's agreement," Douglas said. "Or in your case, a gentle woman's agreement." He chuckled. "You will be escorted to the holding area to appease the honorable Officer Ramirez while I fill out some paperwork. It won't take long. By the time I'm finished, your friend should be here, and you may return to your hotel."

A younger man came through the doorway and motioned for me to follow him. We shuffled down a short hallway where he unlocked a heavy metal door and ushered me in. A narrow passage ran through the center of the long, dark corridor. We passed three individual cells on both sides. My jailer stopped at an open enclosure smaller than my walk-in closet at home. A chill came over me as he clanged the door shut, leaving me alone in my cell.

CHAPTER 24

A cot with a grungy mattress was shoved against one wall, and a rust-stained sink next to a toilet without a seat took up the other. The air was dank and stale, with the tang of disinfectant and urine clinging to it. If there were other prisoners, I couldn't see or hear them. The thick silence was more frightening than being surrounded by angry hookers.

I had no cup to rattle against the bars, so I sat on the edge of the cot. Some other poor captive had drawn a heart with the name Raul in the center. The artist had stuck a dagger between the "a" and the "u." I remembered an article claiming most women in US prisons were there for committing crimes connected to either men or drugs, often both. I suspected this wasn't only an American phenomenon.

I decided I had two options. I could sit on this miserable mattress and feel sorry for myself, or I could try to figure out why I was sitting here and what I could do about it.

Option one felt good, but it was also too familiar. Hadn't I been wallowing in my pain ever since I caught Ben and Stella frolicking in the shower? True, they had betrayed me in the worst way, but hadn't I exhausted my share of self-pity and bitterness? I now had a healthy serving of guilt on my plate for not forgiving her before her death. No, I'd spent more than enough time festering in my own sorrow.

I chose option two. I would sort out events since my arrival to determine what they might tell me about how and why my sister died. The problem was Ben. Our last visit hadn't pleased him.

Ever the gamesman, he expected to charm his way into my heart—and various other body parts—while blaming his wife for their bad behavior.

He believed we would pick up where we were before he married my sister. I wished I could have dismissed this idea as ridiculous. What self-respecting woman would take back a man who cheated on her in such a demeaning way? But if I were being honest with myself—something about sitting in a jail cell encouraged unfettered reflection—I would have to admit the old Grace might have considered rekindling our romance. Not so much because I loved the bastard, but because losing Stella had left a gaping hole in my heart—one I was terrified I would never fill.

So, it wasn't crazy for him to imagine a reconciliation. And it wasn't illogical that when I hadn't followed his script, he went berserk. I pictured him struggling up, eyes inflamed from the blast of Mace, and how furious he must have been knowing I won that round. But he would never concede the game so easily. No, he would plan his next move.

That's when it hit me: Ben was having me followed. He knew I'd met with both Eva and Adelmo. He had been the one who sent the sheriff to arrest me. And if he had enough pull to do that, it wasn't a stretch to believe he had manipulated Stella's investigation to go his way.

I had to get out of this stupid cell and do something.

Before I could determine what that might look like, footsteps sounded in the corridor. The same guard who locked me up released me.

Justin and Ramirez stood behind the reception desk. Justin's mouth was set in a thin, grim line. I could almost hear his teeth grinding.

"You are free to go for now, Señorita Burnette. But you are forbidden to step within one hundred feet of Señor Ben Wilcott."

I gave Ramirez what I hoped was a disdainful glance, brushed past the men, and sashayed into the warmth of blinding sunlight. It had been less than two hours since I'd entered the local jail, but it seemed much longer. I sucked in deep gulps of freedom.

Justin passed me without speaking. I followed him to the rental, and he started the ignition before I was inside, barely giving me the chance to shut the door before he gunned the engine. His tires squealed as he cut the wheel and sped onto the main road, sending gravel spraying in our wake.

After we were on the main road, I gave him a side-eyed glance and saw the muscles in his jaw twitching. Aviator sunglasses hid his eyes, but the crease above the bridge of his nose was deeper than usual.

I cleared my throat. "I appreciate you —"

"Do. Not. Speak." He pressed his foot on the accelerator, snapping my neck into the headrest.

Clumps of wildflowers and shrubbery blurred as we flew toward the villa. I wondered what had happened with Justin. Had Prez's contact given him any real information, or had he wasted his entire morning? By now, I was sure he was aware both he and Harry had been sent on fools' errands. Shit! I'd forgotten about Harry.

I remembered the expression on Luis Cordoza's face when he told us there were no pictures in Stella's file. If it was procedure to photograph the body, why would my sister's case have been different? I suspected there had been photos and somehow Ben had gotten possession of them.

Justin screeched into our parking spot at the villa and hit the brakes hard. When I reached for the door handle, he spoke.

"Hold on," he commanded. "I need a minute." He exhaled and continued. "What the hell were you thinking? Sending me off to talk to some stoner about buying weed from the locals while you were off doing God knows what with that lunatic Allen!"

I started to answer, but he hadn't finished.

"And what about Harry? Is he chasing his tail in Guayaquil so you could play Nancy Drew?"

"Well, I —"

"And getting arrested in a foreign country? You realize you don't have any rights here? They could lock you up and throw away the key. That's what I should have let them do. At least, I'd know where you were."

He scowled at me. I expected a second wind, so I saw no need to respond.

"I was worried sick when I realized you'd gone off by yourself. Which I figured out as soon as I met that dimwit boy Prez tried to pass off as a local gangster. When I got to the hotel and you weren't there, I was sure he tricked you, too. A maid told me you and that jughead took off after I left and I thought, *Oh, no! Grace might be in trouble running around with that hippie imbecile.*" He pounded the steering wheel and glared at me. "And I was right; you were in trouble. But not because Prez was a threat. Oh, no. Because you went along with him willingly without a clue of what he might do to you. And you didn't tell me anything."

He took off his sunglasses and waved them close to my face. I scooted as far away as possible.

"If you'll let me explain," I began.

"Oh, you're going to explain, all right. But not here. Come on. Let's go."

He released the auto-lock and shoved his door open. I trailed behind as he stormed down the path.

He went straight to the refrigerator, removed a bottle of aguardiente, opened it, and poured it into a juice glass. He drank and shuddered. Then he poured another and handed it to me.

All I wanted to do was wash the jailhouse off me but refusing him didn't seem to be an option. I sipped and gasped as the fiery liquid blazed its way down my esophagus. A droplet slipped into my windpipe, and I began choking. Justin sat at the kitchen table where he watched while I sputtered. After several seconds, I caught my breath.

"Jesus! This stuff is terrible." I fanned myself.

He ignored my beverage critique. "Hey, if you're tough enough to get thrown in jail for assault, you're tough enough to drink a little guaro, right?"

I intended to be contrite when I explained how Prez said Stella's housekeeper would only speak to me, but I was getting sick and tired of his high-handedness. Sure, his morning had been a waste, but at least he hadn't gotten arrested and thrown into a Third World jail.

I braced myself and tilted the glass. The second swallow was just as awful, but since I knew what to expect, I relaxed a bit as the heat radiated through me. I set it on the table and stared at him.

"Are you ready to hear my side?" I asked.

For the next ten minutes, I recounted my conversation with Prez and Eva's insistence I come alone. I explained how Ramirez interrupted us and finished with how Prez's lawyer friend negotiated my release. Then I thanked Justin for bailing me out and apologized for wasting his morning.

I kept my meeting with Adelmo a secret.

"You did more than waste my time, Grace." He stood and looked down at me. "You showed a complete lack of faith."

His expression made me forget how obnoxious he'd been earlier.

"You trusted some burned-out beach boy more than you do me and Harry."

I felt another round of remorse.

"It's not that I don't trust you," I began.

"Don't give me that bullshit! You haven't been honest with me this entire trip."

"Honest? You're mad at me because I haven't been honest? You tell me my mother hired you to kill someone and then never say whether you plan on doing it. How could I trust you?"

He slammed his palm on the table.

"How could you believe I'm a stone-cold killer? Is that who you thought I was yesterday in the car? Does being with a potential murderer turn you on?"

"Please, I need some time to think." I stood and pushed away so quickly my chair tipped and crashed onto the floor. I stumbled past it and ran toward my room, but he was too quick and caught me at the doorway.

He held my shoulders and glared. "I'm not a killer, Grace. Your mother was half out of her mind when she found out what happened. She told Mike she intended to find someone to settle the score. Said she knew some tough guys from her old neighborhood—hillbilly Mafia types. He was afraid she'd ask the wrong person and get arrested, or worse, so he called me. I agreed to go along so things wouldn't get out of control. You weren't supposed to know anything about it, but I can't seem to keep my mouth shut around you. It's awful what your sister and Ben did to you. But someday you're going to have to learn to trust people.

I dissolved into his chest, warmed by his heat. He crushed his body against mine, then covered my mouth with his. The kiss was soft, moving from my mouth to my neck. I pulled him close and gasped as his lips touched flesh.

He leaned away from me. "Are you sure you want to do this?"

I couldn't remember when I'd been more certain of anything. I nodded and led him into my room. We stood beside the bed. He guided my body to his and began kissing me again, more insistent now, as he cupped the fullness of my hips.

When I glimpsed our reflection in the mirror, I panicked. I had very little confidence in the love-making department. Before Ben I'd only had two serious relationships, my college boyfriend and an accountant I met through a friend. Sex with the first one was enthusiastic but bumbling. With the second, it was thorough but systematic and uninspired. Sex with Ben had been a production. Rose petals strewn across the bedspread, champagne on ice, expensive lingerie. But it became clear he was the star of the show.

My initial clue was the oval mirror mounted on the ceiling above his bed. The first time we had sex at his place, the lights were mercifully low, so I hadn't seen it. I had too much wine in anticipation of being seduced and threw myself into the act with my personal imitation of reckless abandon. Things had been progressing nicely when he started barraging me with a series of dirty questions. Did I like it when he did that? Or this? Maybe I wanted that? I was at a loss for responses. Later, I learned it had nothing to do with my answers. It was about the interrogation, a sexual grilling. I was so busy trying to process information, I didn't realize we finished. It wasn't until the next morning, when I had the creepy notion we were being watched, that I noticed my naked reflection gazing down on me.

When I told him I was uncomfortable performing with myself as an audience, he explained that he loved seeing me from every angle. I ignored the fact that the mirror had preceded me or that he got more time in front of it than I did. He assured me I would come to love looking at myself. I never did.

I always wondered how the script had changed when it was Stella's body hovering over him. My sister was not a supporting actress.

Justin's hands moved from my hips to my breasts, brushing over my nipples. I moaned and guided his hand inside my blouse. He sat and pulled me onto his lap. I wrapped my legs around his waist, and thoughts of Ben and the past disappeared.

CHAPTER 25

I woke alone in tangled sheets and heard Justin talking in the other room. I slipped into my clothes and joined him.

"It turns out Harry's trip to the city wasn't a complete bust. Cordoza gave him the name of the guy who took photos of the accident and Harry met with him." He paused before adding, "He has the pictures, Grace."

"Oh." I had trouble speaking. Guilt surged over me. For the past few hours, I hadn't thought of Stella at all. I had been behaving like some college coed on spring break. But the knowledge I would soon see the last photographs ever taken of my beautiful sister brought me crashing head-on into reality.

He wrapped his arms around me, and we stood together for a moment before he spoke. "Harry won't be back until late. Why don't I make dinner? Then we can get some rest and look at the pictures in the morning."

I watched as he scrambled eggs and fried bacon. The image of Adelmo's burning eyes turning cold when he promised to find out what happened to my sister came to me. Stella's lover was another example of the dual nature of this beautiful but dangerous country.

"Hey," Justin said as he placed my plate in front of me. "You seem a million miles away."

"I'm just tired." I dragged my fork through the eggs, then put it down.

"I've heard doing hard time is exhausting." He rested his fingertips on mine. "You'll feel better if you eat," he urged.

I choked down a few bites before giving up. "It's good, but I guess I'm not as hungry as I thought. I think I'll go to bed." I stood and picked up my plate.

"I'll get that." Justin eased it from my hand. "You rest. Tomorrow could be rough." He kissed the top of my head.

If it disappointed him I didn't invite him to join me, he didn't show it.

I showered, changed into pajamas, and fell onto the bed. Thoughts of the tiny blonde surfer at lunch reminded me of the last time Stella and I had gone to the Gulf, the summer she was almost fourteen and I was a few weeks from my nineteenth birthday. I told her I was too busy for a family vacation, but she begged and I gave in.

Always precocious and moody, at thirteen Stella seemed to be fighting a war with herself. One minute, she was childlike and charming. The next, paralyzed with sophistication. But when it was just my sister and me, she was still Stella Star. Our last night at the beach, we sat on the sand with the tide coming in. We dug our toes in and squealed as the warm water eroded the solid ground around them. She turned to me and said she wished we never had to leave. I was surprised at how sad she sounded and tried to comfort her by saying we'd be back next year and the year after. But she stood and shook her head.

"We won't, you know." Her words returned to me as clearly as if she were standing beside me now. "This is our last beautiful summer."

Then she ran into the surf, away from the light of the shore. For a few seconds, I hadn't been able to see her and had called out to her in fear. Instead of coming back to me, she dashed straight into our small cottage without saying another word. And for the usual reasons — busy schedules, conflicting interests — Stella had been right. It was our last beautiful summer.

·   ·   ·   ·   ·

The smell of coffee woke me. I joined Justin in the kitchen.

"I think it was after two when Harry got in, so I thought we could just let him sleep."

Sitting with him at the table, like an actual couple, I had forgotten about Harry and the photos. Now I closed my eyes and rubbed my temples. I was no closer to understanding why my sister was dead than when we started. I was certain Ben was responsible; but even though I knew his kind of abuse could escalate, I still had trouble imagining him going that far. And there had been easier ways to cover it up than faking a boating accident.

"Hello." Justin was holding the pot over my cup. "More coffee?"

"Sorry. I just keep thinking about Stella." I nodded and watched as he poured, remembering how strong, but gentle he had been.

"Yesterday was fantastic," he began, taking my hand and tracing his finger across my palm.

Alarms sounded in my head. His next words would be something along the lines of how we had to put all that sex stuff behind us and go back to a businesslike relationship.

"It was great," I echoed, cutting him off. "But I got caught up in the moment. I don't regret anything about last night, but we shouldn't get distracted like that again."

"So, it was a distraction for you?" Justin asked and released my hand.

"Not just a distraction. I mean it was terrific and all, but nothing serious."

"I get it. Don't worry. You're right. We need to stay on track." He stood abruptly, walked to his room, and shut the door.

Well, that was a record for me: screwing up what might have developed into a relationship in less than twenty-four hours. Of course, I was lying about it only being a distraction. The good news was Justin could hardly avoid me since we were staying together, so I should have a chance to make things better. The bad news was I would probably find a way to make them worse.

I considered following him, but it wasn't the time to get into a long discussion about our non-relationship, not with the missing pictures hanging over my head.

I borrowed Harry's laptop and checked my email. Nothing from Mom, but Mike had sent a quick message telling me Lesroy dropped by with Scarlett, and the dog had stopped growling at my cousin. He also let me know my mother was eating more and missed me. I told him about talking to Eva and not getting much in the way of information. I avoided telling him the local authorities had tossed me into the pokey.

My stomach rumbled, so I headed to the kitchen where Harry stood at the counter making coffee.

"I never sleep this late," he said, pouring a cup for me. "Guess I'm not as spry as I used to be."

I felt terrible about misleading Justin, but at least Harry hadn't been part of the deception. I heard the door to Justin's room open and tried to act natural when he joined us.

"This guy tells me you had quite the day yesterday." Harry grinned over his coffee. "It's been a while since I had breakfast with an ex-con."

I tried to smile.

"Too soon?" he asked. "Sorry. What did you find out?"

I replayed my conversation with Eva, then came clean about my meeting with Adelmo.

"But she wasn't the only one I met with yesterday." I turned toward Justin. "I should have told you before, but the timing was off."

I took a deep breath and explained about the detour Prez had taken on our journey. When I got to the part about our trip to Puerto Lopez, Justin jerked upright and sat on the edge of his seat. When I got to the point when Adelmo approached me on the beach, he jumped out of the chair and began pacing in front of the patio door.

"Please, do not tell me you left with that thug!" he said through clenched teeth.

"He's not a thug. At least, I don't think he's a thug. And I didn't go off with him. We went to a museum to talk." There was no reason to tell him no one else was at the museum or how long we sat in the garden. "Could you please sit down? You're making me nervous."

He sat.

I summarized my conversation with Adelmo, leaving out the part about his ominous promise to make things right. When I finished, no one spoke for what seemed like forever. Harry broke the silence.

"So, Balsuto claims he's working on uncovering what happened to your sister."

The way he said "claims" made me remember Adelmo's warning about not believing everything I heard. Could he have been referring to himself in his warning? Did Harry suspect Adelmo of direct involvement in Stella's death?

"I still can't believe you were alone with one of the most dangerous men in the country." Justin sounded angry but seemed to be losing steam. I ignored him and responded directly to Harry.

"Do you think he's lying about not knowing anything?"

"It's hard to tell. Luis tells me not much happens around here that gets past him. And he and Ben were into some very shady business. That doesn't mean he was in on whatever was going on with your sister. But the part about not seeing Stella for months seems strange to me. Does that sound like her?"

That part of Adelmo's story had puzzled me, too. "Honestly, I'm not sure what Stella might have done."

The truth was the Stellas described by Ben and Adelmo were both different from the woman I'd known. Being discontent with the luxury Ben had provided, protecting her family from him—neither sounded like the Stella who had no qualms about marrying the man I loved. And the garden museum didn't fit into the type of place my sister would want to hang out. Even eating cookies with Eva wasn't something she would enjoy. Was it possible she had changed, or had I never recognized what she could have been?

Once in high school she got wasted at a party, somebody called the cops, and they took everybody in. I was at college but offered to come talk to my errant sister. Mom told me to stay put. She said Stella needed to face up to what she'd done and if I came home, I would shift the responsibility to someone else. She said I was like predictive text for her, always completing her words and thoughts to make her into the person I wanted her to be. Maybe being on her own in a strange place, away from me, let her become her own person.

The weight of my loss pressed down on me, and I could think of nothing more to add.

Justin slumped back in his chair, then leaned toward me.

"I hate that we have to talk about our conversation with Harry's source right now, but we're running short on time."

Our return tickets were open-ended, but we planned on wrapping up our business in no more than a week. It seemed the more we found out about Stella's life, the less we understood. Maybe she left the important clues behind with her body.

"You have the pictures?"

"We do," Harry responded. "But we're not sure it's a good idea for you to see them."

My stomach turned at the implication behind those words. "Is it that bad?" I whispered.

Justin rose from his chair and sat beside me. He put his hand on my knee. "It's not that. It's just once you see it, you can never unsee it. When you think about your sister, all the memories you have will fade into the background. Instead of Stella when she was a little girl or at her first dance or even when you were the maddest at her, it will be the Stella in these photos."

I imagined Justin had seen quite a few last images during his stint in the service, and a part of me wanted to tell him to put the pictures away. But if I didn't see for myself what had happened to my sister, it would be too easy to give up and go home. To pretend I believed Stella's death had been an accident.

"I have to, Justin."

He walked to his room.

"He's right, you know," Harry offered. "Why don't you let us take things from here? The photos might be enough to insist on further investigation."

"I want to. I do. But ever since Mike called about them finding her body, I've kept waiting for someone to say it was a terrible mistake. That a young woman washed up on shore, and she looked like Stella, but it wasn't her. I'm very sorry for the family of the real accident victim, but what a relief to discover my sister had been hiding from Ben. Or she had gone into rehab. Or a hundred other happy endings. Then I could tell her I forgive her." Tears trickled down my cheeks, and I wiped them away with the back of my hand.

Justin returned with a thick envelope. He sat beside me and opened it.

"There are ten photos, all from different angles. You can see them all if you like, but I'm going to suggest you only look at these two." He laid them on the coffee table, face down.

My hands were shaking when I turned one over. At first, I couldn't separate Stella from the surface beneath her. She was halfway on her side, her pale body sunk into the frothy sand, fossil-like. Seaweed threaded through long, blonde hair that covered half her face. From the exposed side, one milky, sightless eye stared up at the camera. The straps of her sundress had fallen low on her forearms, and her skirt had ridden up, exposing bare hips and splayed legs. I dropped it onto the table.

"Are you okay?" Justin asked.

I nodded and turned over the second photo. It was a close-up of the marks on her body, a body mottled with dark purple splotches. I picked it up and focused on my sister's neck. The bruises formed a cruel necklace of blurred fingerprints around her throat.

"It's her," I said. There would be no surprise happy ending for me and my family.

The force of pure grief, unadulterated by anger and bitterness, crushed me. I'd been running on the power of my fury for years. Without it, the weight of my sorrow was paralyzing.

Justin touched my cheek. "Are you all right?"

The earth skewed, but I nodded and assured him I was fine.

"Of course, you're not fine," he whispered. "Just let me take care of you for a little while."

One of the many terrible things about grieving is the fear of getting lost in that grief. It's as if naming your pain gives it power over you, defines you. The only way to survive is to refuse to admit how lonely and afraid you are. You pretend you are in control. For the first time since I learned of Stella's death, I didn't care about being in control. I wanted someone to take care of me. Not forever but for a little while.

"It's just seeing her like that," I leaned back on the sofa pillow.

Harry handed me a glass of water. "Honey, nobody can look at pictures like that without—"

"It's okay. We have to talk about them and what they mean." I held out my glass. "I know it's early, but do you think I might have something a little stronger?"

"Hell. It's five o'clock somewhere." He headed for the kitchen while Justin sat holding my hand.

He returned with a snifter with less than an inch of amber liquid. "It's brandy. Sip it slowly."

The last time I had brandy was at one of Ben's fancy parties. I didn't like it any better, but after the second sip, it had a steadying effect.

"Your sister's injuries didn't happen from falling off a boat," Harry began. "Luis put me in contact with one of his friends, the kind of guy who knows people from both sides of the law. He's going to check into Ben's troubles with Balsuto and find out why the authorities ruled the death accidental in the face of contradictory evidence."

I continued to reject the possibility Adelmo had something to do with Stella's murder. No one could fake the kind of misery he was in. But wouldn't a man in his line of work have to be a convincing liar?

"We contacted Mike to let him know we'll be here longer than we expected. He said your mother's better but still not talking much."

Other than sending a few quick emails, I hadn't communicated with Mom since she sent me on her revenge mission. But I would only disappoint her with anything other than news of Ben's death.

"We can't just sit around waiting to hear from Luis's friend." I swirled the contents of my glass.

"Harry and I are going to give the local authorities another shot after we make copies of the pictures and put them in a safe place. We don't want them disappearing again. And Mike got in touch with a friend who runs an independent security group that does business with both local and US governments. He's going to present the photos in Guayaquil and pressure the authorities to reopen the investigation."

"I guess it's just me who'll be sitting around doing nothing."

"That's what I'd like for you to do, but I know you aren't going to listen to me, so we thought you might try to get back in touch with Eva."

I did need to talk more with Stella's housekeeper and friend. Since Prez was the key to finding her, we had lunch at the hotel bar. But a pretty, dark-haired woman was working in Prez's place. She scowled when I asked if she knew how to get in touch with him. When Harry slipped her a ten-dollar bill, her smile returned, and she agreed to let Prez know we were looking for him.

Back at the villa, Harry touched base with some of his employees, leaving Justin and me standing awkwardly outside my bedroom door.

My judgment in matters of the heart had been unreliable even when I wasn't dealing with the complications of grief and danger in a foreign country. Should I reach out to him or leave things as they were? He made the decision for me, by patting me on the shoulder and suggesting I rest.

I liked the idea of a power nap but fell into a deep sleep instead and dreamed of my lost sister.

We were in a church filled with pink and coral tea roses. An instrumental version of "This Will Be an Everlasting Love" played in the background as a little girl with curly, black hair skipped up the aisle, scattering petals. I followed her. Every time I stepped on a blossom, it smoldered into ash. Two men in cream-colored tuxedos waited at the front, a smoky haze obscuring their faces. I joined them, and the traditional wedding march began.

A young woman in a white dress with a bright red veil came toward me. She was accompanied by an older man in a black tuxedo and an old-fashioned top hat. I expected to see our long-lost daddy beside the bride, but it was Uncle Roy looking stern and sober. He stopped, turned to the woman at his side, and lifted her veil.

I looked away to where Ben stood next to Adelmo. Ben mouthed the words, "It should have been you."

I bolted for the exit, but my heel caught the hem of my dress, and I plummeted into darkness, awaking with a jolt. Drenched in sweat, I threw off the covers and checked the time. It had only been a little over an hour since I fell asleep. I lay back for a moment, watching the ceiling fan perform its sluggish rotation. Ben's words echoed. I was furious because it should have been me when Stella and Ben eloped and again when they left for Ecuador. And when my sister died? I felt as if my mother had been thinking those same words: *It should have been you.*

I threw my legs over the side of the bed, walked to the kitchen, and saw a note taped to the refrigerator.

Harry's guy had time to see us this afternoon. Should be back in time for dinner – Rest and feel better. Justin.

The walls narrowed around me, and I rushed to the patio to take a deep breath of ocean air. No way would I be able to sit around waiting for the men to return. I remembered Prez might have left a message about contacting Eva, so I hurried to the front desk. A female employee I'd never seen told me I had no calls.

By now it was after two. The sun slipped in and out of the clouds. The air was heavy and hot. Beads of perspiration dotted my forehead, and my sunglasses slid down on my nose. I could see the shoreline from the pathway and remembered Justin's suggestion I take a walk or go shopping. The idea had annoyed me at the time, but now there really wasn't anything useful for me to do. It was a good time to walk along the beach and wander around town.

I stopped at the room, stuck a bottle of water in my bag, slathered on some sunscreen, and grabbed a straw hat before setting out. I strolled along the path, marveling at the panoramic view below me. Surfers defied the laws of gravity as they popped out of the sea and catapulted into the air. Striped umbrellas dotted the beach, and groups of children built forts and castles.

By the time I reached the sea, sweat and sunscreen ran in rivulets into my eyes and my clothes were damp. I took off my sandals and walked ankle-deep into the water. A slight breeze offered some relief from the heat. When I stumbled into a shallow drop-off, a wave twice my size knocked me off my feet. I stumbled up and raced to the shore.

Feeling like the loser in a wet t-shirt contest, I ventured into a rocky area and stretched out on a coffin-shaped stone to dry out. A sailboat glided across the sparkling surface. Beyond it, a fishing boat bobbed in the rough water. Peace descended over me for the first time since Stella's death. I wanted to stay in this exact spot forever, forgetting the ugliness that propelled me into a world where a woman like my sister could be broken and tossed aside.

After my clothes dried enough to lose their transparency, I threaded my way through the rising tide and across the rocks to shallow water, where I knelt to rinse sand off my legs. A heavyset man several yards behind me stopped at the same time I did. When I looked in his direction, he pulled his white baseball cap over his eyes and bent over as if searching for shells.

He is looking for shells, I told myself. Just because the police had tracked me to Eva's didn't mean I was being followed today. Mr. Fat Cap was most likely some harmless tourist out for a relaxing walk on the beach. The fact he was now walking toward me was nothing more than a coincidence.

CHAPTER 26

No need to panic. I moved away from the waters' edge and weaved through the maze of sunbathers on blankets and towels. Comforted by their presence, I reached the pavement, dusted the grit off my feet, and slipped on my sandals. My shadow was nowhere in sight.

Vendors selling everything from fresh oysters to tacos and ice cream lined the street, but I kept walking until I came to a small building with an elaborate thatched roof. Cheap T-shirts and swimsuits hung from racks on the walls. I walked to a carousel of sunglasses and tried on a pair, using the mirror to scan the throng of shoppers. There was still no sign of him. I exhaled and returned to trying on sunglasses. A flash of white caught my attention. Head down next to a row of clam-shaped ashtrays, my friend was back.

I modeled more glasses before grabbing a pair with faux tortoise-shell frames. Then I moved to a rack of cheap sundresses in vibrant jungle colors. I selected an orange one with a parrot perched across the skirt. At the register, I asked the clerk if there was another exit. He motioned to the back, and I ambled out into a narrow passage between the shops. A few feet away, an elderly man in flowered shorts and no shirt smoked a cigarette. He ignored me as I ran past him.

I ducked into the shop a few doors down and found myself face-to-face with Bob Marley, all sunglasses and serenity on a bright red, yellow, and green flag. Below him sat the biggest bong I'd ever seen. A dark-skinned man with dreadlocks beamed at me with a gap-toothed grin. I asked for directions to the ladies room. There I removed my T-shirt and slipped the sundress over my shorts. It was at least a half-size too big in the top, and the straps kept slipping off my shoulders, but it would have to do. I stuffed the clothes in my bag and gathered my hair into a bun.

I exited the shop and walked toward our hotel. Before I rounded the first corner, a whisper tickled my ear.

"Please, Señorita, I do not wish to hurt you. But you must come with me."

Instead of the heavyset man from the beach, I faced a young boy whose dark hair hung over the side of his face. When he pushed it back, he exposed the half-moon on his wrist. It was Ben's houseboy.

"Eduardo! What are you doing here?"

"I'm sorry to frighten you, but it's better if no one sees us talking. Please, come with me."

Fearful the man from the beach was still following me, I glanced over my shoulder. The street was clear, but a more private location seemed like a good idea.

We wound through side streets, and I speculated on his need for secrecy. Could he be working with Ben, luring me away from the crowds to shut me up? From his reaction to seeing his boss shrieking on the floor, I didn't sense a closeness between employer and employee. Next to Eva, he was the most likely person with insights into what Stella's last days had been like. I had to trust him.

He stopped at the back entrance of a restaurant and held the torn screen door open. I stepped inside, where the rattling of pots and pans threatened to drown the hum of nearby voices.

"This is where my cousin works," he announced and led me to a walk-in closet filled with cleaning supplies. He pulled out a step stool from underneath a shelf and requested I sit.

"I hope Ben didn't fire you because of me."

Eduardo smiled. "No. I still have my job, but Señor Wilcott has been away on business. He left the morning after your visit. He is expected back later today. That is why I needed to see you now.

"I'm sorry to say I cannot help you with how Señora Stella died. But I can perhaps explain to you what happened earlier. A little over two months ago, just after Señor Wilcott fired Eva, your sister left her home. The señor was very disturbed. He sent men to search for her, but they had no luck. He insisted I go to Eva and she return to answer his questions, but she also was not to be found. I feared he suspected Señora Stella had run away with a lover, but I knew she had not."

"You did? Please, tell me how."

"Because Eva had taken her to the home of her sister in Ibarra." He explained she was from the remote town between Guayaquil and Quito.

"But why would Stella leave like that? And how did you find out?"

"I cannot say why, but I know it was true because Eva is my aunt." He grinned. "Señor Wilcott is not aware of our connection."

I enjoyed the thought of Ben blustering around trying to discover where Stella had gone while the answer was literally at his door. Yet, I wasn't sure the boy was being completely transparent.

"She may not have run off with a lover, but she had one: Adelmo Balsuto."

His eyes widened. "I cannot help you."

"Please, Eduardo. It's important. Was Señor Balsuto aware of where your aunt and my sister had gone?"

If Adelmo had known where they were, it was likely he had helped Stella hide. If he hadn't, she might have been hiding from him. Either way, he had misled me.

"They did not tell me that. Only that Señor Wilcott did not and could not find out where they were."

"They may not have told you, but you are a very clever young man. What do you think happened?"

"It is not for me to say." He looked over his shoulder. "But you must believe me. Señor Balsuto would never cause harm to come to your sister."

"If you're so sure it wasn't Adelmo she feared, you must have an idea who would. Was it Ben?"

"It is not good to make guesses about such things here in Montañita. But your sister did not plan to return to her home here. My aunt told me she wanted to go back to her own country. Something happened that brought her back to Montañita."

I begged him to tell me what the something was that had resulted in her death, but he claimed ignorance. I had no choice but to believe him.

"Please, be careful, Señorita Burnette. Señor Wilcott was very angry when you ran from the house. Regardless of whether he was the one who killed her, he is a dangerous man. You should go home before it is too late."

He stepped out of the small room, signaling our meeting was over. We didn't talk as he led me to the busy street. He left without saying goodbye.

I watched him walk away and bit my lip to keep from screaming in frustration.

The more I learned about Stella's last few months, the more questions I had. I was sure Adelmo had helped her get to Ibarra, which meant he had lied to me earlier, but why? And why had Eva gone with her? If my sister wanted to come home, why hadn't she? And most important of all, why had she returned to Montañita?

It was almost 5:00 when I began walking to the villa, still trying to make sense of what Eduardo had shared. Clouds like black smoke hung low, trapping the heat between them and the beach. My bun had fallen out, and my hair expanded into a bird's nest of curls. I had done nothing to prepare for afternoon showers but wasn't worried about getting wet. It was the rumble of thunder in the distance that made my heart race.

Sand sucked at my feet and lightning crackled. I hesitated on the shoulder of the narrow road, considering an alternate route. There was a rustling behind me. Before I could turn, a hairy arm snaked tight around my waist. Something cold and hard jabbed into my ribs and a pair of rough, wet lips brushed across my neck.

"You should pretend we are old friends, Señorita." I twisted away from his sour breath and caught sight of the ball cap. He jerked me back and squeezed me even closer. Together we did an awkward two-step toward a waiting car. The door behind the driver's side was open, and my companion shoved me in.

"You shouldn't be out in this weather, Grace." Ben smiled at me from inside. "Do you hate storms as much as our Stella did? I know they terrified her."

CHAPTER 27

My abduction happened so quickly I hadn't had time to be frightened. Sitting beside Ben in the back of a car driven by his hired thug, I now had the time. But the last thing I wanted was for him to sense my fear.

"You could have invited me over." I clenched my fists to keep my hands from shaking. "Oh, that's right. You took out a restraining order. Awkward."

His face reddened, but he kept smiling. "You always were a smart ass, Grace. One of the many reasons I chose Stella over you."

"And how'd that work out for you?" A few months ago, his remark would have devastated me. Now, I felt only contempt. "Why don't we skip the small talk and get down to the basics of why you kidnapped me?"

"Kidnapped? That's a bit strong, wouldn't you say? It's more like finishing our conversation."

"I said all I have to say, but it doesn't look as if I have much choice in the matter. So, please, let's get it over with, so I can get back to the hotel. My friends will be expecting me."

"No need to rush. We have all the time in the world. But first," he retrieved my purse from the floor where I dropped it, "We should make sure you don't have any nasty surprises." I left the Mace in the rental car during my make-out session with Justin, so there was nothing of any use to me in the self-defense department. He tossed my cell phone out the window, then rummaged through my bag before dropping it. I picked it up and clung to it like a security blanket.

He called out to the driver. "Javi, turn the music up."

The smooth sounds of a saxophone drifted from the speakers, and I stiffened at the sound of Kenny G, Ben's go-to seduction track.

He squeezed my knee. "Relax, sweetheart, and enjoy the drive."

I tried to block out the raw timbre of the sax and what it reminded me of. I needed to concentrate on making sense of the scenery. Torrents of rain transformed the landscape into a smear, and the darkened windows made it difficult to tell which direction we were headed. An occasional glimpse of the rocky roadside terrain indicated we were moving away from the ocean into the hills. Wind pummeled the car, threatening to wash us off the curving road. After what I estimated to be about twenty or thirty minutes, Javi turned up a steep drive. He opened the garage, pulled in, and came around to open my door. The same man who stuck a gun in my back now held out a hand to assist me in getting out.

This casual courtesy frightened me more than anything so far. His cool detachment showed a lack of empathy: demonstrating good manners or good marksmanship would be the same to him. My legs were unsteady, but I clutched my purse closer to my chest and climbed out without his help. Ben stood at the front of the car.

"Welcome to the highest spot in Montañita, unimaginatively named the Point. The natives here are pretty simple." If Javi took offense at the comment, he didn't show it. "This is a business associate's home. He's out of the country and won't mind if we use it." He grabbed hold of my elbow and guided me to the door where he punched in a code and said, "After you, my dear."

We were on the ground level of the house in an elaborate man-cave. A claw-footed pool table dominated the center of the room. Dark paneled walls, probably the last of a rare wood from a nearby rain forest, gleamed, as did the bar that stretched across the back wall. The brown leather sofa with matching recliners sat in front of sliding glass doors, overlooking the mist-covered ocean far below.

"May as well enjoy ourselves," he said. "Javi, Scotch and soda for me, vodka tonic for the lady."

He walked by the pool table and sat on the couch, then patted the seat beside him. I slid past him to the recliner. While we waited for drinks, he checked his cell phone before turning it off.

"Interesting outfit." He leered at me.

I tugged my straps up and crossed my arms over my chest.

Javi delivered our drinks and disappeared up the long staircase beside the bar.

Ben took a deep swallow and sighed. I pretended to sip mine but had no intention of dulling my senses. I didn't know what he had in mind but didn't plan to stick around to find out. Getting away from him would require a clear head.

"You really hurt my feelings the last time I saw you." He finished more than half his drink before continuing. "I'm sure you can understand I can't let something like that go unpunished." He stared at me, his top lip quivering. "But I'm not an unreasonable man. That was part of the problem Stella and I had. She never could get what a reasonable man I am." His eyes reminded me of ones I'd seen on a shark in the tank at the Atlanta Aquarium. "If you answer a few questions, we can come to an agreement that won't be too painful for you."

I fought against rising bile in my throat, tipped my glass, and let the ice touch my lips.

"What's the matter, Gracie? Cat got your tongue?"

Something Ben had said once about his interrogation skills in the courtroom came to mind. How he enjoyed intimidating opponents until he could smell their fear.

"What the hell are you talking about? Whatever it is, I'm sick of sitting here watching you puff up like an overweight walrus in heat. Get to the point or take me home." I took a sip of the vodka for real this time and waited for the explosion.

I had underestimated my ex-fiancé, though. Instead of blowing up, he downed the rest of his drink and rambled over to the bar to make another one.

"Okay, Pumpkin." I hated when he called me that. He returned to his place on the sofa. "What did you hear after you left my house?"

"Ben," I began, wondering if the man had lost his mind. "I have no idea what you're talking about." I carefully enunciated each syllable.

"This is what I'm talking about, you bitch!" he shouted, then reached into his pants pocket. He stood and shoved his fist in front of my face, opening his palm to reveal a small, round disk. It was the mic I dropped while running out of Ben's house.

"You can't deny you bugged my place. Now tell me or I swear to God…"

He waved his fist at me, and I cringed into the chair as far as possible. Then I recalled the rush he got from bullying a witness and how weakness in an opponent excited him. I sat straight and laughed at him.

"That mic died as soon as I dropped it. The last thing Harry and Justin picked up was the sound of you screaming like a little baby. They were on their way in when I ran to the car."

His face darkened to a shade of rotten plum. "You're lying." He leaned in close, eyes bulging. "Now tell me what you heard, or I'll get Javi to help you remember."

"Seriously, Ben. I only wore the mic in case you flipped out. Once I was out of your reach, there was no need for us to keep listening." I was frightened but also curious. What was he so afraid we picked up? It had to be pretty damning for him to be so worried.

"I want to believe you, Grace. I really do, but you have to admit you haven't given me much reason to trust you." He licked his lips. "Maybe if you were a little nicer to me, I might accept what you're saying as the truth."

Like one of the lightning bolts Stella and I hated, it hit me: Ben's Achilles' heel. Achilles's penis was more accurate. The thing you could always count on was that the man was in a constant state of dormant arousal, awakened at the slightest provocation. Although allowing him to touch me was nauseating beyond belief, my survival instinct was stronger than disgust.

His breathing quickened. "Why don't you come a little closer?" He patted the space beside him.

I glanced around the room, searching for something to use as a weapon. My best option was a heavy square-shaped bottle of tequila on the counter.

I got up but kept my distance. If I gave in too quickly, Ben would suspect my sincerity, but if I played it too cool, he might lose patience. I wasn't sure what that might mean, but he was capable of anything.

"I can't do anything until I use the little girls' room." I shifted from foot to foot and gave him a desperate look.

"It's down the hall on the left. Don't take too long."

I brought my face close to his, trying to ignore the stiff black hairs sticking out of his pores. He parted his lips, but instead of kissing him, I squeezed his upper thigh. He moaned and reached for me, but I danced away.

"I mean it, Grace," Ben growled. "No stalling."

Still holding on to my purse, I hurried to the bathroom, then shut and locked the door. I searched my bag, frantic for something to defend myself with. My hairbrush was too flimsy. I might do some damage with the hotel pen, but it would most likely only further enrage my captor. That's when I noticed the pillbox where I'd stored the Xanax from the lady on the plane along with Mom's Ambien. If I could get them in Ben's drink, I should be able to, at the very least, disable him. There was a possibility the drugs and alcohol would kill him, but that was a chance I was willing to take. Before I had time to proceed with my plan, heavy footsteps pounded above me, followed by shouting and the crash of broken glass.

I crouched beside the toilet and waited for the noise to die down. Then I peeked out of the bathroom before walking toward the den. The room was empty. I hurried to the sliding doors and found they were bolted shut. I could try to make it to the garage, but that could be another dead end, and I had no idea where Javi or he might be.

From overhead, I heard footsteps and surveyed the room for a place to hide. I noticed a handle on one of the panels beneath the stairway, opened it, and discovered a small storage area. The steps grew louder. I squeezed myself inside and shut the door behind me. Blinking in the thick darkness until my eyes adjusted, I identified a rolled-up throw rug, a painting, and a tennis racket.

My heart pounded so loudly I was certain the person above had to hear it. A series of harsh, popping sounds ended the silence. Someone shrieked, and I realized it was me. I moved deeper into the storage closet but stopped when something poked me in the back. After feeling around, I discovered the sharp object was a broken pool cue.

The footsteps resumed, much closer now. I held my breath, but the walls closed in, and I gasped. Sweat trickled between my boobs as I fought the urge to kick open the door and make a run for it.

Stay still, stay still, stay still. I repeated my silent mantra. And it worked. The walls receded, my breathing settled, and my body cooled. That's when something squirmy and hairy brushed against my cheek, dropped onto my shoulder, and skittered down the back of my dress.

Wave after wave of uncontrollable screams echoed around me as I tugged at the straps of my sundress and yanked it down to my waist. I lifted my hips and slithered out of it. The warm, fuzzy thing continued to scamper around on my back, and I flailed my arms over my shoulders. I didn't hear when the door opened. Light flooded my hiding place. I reached for the pool cue and jabbed it in front of me.

Blinded by the flashlight beam, I didn't recognize him until he spoke. "Easy there, Grace. It's me, Prez. There's no reason to be scared. I'm not going to hurt you."

About that time a fat, hairy spider scuttled to my side. His long legs ended in what looked like pink booties. I threw the pool stick toward Prez and scrambled out of the closet on all fours, running straight into a pair of bright orange and purple tennis shoes.

He helped me up, then glanced down at the creature who had terrified me. "Not to worry, Grace. That's only a pink-toed tarantula. They're all over the place here. The little guys are pretty chill. He didn't bite you, did he?"

"I don't think so." I stood behind him, wearing only my bra and shorts. "Would you mind?" I pointed to where my sundress lay in a wad.

He tossed me the wrinkled garment. "Even if you got bitten, you'd just get all swollen and nasty. People almost never die except in the case of a super bad reaction."

Before I slipped the dress over my head, I thought of the gunshots from the upper rooms.

"How did you know where to find me?" I asked, trying to sound calm.

"It wasn't too hard. This is where Ben said you'd be."

Then I saw the gun in his hand.

CHAPTER 28

Unable to reconcile Prez, the ultimate hippy, with Prez, armed and dangerous, I could only stare at the dead-eyed man while trying to make sense of it all. Why would Ben tell him anything?

Regardless of their relationship, it was obvious Prez hadn't come to rescue me. I glanced toward the stairwell, looking for the broken pool cue. It was too far to reach and would be of little use against a gun. The bottle of tequila still sat on the edge of the bar. If I could get to it, I could hurl it at his head and make a break for the stairs. Then I could grab the pool stick and run. But to do that, I had to take him by surprise.

"I don't understand," I said, hoping to distract him with conversation. "Why would he tell you where we were going?"

"It's a long story, and I'm not sure we have time right now. Your ex and I were both working for your sister's friend, Balsuto. He handled legal shit for him, and I," he said, laughing, "handled illegal shit for him. Pretty much everything about that dude is illegal, but that's beside the point." He checked his watch.

"Anyway, we worked a few deals on our own. But you already know about that, don't you, Grace?" He grinned.

A separate deal between Ben and Prez, somehow double-crossing Adelmo—that was what they thought I'd heard. But why did it matter? I had no proof, and the local police wouldn't be interested if I did. And shouldn't they be worried about Harry and Justin having the same information? But they hadn't had private communications with him. Only I had. So, it wasn't the authorities they feared; it was Adelmo.

"What if I do?" I asked, trying to determine what he wanted from me.

"Don't get smart with me," he snarled.

Outside, the wind gusted, and a glass door shattered. He leaped toward the sound, firing his weapon several times. I dove for the tequila bottle. Never much of an athlete, I had a few shining moments as junior varsity pitcher on my high school softball team. I had the lowest batting averages and could never get the hang of sliding into a base, but I had a mean arm. I prayed I hadn't forgotten how to put one over the plate.

Prez stopped shooting but continued to scan the room. I aimed and hurled the tequila straight at him. He glanced up just as the bottle smacked him on the bridge of his nose. After giving me a puzzled look, he touched his injury and wiped at the blood dripping down his chin. Then he howled.

I didn't wait for his next move. I grabbed the pool stick and took the stairs two at a time. Inside the main house, I latched the door and surveyed the area. I was in a brightly lit kitchen with stainless-steel appliances. In front of the enormous sub-zero refrigerator, a gaping hole in his forehead, lay Javi.

Blood pounded in my ears as I ran past his body into a high-ceilinged formal living area. Like the room below, a wall of sliding glass doors provided a view of rocky cliffs above the ocean, barely visible in the whipping rain.

Please don't be locked. Don't be locked. Thank God, they weren't. I rushed through them onto a deck that ran the full length of the house. Metal recliners and tables stacked at random angles complicated my search for an exit. I spotted stairs at the far end and bounded toward them as fast as the cluttered surface allowed.

A wave of vertigo brought me to an abrupt stop. Thick clouds of mist hovered over the faraway ground. The banister seemed sturdy, but if I made a false step on the slippery wood, I would crash to the bottom. Like a tightrope walker without a net, I took hold of the rail with one hand and held my cue stick with the other. Only the sound of the sliding glass door kept me from turning around and crawling back to the balcony.

The rubber soles of my sandals squeaked as I descended, and I was sure Prez heard every leaden step but was too worried about losing my balance to risk a backward glance. The last few planks were spaced at odds from the others, causing me to stumble and lose my footing. When I reached the ground, my knees slammed into sharp little pebbles, but I held onto the pool stick.

"Come out, come out, wherever you are!" Prez's eerie, childlike command echoed overhead. Without stopping to think or catch my breath, I darted underneath the stairs. I prayed the blow from the tequila bottle had done more than bloody his nose — that it had addled him. Addled or not, he was making his way down. My eyes adjusted to the dark, but he had the advantage of having been here before.

Don't panic, don't panic, I told myself while searching for an escape route. Even if I found it, I doubted I could outrun him. My best option was to slow him down and return to the main road.

From my hiding place, I wriggled my way close to the landing and waited, pool cue in hand, for him to reach the last three steps.

"There's nowhere to run, Grace." He stopped inches from me. I held my breath. "This is not cool. I only want to talk." He resumed his descent, and just as he reached the third step from the bottom, I jabbed the stick upward. He let loose a guttural cry, and I slid it sideways, then cracked it across his ankles. Now his scream was more of a high-pitched squeal. His feet slipped, and I heard a sickening thud as he bounced off the rail and flew down the last few steps. There were no more screams.

Without checking to see if he got back up, I bolted toward the front of the house. The driveway was as steep as I remembered, so I scrambled crablike down the incline and rushed to the road, hoping I could make it before he recovered.

Continuing along the rough shoulder, I moved as fast as I could. A motor roared around the curve, and I resisted the urge to flag down the approaching vehicle. If the car was headed to the house where Prez and Ben held me captive, the driver was more likely foe than friend. I hid behind a cluster of boulders and waited. Glaring headlights made it impossible to identify until it was beside me. It was Harry's Bronco.

He skidded to the side of the road, and the men jumped out.

Justin reached me first and crushed me to his chest.

"Jesus, Grace! What happened to you?" Harry asked.

Justin relaxed his grip and held me at arm's length, surveying what must have looked like heavy-duty damage.

My hair was matted to my head. I could feel grit on my face and arms and realized my sundress was hanging by one strap, exposing what was once my sexiest bra. Now it was mud streaked and sad. My skirt was torn and covered with dark red spots from my shredded knees, and somewhere along the way I lost a sandal.

"I'm not sure, but I might have killed someone," I confessed before my legs buckled. Justin got me in the car, and I explained what had gone on since I'd seen them.

When I finished my story, no one spoke for a moment. Then Justin said, "I think we should go to the villa."

"I'm not sure what happened to Ben, but Prez could need an ambulance." I protested.

"It's not a good idea for anyone to see you here," Harry said while turning the car around. "Remember that restraining order? The authorities might not believe the man who took it out would want to kidnap you."

I hadn't thought about that. In my defense, I hadn't had time to think about anything other than getting away. But they were right. Leaning against Justin's body, I tried to shut out the image of the hole in Javi's head.

"Wait. How did you guys know where to find me?"

"Eduardo. He watched as you started toward the villa and saw the guy shove you into Ben's car. He wasn't sure where they'd taken you but had heard about the Point house. It was our best bet, so we came."

It was after midnight when we returned to the hotel. I sat on the sofa while Harry cleaned and bandaged my knees. Justin watched with a grim expression on his face.

"So, Ben's missing and Prez is disabled, maybe dead," Harry surmised, putting the finishing touches on my bandages. "The two of them were at odds with Balsuto. Could he be aware of the double-cross?"

"I doubt it. Because if he was, I don't think they would be around to talk about it." Justin turned to me. "You wouldn't either."

I couldn't get past the notion Aldelmo would hurt me or Stella but didn't argue the point. Instead, I reminded them about what Eduardo had told me and insisted finding Eva was more important than ever now that we knew she had been with Stella before she died.

"You're right, Grace. But I think we all need to get some rest before we decide what to do next," Harry said.

"I agree." Justin stood and offered me his hand. "You've had a busy day." He pulled me to my feet. He led me to my room and shut the door behind us.

"Please don't be upset with me. All I meant to do was shop."

He put his finger to my lips and said, "I'm just glad you didn't get killed. But you're muddy and exhausted. You take a quick shower, and I'll sit here to make sure you're okay. We can talk tomorrow."

As tired as I was, I wanted to invite him to join me. But I remembered his reaction when I said what we had was no big deal. So, I showered alone, checking for any additional injuries sustained during my ordeal. I was in surprisingly good shape, with only a few sharp pains in my shoulders when I pulled my gown over my head.

When I finished brushing my teeth, I found Justin snoring on top of the covers. I turned off the lights, slipped under the blanket beside him, and fell asleep faster than I had since we arrived in Montañita.

When I awoke after ten the next morning, I heard the men talking from the other room, pulled on my robe, and joined them.

"We ordered in earlier, but you were out," Justin said. He motioned to a platter of assorted pastries. "Saved some for you." It had been over twenty-four hours since my last meal, and I was starving. I took a turnover dusted with powdered sugar and bit into it.

Harry poured coffee while I demolished the first pastry and chose another one. Justin watched and smiled at me from across the narrow table. He picked up a napkin and reached over to wipe some fruit goop off my chin. "I forgot what a dainty eater you are."

The intimacy of the gesture brought a lump to my throat. When Stella was little—and sometimes not so little—I would laugh at how enthusiastically she dove into a piece of cake or pie. Like Justin, I would clean errant crumbs or cream from her face.

My expression must have revealed the tidal wave of emotion because he drew back his hand and dropped the napkin by his plate. "Hey," he said. "I was kidding. Are you okay?"

Not only was I not okay, I might never be. I couldn't imagine a time when random thoughts of Stella wouldn't pierce my heart.

"I'm still just a little out of it." I stirred cream into my coffee and watched it lighten. Harry sat beside me and put his hand on my shoulder.

"You're entitled. You had a hell of a day."

I sipped the coffee, then remembered that I hadn't asked how things had gone for them. "What did you find out from your source?"

Harry started the update. "Luis's union guy tried to track down the personnel at the local morgue when they brought the body in. Funny thing about that. The two guys on duty have disappeared without a trace. Probably got a pay-off and changed careers. Word is somebody's been trying to move in on Balsuto's operation, but he wasn't sure Ben was involved. Your visit with him answered that question."

"So, your friend wasn't much help." I sighed.

"No." Justin took over the narrative. "But the government guy in Guayaquil made some calls and found out where they sent your sister's body to be, uh…."

"You mean cremated." I helped him out. "And?"

"And Ben never picked up her ashes." He stood, walked to his room, and came back with an ornate gold-plated urn. "We got them. It's not much, but at least your family can have some closure." He placed it in the center of the table. I wrapped my hands around the cold metal.

"It's a lot," I said and wiped at my eyes.

He handed me his handkerchief. That old-fashioned gesture made me feel warm and safe. Without thinking, I blew my nose with it.

Harry cleared his throat. "I'm not sure what our next step should be. We've figured out what Ben and Prez were hiding. The question is how does Stella fit in. Sounds to me like your sister's housekeeper knows more than anyone else about the situation. I'll work on tracking her down. You guys see what the cops know about what happened at the Point."

Justin agreed and Harry set out, leaving us alone with the harsh reminder of Stella's death. Even more than those horrible pictures, that urn signaled the finality of my loss.

"I don't have a clue how Stella would feel about the whole cremation thing. We never talked about dying." I ran my fingertips over the bronze container. "There are so many things we never got the chance to talk about."

"Oh, God, Grace." He wrapped me in his arms. "I can't stand to see you hurt like this."

He rocked me back and forth the way Gran had whenever I suffered a fall or a broken heart. I wanted to stay there forever. But I would find no peace or safety with Justin until I answered the questions left from Stella's death.

I placed my hands on his chest. He tilted my chin up and looked into my eyes, then brushed his lips across mine and kissed me on the forehead before releasing me.

I excused myself to get dressed. I winced when I saw my reflection in the bathroom mirror. My hair was sticking up in weird angles all over my head. And despite sleeping in, the dark circles under my eyes transformed me into a frumpy raccoon. I needed concealer and fast. I scanned the room for my make-up bag, and my stomach flip-flopped.

My sandal wasn't the only thing I'd left behind. My purse was still sitting in the bathroom of the house on the Point.

CHAPTER 29

Justin sat on the patio waiting for me. The sun was out, but the air was thick and wet. I sat on the wicker chair beside his recliner. "We've got a problem." I told him about my missing purse.

"Shit! It won't be good if the police, or anyone else finds out you were there. There's been nothing on the news, so there's a good chance no one has discovered the bodies. If I go now, I can get in and out without drawing too much attention."

"That sounds like a great plan, except I'm going with you. I'm familiar with the layout. Plus, you need a lookout."

I expected him to protest, but he shrugged and said, "At least that way I'll know where you are."

Around us, greenery glistened. The sweet, heavy fragrance of Montañita's version of honeysuckle saturated the air, reminding me of Georgia summers. Lesroy, Stella and I would pick blossoms from the vines and suck nectar from them. She pretended she was a butterfly, laughing and prancing from vine to vine. The memory soured as I remembered reading that butterflies like the taste of blood.

His voice brought me back to a reality where my sister would never laugh again.

"I'm going to grab some water from the lobby." He tossed me the keys to the rental. I rolled down the windows, blasted the air conditioning, and waited.

When he returned, he handed me a bottle and took hold of my hand as I reached for it. "You look better this morning. Maybe a little worse for the wear, but not too bad." He grinned.

"Thanks a lot." I dreaded returning to the scene of my captivity, fearful of what I might find. I wasn't about to give Justin an excuse for dumping me, though, so I smiled and gave him a playful punch on the shoulder.

After an exaggerated wince, he asked if I could find something on the radio that wasn't salsa or reggae.

It wasn't an easy request, but I located an oldies station, and we listened to Aretha belt out her demand for respect. I recognized the rocks lining the right side of the road, but today I saw wildflowers blooming and armadillos scuttling by.

A cloud came between us and the sun, and I flashed back to the pitch-black surrounding me in my hiding place under the stairwell. I hit the automatic button on my window and stuck my head out, inhaling deep breaths of air the way Stella and I had sucked the nectar from those delicate petals so long ago.

The terrain got rockier as the road narrowed, and I recalled the sensation of bumping along the same route less than twenty-four hours ago.

"That's the turnoff to the house." Justin pointed up a steep drive lined with manicured shrubbery. "I'm thinking we should park the car and walk if you're up to it. We can duck behind the bushes if we see anyone approaching."

He removed a gun from the glove compartment, then unsnapped the holster and stuck the weapon into the back of his waistband. Despite my mother's and grandmother's predilection for guns, I hated them. After my experience last night, however, I could hardly question the sensibility of being armed. We climbed out of the car and started toward the house. By the time we reached the summit, I sweated the band-aids off my scraped knees.

"The stairs to the deck wrap around the side of the house. You can't see them from here, but if I've got my bearings right, Prez fell just behind those flowery bushes."

"It doesn't look like anyone's here," he said, removing the gun from his waistband. "Let's go around back and try getting in through the doors to the deck."

We followed a stone-paved pathway I missed the night before. I stopped at the corner of the house, dreading the possibility of seeing Prez's body sprawled at the foot of the stairs.

"Why don't you wait here?" he suggested when he noticed I wasn't right behind him.

I shook my head and resumed walking. Prez wasn't lying dead on the ground below the deck. Justin examined the decorative pebbles. "No blood, but it looks as if someone smoothed the gravel here."

We climbed the deck stairs. When we reached the top, he pulled me into a crouch beside him. It was a short distance to the glass doors, but out in the open the way we were, it seemed to take longer than our hike up the hill. He reached the entrance first, covered his hand with the bottom of his T-shirt, and pushed the door open.

Except for the hum of the air conditioner, the room was silent.

"The kitchen's that way," I whispered and braced myself for the sight of Javi's bloody body. But the kitchen was empty. Every surface—granite countertops, stainless steel appliances, hanging light fixtures—was so clean it sparkled. There was no blood and gore smeared on the built-in refrigerator. If not for the scent of bleach in the air, there was nothing to suggest anyone had been there.

"I don't understand. Javi was right there." I froze at the spot where Ben's henchman had slumped against the fridge, mouth open as if his friends had just popped up to yell surprise. "How did they get the place so clean so fast? They must have had a team of mini-maids in here before dawn."

Justin pointed to the door leading downstairs. "This way?" he asked.

He held the gun in front of him just like in the movies as we went downstairs. We paused at the bottom. Colorful throw pillows I hadn't noticed the night before covered the leather sofa. I walked to the place where I had smashed Prez's face with the tequila bottle. No glass, no blood.

"You're right about this being a professional clean-up job. But it wasn't mini-maids. Where did you leave your bag?"

I walked down the hallway to the bathroom and eased the door open. The same cleaning crew must have wiped the counters clean.

There was nothing there. If Harry and Justin hadn't found me careening down the hill last night, I might have thought I imagined everything.

"No purse?" I jumped at the sound of Justin's voice. "Sorry," he said. "After the job they did on the rest of the house, I'm not surprised. Come on; let's get out of here."

We left the way we came. I froze at the spot where I saw my first murdered thug. Still no Javi.

"I don't understand," I said, as we drove down the mountain. "How could someone wipe away everything that happened last night?"

"One thing's for sure," Justin said. "It wasn't the police. What worries me is that goddamn bag of yours. Whoever has it knows you were there last night, and that you witnessed a murder."

"I didn't actually see anyone get shot. Just because Prez came down after I heard the gunshots doesn't mean he killed Javi."

"Right. But odds are he did. Besides, professionals did this clean-up job. And they don't leave loose ends. You're a loose end."

I turned up the radio. Gloria Gaynor was belting out "I Will Survive." I wondered if I would.

We stopped at a Mexican cantina and picked up tacos to go, then ate on the patio of our villa. We were sitting there, staring at the ocean, when Harry joined us with a six-pack of beer.

"Not much luck tracking down Eva. No one's seen her since your visit, or no one will admit seeing her. How about you guys? Did you get the bag?"

The prospect of listening to Justin recount our morning was more than I could take. I excused myself and went to lie down. With the blinds drawn, the room was cool and dark, so I didn't notice it until I turned on the bedside light. Dead center on top of my bed sat my missing purse.

CHAPTER 30

I rubbed my arms against the chill bumps popping up in response to what seemed like a ten degree drop in temperature. Shivering, I wracked my mind to come up with an explanation for the bag's return.

Instead of a logical reason, I thought of the year we discovered Stella's involvement in a series of petty thefts. Although I knew it was impossible, I was certain she was the one who had engineered the reappearance of my purse.

When my sister was five, we called her magpie, not because she was chatty or quarrelsome. Because she liked to steal bright, shiny objects and hide them. She started with random articles from around the house: Gran's clip-on earring, a jeweled crown from my one and only ballet recital, a lipstick from my mother.

Mom discovered the stolen items in a shoebox underneath Stella's bed. When confronted with her larcenous behavior, my sister seemed surprised at all the fuss. She didn't understand why it was a big deal. We explained it was wrong to take things that belonged to other people.

For months it looked as if Mom's talk registered, and in a very literal way it had. Nothing went missing at home, and we thought our mother had successfully nipped Stella's criminal career in the bud — until her distraught kindergarten teacher called.

We discovered what she had learned about not lifting stuff from family members had not translated into the classroom. She comprehended the law itself but not the spirit. Her classmates reported missing pencils, notebooks, even jackets and gloves. Rather than keep them, she always returned the confiscated booty to its rightful owners. There had been no question she was the thief because the teacher caught her red-handed—not in the act of theft, but while sneaking a stolen crayon box back into a little girl's backpack. The woman was at a loss since she always returned what she had taken, but the behavior disrupted the daily routine and had to stop.

It was one of the few times I remember Mom spanking Stella. Later, I asked my sister why she stole from her classmates when she didn't want the stuff she took. She smiled and said it was fun to see her friends searching for the missing objects. And it was a blast to watch their joyful reactions when they recovered their lost treasures.

She never got in trouble for stealing again, but I doubted she had stopped. She just became better at it, and after she stole Ben, she no longer returned stolen goods.

Until now.

Except I didn't believe in ghosts. Stella was gone, and she wasn't coming back. She had nothing to do with the reappearing purse. To think she did was nothing more than wishful thinking or a result of my guilt. Neither of these reasons accounted for my continued shivering. I grabbed a sweater from my suitcase and called for Justin.

"What's wrong?" He appeared within seconds, Harry close behind.

I pointed to the bed. "It was here when I walked in."

"Don't touch it," he commanded, then left and came back with a broom. We watched as he poked the bag as if he expected a bomb or poisonous snake to be in it. But there was no explosion nor slithering reptile. He hooked the handle through the straps, lifted it off the bed, and carried it outside.

"Really, Justin," I said, following him through the patio doors. "It's not booby-trapped." But I didn't protest when he dumped the contents onto the thick glass table.

"Is anything missing?" he asked, using the broom to move stuff around.

If there was, I couldn't tell, nor did I notice any additions. Satisfied the bag posed no threat, he allowed me to put my things back in order. Then we walked inside.

"Here's how I see it," he began. "The only people who could have returned it are Ben, Prez, or whoever cleaned up after them. But Ben and Prez wouldn't have wanted anyone to know you were there. So, they would have ditched it, not gone to the trouble of sneaking it into your bedroom." He sat beside me on the sofa and put his arm around my shoulders.

"It could be a message," Harry said. "They want to make sure we realize how easy it would be to get to us."

"More of a threat," Justin said.

"But what if it wasn't them or their men?" I asked.

"There's only one other person who would be interested in last night's activities at the Point." Justin paused before adding, "Balsuto."

If it was Adelmo, why would he take such care to obliterate all traces of what had happened at the house? Ben and Prez had both disappeared, and Prez could be dead. No one had mentioned that possibility, so I brought it up myself.

"The last time I saw Ben he was alive, but Prez took a nasty fall. He might not have survived. Maybe whoever did the clean-up wanted to help me. Bringing back my purse was nothing more than a polite gesture."

"I'd say it was more than mannerly," Harry said. "But I sure as hell hope that's not the case. Yes, the world would be a better place without those assholes in it. Regardless of the motive behind the cover-up, though, you're involved now, which makes it easier for the authorities to consider you a murder suspect."

The concept I might have taken a life hadn't been real to me until Harry said it out loud.

"I'm more worried Grace didn't kill him, which could mean they're still after her," Justin added. "Because they know what Balsuto's capable of doing if he finds out they were trying to screw him over. That's what they were so concerned about, and they should be. Balsuto's not the forgiving type. They can't afford for you to talk to him."

Had I been a fool to refuse to believe the man I once considered my one and only true love wanted me dead? I had no doubts what Prez had in mind for me. I suspected he might have not only wanted me out of the way but had planned to shoot Ben, too.

"Maybe we should go home, leave all this insanity behind," Justin suggested. "There's a chance Javi is the only casualty from last night, and Grace had nothing to do with that. Regardless, it's a good idea not to be here if bodies start turning up."

I knew he was right, but we'd discovered almost nothing about my sister's murder.

"I'm not worried about getting arrested. The only people who know for certain I was even in that house are dead or involved in bringing me there against my will. They can't very well go to the police. Please, Justin. I could never face myself, not to mention my mother, if I left now."

"Would she want to lose another daughter? Forget it. You won't change your mind. So, I'll just fix myself a strong drink and pretend everything's going to be fine."

"Make that two." Harry and I said in unison.

He was overly generous with the vodka, but I didn't complain.

Harry talked more about his unsuccessful attempts to find Eva or her nephew, but I had trouble listening. We'd been in Montañita less than a week, and I'd seen and perpetrated more violence than I had in my entire life. And it was the Christmas season.

I noticed no one was talking and that both men were staring at me. "I'm sorry. I blanked out."

"Harry was saying he thought the two of us should go back to Ben's this afternoon to see if he made it home and talk to Eduardo. It's too dangerous for you to come, but we don't want to leave you alone."

"Stop right there. If you remember, I handled Ben, not once but twice. And after a pool stick to the crotch, Prez won't be moving very fast." If at all, I thought. "And there's no good reason for Adelmo to hurt me. Even if I overheard something, who would take my word over his?"

Justin looked as if he wanted to speak, but Harry put a hand on his shoulder. "She's right."

"Okay, okay." He ran his fingers through his hair. "But could you please promise to stay inside and keep the doors locked?"

I promised to try.

Harry glanced at his watch. "I need to see a client just outside of town about a problem he's having with the security system we set him up with a few months ago. It shouldn't take much more than an hour."

After he left, Justin went to the patio to check emails. I sat at Harry's laptop intending to send an email update to Mike but felt guilty about not talking to them in person since arriving in Ecuador and called instead. The call went to voicemail. After leaving a rambling message about how we were trying to piece together Stella's last months, I told Mom I loved her and would get back to her later. I made no mention of my kidnapping or the possibility I was a killer.

When I finished, I joined Justin on the patio.

"I forgot to thank you and Harry for rescuing me the other night. There's no telling what would have happened to me if you hadn't showed up."

"Somehow, I think you would have been just fine."

Only I didn't want to be fine without him, couldn't or wouldn't imagine being without him. I understood how reckless it was to experience such strong emotions after the short while we'd been together. But losing Stella a second and final time had taught me to reassess my life.

Before I could tell him how I felt, he came to me and traced the outline of my chin with his index finger before crushing my lips with his. The suddenness took my breath. I wrapped my arms around him, desperate to melt into his body. He slipped his hands up my back, and I trembled. After nibbling my earlobe, he kissed the hollow of my throat, bringing his mouth lower until he reached the top of my breast.

Without warning, he released me, and I stumbled into a chair. When he threw himself between me and the patio door, I saw Harry standing there, tapping on the glass. The roaring in my ears must have drowned out the sound of his knocking. I adjusted my clothes and smoothed my hair while Justin did some adjusting of his own.

"Sorry," he said, as Harry shuffled toward us. "Didn't hear you get back."

Nothing like stating the obvious, I thought, and resisted the urge to giggle.

"Hate to interrupt, but we should go if we want to miss the worst of the traffic." He was blushing. This time I giggled.

I followed the men to the entryway where Justin grazed my cheek with his lips, then gave me a proper kiss.

"I'll start the car. Later, Grace." Harry scurried out without looking back.

"I think we embarrassed him."

"You know you're driving me crazy," he whispered in my ear. "Could you please stay out of trouble or at least not cripple or maim anyone while I'm gone?" He lifted my hair and nuzzled my neck. "God, I don't want to go."

"I'll be waiting for you." I locked the door behind him.

I sat at the kitchen table and checked my email. Lesroy sent a picture of Scarlett lying in the middle of his bed, a leather slipper in her mouth. He added the caption: *Police locate shoe of missing man. Hopes for finding the body are slim.*

His message made me long for home. What if we all just said screw it, packed up, and left? Nothing we discovered or accomplished could bring Stella back. And I had to believe everyone gets what they deserve, that fate or karma or whatever would take care of her killer or killers. But what if I was wrong? What if the people who strangled my sister and treated her body like yesterday's garbage got away with it? I couldn't allow that to happen.

Although they had been gone only a short while, I was restless. I rummaged through the magazine rack until I found an English version of *Star* and curled up on the sofa to catch up on the lives of the rich and famous. I thumbed through the first few pages, tossed it aside, and drifted into a sound sleep.

My dreams weren't about Stella. She just kept turning up in them. In one, Lesroy and I were in my living room, and she came in with a baby on her hip. I knew, in the inexplicable way you know things in dreams, the infant she carried was mine. In another, Scarlett and I were running in a field. The dog stopped and stared into the woods where my sister stood, then vanished into the thicket. The last started on a high note. Justin and I were lying entwined on my mother's bed, kissing and touching. He rolled me over until I was on top of him, and I saw Stella's reflection in the mirror over the dresser.

I startled awake, conflicted as usual about her but also in deep sorrow. Seeing her with my baby—a child I would never have, according to Mom, unless I got with the program—made me think of all the firsts Stella and I would never share. But the one with Justin brought back the bitterness I held far too long.

Dreams, like memories, deceive us. They show a reality we wish was real; then they destroy hope with truth.

I wandered around the room. It was after two, and I was beyond bored. I picked up the TV remote and began flipping through channels, stopping at a telenovela, like American soap operas only more melodramatic. It was in Spanish, but I decided to expand my limited vocabulary. Even without subtitles, I could tell the plot followed a beautiful young woman torn between two men. The story mesmerized me. Close-ups of passionate, open-mouth kisses and fade-to-black sex scenes were hot stuff for daytime television.

I couldn't understand any of the dialogue and didn't realize it was over until the credits ran on a split screen. Frustrated at the realization I'd never know which of the steamy heroes the heroine chose, I reached for the off button as the station cut to the local news desk. A ridiculously handsome man in a tan suit and red-striped tie stared into the camera with the words *Noticias de última hora* flashing below him.

The picture shifted from a shot of the newsroom to footage of police with grave expressions, standing next to a scattering of small boulders at the edge of the ocean. One of them began speaking. I moved until I stood inches from the TV, expecting proximity to improve comprehension. But the only words I caught were *tablista* and *Estados Unidos*: surfer and United States.

When the camera panned in on the base of the rocks, my stomach flipped. I strained to pick up what the reporter was saying, but it was useless. He spoke too fast. The cameras cut back to the anchorman. His solemn expression morphed into a cheerful smile as he transitioned to a commercial break.

I couldn't have seen what I thought I had. I clicked through channels, hoping to find more on the story, but there was nothing. Nothing at all to confirm that quick shot of a bright orange and purple tennis shoe.

CHAPTER 31

I turned off the TV, took a bottle of water from the refrigerator and held it against my head, praying the coolness would provide clarity.

Calm down, Grace. You can't be sure it belonged to Prez. The color on the set isn't great and even if it is the same, Prez Allen can't be the only surfer from the United States who wears orange and purple tennis shoes.

I told myself I was still in shock from my ordeal at the Point and not able to tell the difference between reality and imagination. The trick was to stay calm and not jump to ridiculous conclusions. A soft tapping sound interrupted my reverie.

Remembering my promise to be extra careful, I looked through the peephole where a stack of fluffy white towels blocked my vision.

I released the bolt lock and opened the door. The laundry tumbled to the ground. Instead of a smiling staff member, a bald man built like a linebacker stood there.

I stepped back, grabbed the knob, and tried to shut him out. But he was surprisingly agile for his size. He stuck a booted foot on the doorstep and sidestepped through the entrance, clicking the lock behind him. I continued backing away from him, then bolted for the patio. Once again, he moved faster than expected and took my arm without applying pressure.

"Por favor, Señorita." He released me but stepped in front of me, blocking my flight path. "My name is Marco, and I am not here to hurt you. I have a message from Señor Balsuto. He wishes to see you, but only if you agree to it." A look of genuine concern came over his round face, as he carefully removed a folded piece of paper from his back pocket and handed it to me.

Grace,

If you still want to know who caused your sister's death, I ask that you go with Marco. It is a short distance to travel for the chance to take part in getting justice for our beautiful Stella. I will not have you brought against your wishes, but if you come to me, like the little creatures who crossed our path when we last met, you can be assured of your safety.

Yours always,

Adelmo

I assumed his reference to the colorful crabs we encountered on the way to the museum was to reassure me the note came from him. I wondered what would happen if I refused him. Would Marco leave? Would my refusal end any chance of finding out what happened to my sister?

Adelmo promised he would uncover the truth about Stella, and, while his fervor frightened me, I believed him. I explained to Marco I would go with him but had to write a note for my friends to let them know where and with whom I was going. He smiled but shook his head in response to my inquiry about our destination.

"I am sorry, Señorita. I am under orders not to reveal such information. Your friends must trust you are safe."

Trust. That was the issue. Justin said Ben destroyed my ability to trust, and until he came along, that was true.

Adelmo was a different story. I shuddered at his obsession for vengeance when we first met but had come to understand it. I even experienced a strange connection whenever I was with him. While lack of fear might not be the same as trust, it would have to do.

Marco waited while I found paper and pen. I supplied as many details as I could about who had summoned me and why I was going. I emphasized Adelmo had guaranteed my safety, and that I took him at his word.

My escort held the door open and guided me to a long, black limo. I sank into the dove-gray leather seats, wondering if I had made the right decision. While I believed my sister's lover wouldn't harm me, I suspected his information about Stella's last hours would devastate me. And the line in his note about taking part in delivering justice for her might destroy me.

I closed my eyes. The image of a bright orange and purple tennis shoe flashed through my mind. I trembled at the possibility I had already played a role in settling the score for Stella. But if Prez had killed her, I wasn't sorry. Besides, my actions at that hellish house were more self-defense than murder. Adelmo talked about getting justice, but what if it was more like revenge? If so, did I care?

The Grace Burnette who landed in the Guayaquil airport less than a week ago had been determined to protect Ben from violence, regardless of his culpability. But I wasn't that woman anymore. I'd been bullied and terrorized, had seen brutality up close and personal in the form of my sister's destroyed body. And I had faced the fact I would never get the chance to tell her that, despite all the heartache between us, I had never stopped loving her. She was and would always be my flawed, but beautiful, Stella Star.

So, the answer was no. I didn't care whether it was justice or revenge.

I had no sense of how much time had passed before the limo slowed to a stop. Marco came round to my side and opened the door. Unlike Javi's indifference, his demeanor suggested he cared about me, didn't want to terrify me. When he offered his hand, I took it.

The glare from the sunlight stabbed at my eyes. Marco had parked on the edge of a construction site. Developers had bulldozed the land, creating an artificial clearing for the foundation. Several car lengths in front of our limo, a black sedan sat beside a small trailer.

"Señor Balsuto is waiting," Marco said.

"You're not coming?"

"No, Señorita. My instructions are to wait here."

I squared my shoulders and stepped up to the makeshift cement block stairs. An air conditioning unit jutted from a side window. It wheezed and dripped water onto the ground, forming a puddle in the rutted earth. After inhaling and exhaling, I tapped on the aluminum door.

I almost didn't recognize the man in front of me. He'd shaved his thick beard, leaving a heavy five o'clock shadow in its place. Beneath it, his skin had a grayish tint, suggestive of someone suffering from a long-term illness. Deep lines creased the corners of his bloodshot eyes. But his smile was as seductive as before, and his hands were still warm and strong.

"I am so glad you came, Grace." He ushered me in and closed the door.

Despite the sputtering contraption in the window, the air was damp and clammy. It was so dark I had to stop, unable to get my bearings. He flipped a switch, but the dim light did little to illuminate the room. Then he led me farther into the trailer. It wasn't just the poor lighting that made the room seem more like a cave than a civilized dwelling. The paneled walls were a dull brown, providing little contrast with the worn carpet. The only furnishings were a broken-down desk, a plaid recliner with stuffing sticking out of the seat, and a rickety kitchen chair.

"I apologize for the conditions of our meeting place, but privacy was more important than appearance as you will soon understand. But first, what may I bring you? Water or soda? Something stronger if you prefer?"

"Water's good, thank you." I watched as he dragged a cooler from beneath the desk and removed two bottles.

"I appreciate your coming. It cannot be easy for you to put yourself in the hands of someone you do not know so well. But from the moment I saw you, it was as if we had known each other for quite some time. Like my beloved Stella, you are a very old soul. Perhaps you and I were close in some earlier life."

He stopped to stare into my eyes, then shook his head and continued.

"I felt the same about your sister, only much stronger. It was as if she filled some part of me I never knew was empty. I won't lie to you, Grace. I have wanted many women. Once I possessed them, my desire faded. But Stella was different. She was an irresistible combination of passion and sorrow. Just when I thought I had seen all of her, I found another level to her soul. The more I made love to her, the more I had to have her. Each time we were together, I traveled deeper into undiscovered territory, both in her body and her spirit. I know she wronged you, and I understand your anger."

Adelmo slid closer and reached for my hands again. I let them rest in his.

"Stella also understood. She told me she had vowed to change, to become a better person, one deserving of your forgiveness. Unlike others who make such promises, I watched as she kept hers. And I fell deeper in love with the woman she became."

His voice thickened as he brought my hands to his lips, the same way he'd done in the museum garden. He seemed confused for a moment, as if he wasn't sure who I was, and for the first time since I'd entered the little trailer, a sense of dread overcame me.

"Your sister was a woman with many secrets. Some we shared and some I only sensed. Just as I promised I would find the truth about what happened to her, I made promises to her as well." He let go of my hands and sighed. "But we will save that for another day. Today, I keep my promise to you." He motioned for me to join him as he stepped toward the back of the trailer.

Had I made a mistake putting my faith in a man of such drastic extremes? His love for my sister bordered on obsession. And while he never exhibited violent behavior in my presence, both his intensity and reputation hinted he was capable of bursting into uncontrolled rages. But were these actual contradictions? Weren't they more like points of continuum on the line of human emotions? The problem was I couldn't be sure where his feelings for me might fall on this scale.

We walked into what had once served as a bedroom. The acrid scent of urine assaulted me. I gagged before covering my nose and mouth. Here, it was even darker. Although he was only a few feet from me, I could only make out his outline. Faint light trickled in from windows, covered with heavy fabric. No trace of wet air conditioning made it to this room where the heat was almost tangible. I could hear him walking farther from me. Once again, I had to give my eyes time to adjust. When they did, I couldn't comprehend what I saw.

In the middle of the room a man in a solitary chair slumped forward, head down, body tied in place with bloody ropes.

Adelmo charged, drew back his thick-booted foot, and kicked hard enough to flip him over backward. Pathetic whimpers drifted up from the twisted lump. Adlemo righted the chair but not before administering another violent attack, this time to the man's stomach. Moans became screams of agony as he struggled to lift his head. Blood, both fresh and dried, lined his forehead like savage war paint. One eye was swollen shut; the other, marked by a wide gash just above the cheekbone.

"What did I tell you about making all that noise?" Adelmo hissed and backhanded his prisoner, who jerked in response to the blow and fell back into his original position: head down, face obscured. But not before I recognized the bloody, beaten ruin that was now Ben Wilcott.

CHAPTER 32

I stared at the horror that had once been the man I loved, then turned to Adelmo and gasped, "What have you done?"

"I have uncovered the truth, my sweet Grace." The naked bulb cast shadows across his face. "And here it is."

He yanked Ben's head back and poured water over him. Ben sputtered and fell forward again. Adelmo jerked him upright by the hair.

"I have brought someone to see you," he said with what could have been mistaken for a benign smile. "You will tell her the story you told me, and then, maybe, if you get everything right, you might make it out of this alive."

I wondered if it was as clear to Ben as it was to me that he had no chance of going home in one piece. But he turned to his captor and murmured something. Adelmo shrugged and whispered in his mangled ear. Whatever he said gave Ben the motivation to speak.

"I'm so sorry, Grace," he began, but Adelmo dug his fingers into Ben's shoulder, causing him to shriek.

"Just explain what happened. Tell her how you killed Stella."

He started his story with a description of the couple's fights: how they had begun as shouting and shoving matches and had escalated into open-handed slaps before culminating with him pushing her down the stairs. At that point Adelmo thumped Ben on the side of his head and grasped him by the neck.

"Please, Adelmo. Let him finish." I wish I could say I'd spoken to spare my ex more pain, but I only wanted him to tell the story without interruption, to get it over with so I could escape the festering air of that miserable trailer.

He continued his account of how he suspected Stella was having an affair and had confronted her. Things had gotten violent, and she locked herself in the bathroom. He admitted to being so drunk he passed out. The next morning, she disappeared, and he didn't see her for over four months. He hired people to look for her, but they found nothing.

After a month, she sent word she wanted a divorce and planned to return to the States. By then, he had given up on the relationship and resigned himself to letting her go. It wasn't as if they'd been making each other happy anyway. But then everything fell apart.

He stopped at this point and requested more water. Adelmo poured the rest of the bottle into the broken man's mouth and nudged him hard.

"I swear I didn't mean for it to happen, Grace." He gasped for breath. "There was no reason for her to come back. I didn't even know she was there." He made a gurgling sound that might have been a sob. Then he faced Adelmo. "It wasn't my idea. None of it. You have to believe me. It was all Prez's fault."

Adelmo twisted his mouth into the semblance of a smile and nodded.

"Prez was at the house. He got involved with some Colombians and wanted to set up a deal with them cutting Adelmo out of the picture." He winced and faced his captor. "I swear, I would never have double-crossed you, but he threatened me." His voice had taken on a high-pitched whining quality. I fought the urge to kick his chair over myself.

"We didn't know she was there. I guess we made a lot of noise, and she hid. When Prez left, she came out. Said she just needed to get something from the bedroom and no, she had no idea what we'd been talking about. But I was scared. What if she was lying and planned to go to the cops or found another way to use it against me? I didn't know what to do, so I called Prez. He hadn't gotten far." Ben groaned. "Oh, God, oh, God! What did I do?"

Adelmo gave him a disgusted look, then tapped him on the shoulder, his composure more terrifying than his fury had been.

"Prez promised he was just going to talk to her, find out for sure what she knew. He said I should disappear for an hour, that he would text me when it was safe to come back. I shouldn't have gone." He choked down a sob.

"Go on, please," I encouraged. "Explain how you never thought Prez would put his hands around her neck and choke the life out of her. Tell me all about how you left my sister alone with a sick, sociopathic fuck, never imagining he'd kill her and throw her into the ocean."

"Please, Grace," Ben begged. "I never meant for anything bad to happen to her. God help me, I still loved her. You've got to believe me. If only she'd just stayed away."

"Right. It was Stella's fault for getting killed. I guess you didn't mean for me to get hurt either when you and Prez took me to that house. What were you going to do, Ben? Screw me and then leave me so Prez and I could *talk*? Would that have been on me, too?"

He moaned.

"Did you help dump her body, Ben?"

"How could you even think that? It was all Prez. I didn't know the boat was missing until the cops started asking questions. I confronted him, and he admitted he had taken her body and staged the accident. I found out later he bribed the authorities to cover up the crime."

His lips twisted in a grotesque imitation of his old smile. Even in his wretched state, he held onto the hope I could be charmed into believing him.

"And that night at the Point, I had no intention of hurting you. I was just supposed to find out what you knew. I tried to stop Prez, but he flipped out. The son of a bitch fired on me. That's why I got the hell out of there. I swear I'm telling you the truth. I never meant for any of it to happen. Ask Prez if you don't believe me. Adelmo has him, too. He knows the truth."

Adelmo gave Ben another eerie smile. "I think you have misunderstood me. Prez will not be answering any questions. It seems the poor man was a bit, how would you say, accident- prone? My men found him unconscious at the foot of the balcony stairs, tangled up with a pool cue stuck in his thigh. Sadly, when he regained consciousness, he resisted their attempts to help him. There was a struggle, and somehow his neck was broken."

Ben's eyes rolled back, and blood gurgled from his mouth.

So, I hadn't been the one who killed Prez. Adelmo's men had done it and made his death look like an accident, the way Prez had done with Stella, Adelmo's idea of a little joke.

I guess I should have experienced guilt or at least remorse for my role in Prez's demise, but I was removed from it and from the desperate man in front of me. I wanted to go to the villa and shower under the stingy stream of water. Then I would pack up and leave Montañita forever.

"And now my question to you is what would you like to do with this pedazo de mierda? He may not have been the one who killed our Stella, but he is just as much to blame. Is he not?"

Yes, Ben was equally guilty of murdering my sister.

"I don't know," I whispered.

"I think you do." He pulled a gun from his waistband.

I recoiled. "What about the police? Now that we know what happened, they can find enough evidence to prosecute him."

Adelmo dismissed the idea with a wave of his hand, the one holding the weapon. "Accidental deaths are far more favorable to government reports than murders. And I imagine this man would use his wealth to cut a deal. Or perhaps he would trade information about me for his freedom. Isn't that right, old friend?"

"I would never sell you out, Adelmo. That was all Prez." His whine became a low buzz, like an electric saw losing power.

"Of course, of course," Adelmo patted him on the back, then turned to me. "Even if the police investigated and a judge found him guilty, Ecuador abolished the death penalty long ago."

His tone suggested the matter was settled.

"Adelmo, please." I looked at what remained of the man I'd once loved. "Prez is already dead. Maybe that's enough."

"Are you sorry the man who strangled your sister is no longer alive?" he asked.

When I thought I had been the one who killed Prez, was I sorry? I had been horrified at first. But later? Later I felt nothing at all.

"That's not the point. The point is shooting Ben like this would be straight-up murder. And I don't want to be a part of it."

"That's right, babe." Ben reentered the conversation. "You're not a killer. Stella wouldn't want you to become one either. She — "

Adelmo backhanded him again. "Do not speak her name!" He shouted and raised his hand to strike him again. I held his arm.

"Enough!" I shouted, startling both Adelmo and myself. "I hate saying this, but he's right. Stella wouldn't want me to become the kind of person who could condone putting a bullet in an unarmed man, no matter how disgusting he might be. I want to take our chances with the police. Didn't you say it was for me to decide?"

That wasn't exactly what Adelmo had said, but I hoped he didn't remember.

"You are a good person, Grace. Stella told me you were, but I had trouble understanding how such a good person could not be more forgiving. Now I do. There are some things we cannot forgive."

"But I was wrong not to forgive Stella, and I'll have to live with that for the rest of my life. Please, don't make me live with this." I pointed to Ben.

Adelmo sighed and put the gun back in his waistband. "I understand." He guided me into the front room. Outside the narrow window, the sky had grown dark, and I wondered how long I'd been a guest at Adelmo's little house of horrors. The clock on the dusty microwave read five ten. That was the moment the first rumble of thunder sounded.

Adelmo opened the door and surveyed the clouds. "I believe we are in for a very bad storm. If you and Marco leave now, you might make it down the mountain before the rain comes full force."

"But aren't you and Ben coming?"

"Ah, my sweet Grace. You should know your sister never doubted you would forgive her. She said you were the only one she ever cared about letting down, and she vowed to become the kind of woman you could love again and respect for the first time."

I wiped my eyes and looked away in the distance where an arrow of light burst through the dark clouds. A rumble of thunder followed. The storm was getting closer.

"I am not such a good person. Your sister understood this and loved me despite it. But it was family Stella valued more than anything. She had to return home to show you how much she had grown. I wanted her to stay, but circumstances changed, and it wasn't safe for her to remain here with me, so I agreed to let her go."

Marco watched us from a distance, and Adelmo called out to him in Spanish. He got into the car and started the engine.

"And now you must go. I will remain here with my guest a little longer. Then I will leave the country for a short time. Perhaps I may someday visit you in your lovely country and see where my beautiful Stella was once so happy."

A shaft of lightning split the air, and I screamed as the accompanying thunderbolt sounded. Marco stepped from the car, leaving the engine running. The man who loved my sister more than life kissed me on the cheek and walked toward the trailer. I tried to run after him, but Marco wrapped an arm around my waist and held me.

"Please, Señorita," he said. "We must go. It is not safe to stay here out in the open."

As if on cue, rain pelted the ground, creating instant puddles. Three bolts of lightning shot across the sky in brief terrifying intervals, and thunder blasted. I slipped out of Marco's grip and stumbled onto the ground. He reached down to help me, and a blinding flash of light illuminated the air, bringing with it a scorching heat that rippled through the hair on my arms and neck. It hovered overhead. I could smell bitter smoke almost at the same time resounding thunder deafened me. Then there was darkness.

CHAPTER 33

Sparks flickered against a black velvet surface where I lay listening to faraway voices. What I thought was thunder was more a thumping sound, as if something heavy were being dragged across a wooden floor. I focused on the pinpricks of illumination and discovered it was the jar of fireflies Stella and I captured on the night Rita and Lesroy came running into the house with Uncle Roy in hot pursuit. In all the excitement and the culminating storm, we forgot to set them free.

Stella's solid little body lay beside me in Gran's bed. I eased out from under the quilt. The gentle rhythm of my sister's breathing remained constant as I slid off the bed and tiptoed to the dresser. The tiny creatures clustered near three holes in the top. Only a few blinked out a farewell light show to the world. I got to them just in time.

I'd forgotten what awakened me until it sounded again, this time more of a shuffling accompanied by an occasional female grunt. Because of Stella's aversion to complete darkness, the door to wherever she slept was always left ajar. I stepped into the hallway and felt my way toward the living room, stopping at the entrance, where I could see Gran and Mom standing side by side. At first, I thought they were fighting over a coat or jacket. But it wasn't a jacket they were tugging at. It was Uncle Roy. I thought he was dead, but then he snorted and sniffed in his usual drunken style. A combination of relief and disappointment washed over me as I watched the women drag my uncle through the open front door.

Once outside, they closed the door behind them, and I ran to the window, ducking low to peer out at them. Uncle Roy's head banged on the steps from the porch to the walkway and continued bumping along as my mother and grandmother struggled to haul his body up and into the passenger seat of his truck. Once they stuffed him in, head lolling against the window, Mom walked around to the driver's side, got in, and drove off. Gran followed in our old Chevrolet.

In a late-night trance, I wandered onto the front porch, still holding the imprisoned fireflies. From behind me, Stella's soft little voice drifted up. "We better let them go now." I unscrewed the top and shook the jar. It took a few seconds for the dazed creatures to remember what freedom looked like, but gradually they fluttered away. Stella held my hand as we stumbled back to Gran's big bed and held each other in the dark.

We never saw Uncle Roy again.

CHAPTER 34

A murmur surrounded me as I swam toward consciousness. The constant buzzing in my ears made it hard to understand what the words meant, but I knew I was no longer in Gran's bed. My eyelids were heavy and sore. I opened them only enough to allow the tiniest glimmer of light in. But it was bright enough to send excruciating shards of pain through my brain. I reached for my forehead, but the needle and tube stuck in my hand restricted my movement.

I had to be in a hospital, but where was it, and why was I there?

"Grace? Are you awake, Grace?" A soft voice suppressed the buzzing. "Nurse! Somebody get a nurse, goddammit! She's waking up."

"Please, not so loud." I opened my eyes again and tried to sit.

"Take it easy. Here, let me help." Gentle hands eased pillows behind my back.

"Justin, what are you doing here?" For a second, I thought he was the one in the hospital bed, and I was the visitor. "I don't know where I am," I admitted and convulsed with gulping sobs.

A nurse pushed past him and placed a cool cloth on my forehead. "I'm giving you something for the pain," she explained.

While she and Justin whispered at the end of my bed, flashes of memory returned. I didn't know where I was or how I'd gotten there, but I remembered crouching down with Marco in front of the trailer.

He finished his conversation with the nurse and sat beside my bed, then took my hand.

"What happened?" I hated the foggy sensation permeating my memory.

"It looks like lightning struck the construction shack and it exploded." He rubbed my arm, and I noticed a line of stitches from my wrist to my elbow. "You got hit by some flying debris."

"Oh, God," I groaned and rested my head on a pillow. "Ben was in that trailer."

Justin nodded.

"What about Marco?" I thought about the heavy-muscled man with the sweet face and how he threw himself on top of me.

"He's in pretty good shape—loopier than you, believe it or not, but they expect both of you to be fine."

Justin explained the blast had rumbled through the land, and local farmers had followed the smoke to the construction site. There had been a store of ammunition in the mobile unit, exacerbating the effect of the lightning strike. The men took us to an emergency clinic. The doctor there had us transported to Vernaza Hospital in Guayaquil.

"How did you find me?"

Justin ran his fingers through his hair, and I saw how exhausted he looked.

"When we found your note, Harry and I weren't too worried at first. I thought maybe you were right about Balsuto not wanting to hurt you. But the later it got, the more scared we got. Harry put his security people on it right away. Somebody picked up on an explosion in the hills above Montañita."

He looked away. When he returned his gaze to me, there were tears in his eyes. "We heard there were fatalities but couldn't find out who had been killed." He paused and grabbed my hand again. "I thought it was you." His voice broke.

"But it wasn't," I whispered. "I'm fine." I slipped my hands out of his and touched his cheek, dragging my IV line along. We were in the middle of untangling ourselves when Harry came into the room, carrying flowers, a balloon, and a box of chocolate.

"You're awake!" He dropped his gifts onto a cart by the bed and leaned over to kiss me on the forehead. "It's good to see you looking a little more like yourself."

"Thanks. Justin was filling me in on some details. How long have I been here?"

"They brought you in after eleven two nights ago, so about forty-eight hours," Harry filled a glass with water for the flowers.

Losing two full days transformed me into an unwilling time traveler, as if my body had been bound to the hospital bed while my spirit roamed. And I had journeyed far from this place. I had returned to the night when my mother and grandmother murdered Uncle Roy.

A young man with a stethoscope appeared. His smooth skin looked as if he had only begun shaving, and when he announced he was my doctor, I didn't believe him. He was professional and efficient in his examination, though, and agreed I could go home in the morning if I promised to follow post head trauma instructions. I resisted the urge to pinch his cute baby boy cheeks and promised to do exactly what he told me.

Harry kissed me on top of the head and left, leaving Justin sitting by my side.

"You should get some rest. Have you been staying with Harry or at a hotel?"

"Neither," he replied and titled his head toward the recliner in the corner.

"You didn't have to do that. I'm fine, actually, I'm super fine." My pain meds kicked in hard, and he kept slipping in and out of focus.

"Grace," he brushed his lips over mine. "Shut up and go to sleep."

When I woke the next morning, Justin was snoring softly from the recliner. He helped me dress, and we waited for the doctor's arrival.

He showed up a little after nine with a list of what to expect while recovering from a concussion. I was now subject to a variety of side effects: everything from irritability, depression, and memory loss to chronic pain and personality changes. And, of course, that damn ringing in my ears.

I promised to check in with my doctor when we returned to the US, and my adorable young Ecuadorian physician wished me luck and sent me on my way.

On the drive, I pictured families gathered around crowded tables and wondered how many of those families set a place for missing loved ones. Would my sister be the ghost at our family table every holiday? Or would my mother give up and let us become one of those families who go out for all the meaningful holidays until those special occasions no longer have meaning.

Justin interrupted my gloomy thoughts to explain someone from the villa had done all my packing for me, so there was no need to return to Montañita. I should have been grateful. But despite all the terrible things I'd seen and uncovered during my stay in that beachside party town, I felt a twinge of regret about not saying goodbye to the place. Glass half empty again, Grace.

We passed a deserted construction site and I gasped. I knew Ben had died in the explosion, but what about Adelmo?

I turned to Justin. "Did they find Adelmo's body in the trailer with Ben?"

Justin didn't look at me when he answered. "No, Grace. Balsuto's body wasn't recovered."

CHAPTER 35

Black clouds, heavy with rain, obscured my farewell view of the country where my sister died. When I closed my eyes, vibrant reds and yellows and oranges of the row houses scattered on the hills flashed, then melted into lush greens and blues of the river with the ever-changing currents.

Turbulence jolted the plane and my stomach. I dug my fingernails into the armrests. A flight attendant beamed at us as she demonstrated the proper way to put on our oxygen masks. Her emphasis that we should attach our own before helping others reminded me of my relationship with Stella. I focused on taking care of her and forgot about my needs. Now that she was gone, would I remember how to breathe?

My eyelids burned, and I rummaged through my purse for a tissue. I came up empty, except for a soggy one left from the scene I caused when we said goodbye to Harry, who had insisted on sending Stella's ashes home to my mother. His act of kindness unleashed a flood of emotions I'd kept damned up for over three years. During the past two weeks, cracks developed in the foundation and the damn exploded. My passion for Justin, the depth of my loss, the kindness of people I just met—all of this overcame me at the gate. I clung to Harry, sobbing into his chest. Only his promise to visit me in the States kept me from collapsing.

I closed the window shade. Whether it was an electrical glitch from my brush with lightning or my inability to comprehend how Adelmo vanished, I was having trouble remembering the story.

I tapped Justin on the arm and said, "I know you already explained this, but are you sure nobody knows what happened to him?"

He shook his head and repeated how the authorities insisted that not only was his body not recovered, but no one had seen him since the incident. They credited the trouble he'd been experiencing from both the government and the competing gangs with his disappearance. They speculated the explosion might have given him time to skip the country while everyone thought he was dead.

My sister's lover was an imperfect man, capable of walking into that shack and putting a bullet in Ben's head. But if Adelmo was right and Stella had changed, it was possible he was also a different person. His being alive made me hopeful, as if a part of my sister survived with him. The better part.

"I forgot to tell you we found Eduardo," Justin added.

The name eluded me at first, but I pulled it up. They had wanted to find Eduardo to ask questions about Eva and my ex.

"He was clearing his stuff out of the house when we got there. He agreed to get in touch with his aunt for us. Before we left, he asked us to tell you he was sorry your stay in Montañita was unpleasant, but you didn't need to worry about the Señor."

"Sounds like he didn't expect Ben to come back."

"Not much escaped him, so I would guess that's right. With him out of the way, Eva might talk to you. Speaking of talking, you never told me what happened at the construction site." He traced his index finger over the lines in my palm. "If you're not ready, though, I can wait."

"I'm ready," I said. I started with Marco's knock at the villa and ended with me crouching underneath the man. A sense of shame made me reluctant to share how I asked Adelmo not to kill Ben. But holding back the truth no longer seemed worth the effort. So, I explained how I begged him to let the justice system take care of my sister's murderer. My only omission was that the lightning strike had illuminated the recesses of my memory.

"When it came right down to it, I couldn't do it, couldn't get the revenge my mother wanted. But he loved Stella too much to let anyone else hold the fate of her killer. He had more courage than I do. Or maybe I didn't love her enough."

Justin pushed up the armrest and scooted close. "There's nothing courageous about shooting someone in cold blood, no matter how much he deserves it." In a firmer tone, he added, "I never want you to say that again, that you didn't love your sister enough. This entire trip has been a testament to your love. If you hadn't kept pushing and probing, we would never have learned the whole story."

"But is it really? How can we be sure if we don't understand why Stella disappeared? Or why she came back to the house, or what made her change into the better person Adelmo says she was. And if Eva doesn't call, we never will."

"Isn't it enough she wanted to be an improved version of herself? And that she never doubted you loved her?"

He was right. But for me, the reasons for Stella's behavior held the key to a door I wasn't sure even existed. Yet I couldn't get rid of the nagging feeling I was leaving something behind. Something Stella wanted me to find.

.   .   .   .   .

Midway into our flight, I thought about the contract Mom took out on Ben. I wondered how much money she offered and how she would answer if I asked her about it. Would she insist it was a joke? Or say she must have been out of her mind with grief? That she didn't even remember saying it?

Once upon a time, I would have believed her. Now, I couldn't picture a world where I would believe anything she told me. Because there was no doubt, Gran and Mom drove Uncle Roy, passed out cold in his truck, to the lake and pushed both into the murky water. Not only did I remember seeing them drive away, but I pictured Stella joining me, awakened by the noise. The two of us watched the taillights disappear along with the man who hurt our Lesroy, and we never mentioned it again. Until she asked about it long after we grew up.

My mother's thirst for revenge made sense. She'd been willing to kill to protect her sister. And I hadn't even been willing to accept calls from mine.

I glanced at Justin, who was reading the newspaper. I guessed, to the casual observer, we looked like a married couple, content to be separate, but together.

But we weren't a couple, married or otherwise. And we never had been. Ours was one of those shipboard romances only with guns and explosives. Once we returned to home port, would we resume being strangers? Despite the urgency of our attraction, I knew almost nothing about him: what he did for a living, whether he'd been married, if he wanted kids. More important, did he want me?

Then I remembered something Stella said to me before I met Ben. I complained about how hard it was to find a good man. She told me I didn't think I deserved to find a good man, so I talked myself out of relationships before they began. Or I tried to be what I thought the guy wanted because being myself wasn't good enough.

And she'd been right about my relationship with Ben. He seemed too good to be true. I worried he would wake up, see the real me, and run. So, I remade myself into his perfect partner. I pretended to like fancy wine and playing tennis at the club and all his weird sex stuff. And it worked for a while until he discovered my sister didn't require remolding because she was exactly what he wanted.

Well, Justin had first-hand, worst case knowledge of the real me, and he was still here, sitting beside me.

I realized I was doing what Stella accused me of: thinking of reasons I wasn't good enough to be in a relationship with a man like him. Instead of sitting here going over what wouldn't work between us, I should talk to him and find out what would. She was right. I should stop doubting myself and go for it.

But when I turned to begin the go-for-it process, my seatmate was leaning back on his pillow, sound asleep. I sighed, turned toward the window, and drifted off myself.

When I awoke with my head on Justin's shoulder, the pilot was announcing our approach to Atlanta.

"Glad to be home?" he asked as I sat up.

"I'm not looking forward to facing Mom. Other than that, yes. How about you? Are you happy to be home?" Where was home for him? Would someone be waiting for him? Again, I realized how little I knew about his life.

"Well, it will be a letdown after Montañita. But yeah, it's always good to get back to the States."

I had so many questions I wanted to ask, but people began the dreadful process of disembarking. The man across the aisle leaped up as soon as the light went off, cracking his head as he shoved himself over the woman in the seat beside him. He opened the overhead and dragged out his bag, then stood, tapping his fingers on my hand rest. A mother with three kids put one on her hip and the other two between her legs and inched toward the exit. A married couple tossed pillows and sweaters, searching for the woman's reading glasses, only to discover they were hidden in her fluffy perm.

Justin and I waited until the flood of people turned to a steady stream before gathering our bags. When we reached the gate, I saw the sign before I saw my cousin: *Thank the Good Lord. Grace is back!* Lesroy waved, then spun the placard before he dropped it, raced up to me, and whirled me around.

"Oh, my God, Grace." He released me, and I stumbled against him. Then he looked me up and down. "You're not different at all." He sounded disappointed.

"Why should I be? I've only been gone a few weeks."

"When Mike said lightning struck you, I about lost it. I expected you to glow, or at least have one of those Bride of Frankenstein white streaks in your hair. But you only look peaked, like you just got over a stomach flu or a bad case of food poisoning."

"I did not get struck by lightning. It hit near me and threw me to the ground."

People bustled past, and I suggested we move to the side where I gave a quick correction of the details of my injury and introduced Justin.

The way the guys I dated reacted to my cousin was my litmus test. If I detected any kind of negative vibes, that was it. Ben was the only one who ever fooled me. He pretended to like Lesroy until we got engaged. After I agreed to marry him, he showed his true feelings. By then, I convinced myself I was in love. I didn't like how he avoided being with my magical cousin. But Ben loved me, which meant he would change for me.

Other than Lesroy gripping a little more enthusiastically than usual, the handshake was normal, and Justin seemed at ease. My cousin turned and mouthed, "He's hot!" while fanning himself with the recovered welcome sign.

"I can't wait to hear everything about the trip, but for now," he swept his hand toward the exit, "your chariot awaits."

Gray snow-clouds filled the air with a wet, heavy scent. Justin explained he left his car at international parking and could take the shuttle, but Lesroy insisted on driving him.

My cousin conducted an abbreviated talk-show-style interview on the short ride. I was both embarrassed and grateful since he got answers to most of my questions about Justin's personal life in record time.

He worked for a security firm in downtown Atlanta and rented a house in the Old Fourth Ward, not too far from Lesroy. He came close once, but no, he hadn't married. Dogs were great, but it wasn't fair to have one when he traveled so much. When we pulled up to his car, my very own Entertainment Tonight host had just gotten into recent dating history.

"Enough!" I intervened. "You're wearing him out with all these questions." I unfolded, stepped out, and waited for Lesroy to open the back. Justin transferred his luggage and came to my side of the car where I stood shivering.

"It's freezing out here. Get in," he ordered. He leaned down and kissed me on the lips. "I'm going to give you some time with your family, but I'll call." When we broke apart, he touched my cheek before walking away.

Lesroy waited until Justin started his car before leaving.

"Well, well. It looks like Gracie's got a boyfriend. Tell me all about it, every dirty detail. And don't you dare say there's nothing going on between you two. Don't forget, I have sexdar."

Laughing, I said, "No way am I giving you details of my sex life."

During the rest of the drive, I filled him in on my Ecuadorian journey. When I finished, he shook his head. "My, God, Grace. Who are you and what have you done with my cousin? Spraying deviants with Mace, hanging out with criminals, and engaging in carnal relations with one of the hottest guys I've ever seen. I should have gone with you."

We pulled into the garage, and I ran straight to the kitchen, eager to see Scarlett. When she didn't greet me at the door, I called her name. There was no answer.

Lesroy came in with my bags, and I pounced. "Is Scarlett okay? Is she sick? Did you leave her at the vet?"

"Calm down. Miss Scarlett is fine." He fidgeted with the zipper on his jacket, not allowing his eyes to meet mine. "I, uh. That is your mom, um. Okay, don't get mad. But your mom made me leave Scarlett with her, so you'd come right over."

"Dammit, Lesroy!" He winced and stepped back. "Well, it's not going to work. They'll have to keep her overnight. I am not up to facing that woman. One more day won't make any difference." But the house felt empty without the Doberman's haughty presence.

"Sure, Grace. I understand."

And, of course, he did. First, he knew I would put CNN on as background noise as soon as he left. Then I would check for frozen pipes or signs of a break-in. Next, I would go through the refrigerator to determine what needed to be pitched and what could be salvaged. By then the sound of quarrelsome politicians yammering at each other would be getting on my nerves, and I would long for the clicking of claws on my hardwood floors.

But it wasn't only my co-dependent relationship with Miss Scarlett that compelled me to bite the bullet and go to my mother's house. And it wasn't just the need to give her closure on my sister's death. The memory of the night Mom and Gran killed Roy had tormented me since my memories returned.

I wasn't surprised my grandmother had willfully taken another life. To her, family was everything, and there was nothing she wouldn't do to protect us. Acknowledging that my mother went along with the plan to commit murder, even if the victim was my scum-sucking uncle, forced me to accept she wasn't the woman I thought she was.

Prez's death had troubled me, and I was relieved to discover I bore no responsibility for it. Any injuries I inflicted were the result of his attempts on my life. I accepted my lack of regret about what happened to him as a rational reaction to his part in Stella's death. Still, the thought of him lying on the rocks, his neck cocked at an unnatural angle, wasn't something I could shake. It was a lighter burden than not having resolved my issues with Stella before her death, but it would haunt me. Because when I shoved that pool cue through the slats in the staircase, I hadn't worried if it would be fatal for Prez. Caught in the most primal of all urges, survival, I hadn't cared about anything other than getting away from the man with the gun.

What my mother and grandmother did was different. When they loaded my drunken uncle into his truck, they made a conscious decision. The twenty-minute drive to the lake gave the two-woman caravan plenty of time to recognize the enormity of what they planned to do. And they did it. As I imagined it, they wrangled him into his spot behind the steering wheel, started the vehicle, and watched as it careened down the embankment. My grandmother never did anything halfway. She wouldn't have left until the last bubble disappeared and the muddy water calmed. I pictured Mom waiting in the car, grim and silent, but not disapproving.

Their actions, however, were nobler than my desperate act of self-defense. Theirs was an act of love. At least in their eyes, it was the only way to protect Rita and Lesroy. Because my aunt had a history of taking her husband back, regardless of the pain he inflicted. And Uncle Roy would have only gotten worse.

After about an hour of stalling, I gave up and set out for my mother's.

Although it was only a little after six, it was already December-dark and frigid enough to make my nose run. As usual, every light in the house was on when I got there. Gran was an electricity tyrant, insisting we turn off lights as soon as we left a room. I assumed Mom's extravagant disregard for worrying about the bill was her way of rebelling. Now, I thought it might be less about rebellion and more a fear of what might be hiding in unlit corners.

When she greeted me, I gasped. This shadow-version of my mother was not the woman who had always been invincible in my eyes. Learning about her capacity for deadly action only made her seem more so. But today I saw mortality on her face, and it terrified me.

In the two weeks I'd been away, she had dropped at least five pounds, not a lot of weight, but she'd been thin before Stella's death. Her cheekbones were razor sharp and naked, with no trace of her signature cherry-plum blush. After Gran died, Mom cut her shoulder-length hair into a becoming pixie. She kept it an almost natural shade of light brown and was meticulous about root control. Today, a thick line of gray snaked through her part, and the short strands framing her face were slicked back, accentuating her skeletal appearance.

Any anger or resentment I'd been carrying disappeared. I threw my arms around her. She had always been the one who initiated physical contact, a precise hug and a kiss on the cheek. Affection in my family was more efficient than effusive. As much as I loved Stella, our greetings and departures consisted of little more than quick touches on the shoulders or air kisses. Lesroy said we were emotionally stunted. I insisted we were dignified and reserved. Faced with the actuality of losing my sister and the inevitability of losing my mother caused something inside me to shift, as if an ice flow splintered.

She stiffened, shocked by my enthusiastic show of affection, then hugged me back.

"Let's get out of the cold." She kept one arm around me on the way to the dark- paneled den, as if she feared I would vanish if she let go. From behind the door to the spare bedroom, came a frantic scratching, followed by a low-pitched whine.

"That dog has the worst case of canine depression I've ever seen. Lesroy hand fed her. I had to shut her up in there to keep her from wandering through the house, pissing and moaning."

"You know she's housebroken," I said. Scarlett thudded against the door, knocked it open, and wriggled through. I braced myself for her usual full-frontal attack, but she plopped down, belly up, flopping back and forth like a fish on a dock. I knelt beside her while she yelped two octaves higher than normal. When I stopped rubbing her tummy, she righted herself and began covering my face in fragrant doggy kisses. I wondered if my departure made her feel as if a second sister had dumped her. If so, her uncomplicated joy at my return revealed an enviable capacity for love and forgiveness. It also sent the happy signal she was my dog now.

"That's the first time the poor girl has shown any energy since you left. Lesroy was planning to take her to the vet if you didn't get home soon. Looks like she's fine now."

Scarlett followed us to the den and sat on the floor in front of me. Mike announced he was going to make a batch of lemon drops. I'm not a big martini drinker, but his mixture of lemon, vodka, and a special secret ingredient was irresistible.

Mom draped a sweater over her shoulders and leaned toward me. "I need to know everything that happened over there. Mike's been sharing information, but you know how protective he can be. He doesn't realize it's worse not knowing. But you understand."

I wondered if she was referring to recent events when she said I understood. Either way, she was only half right. It could be better and worse at the same time. As a woman who knew what it felt like to take a human life, however, she should be capable of handling the truth.

Scarlett scooted closer and laid her head on my knees. I rubbed her silky muzzle and scratched behind her ears.

I started by telling Mom as much as I could remember from Stella's letters explaining someone had stolen them, that it was most likely Prez, but we'd never been able to verify that. I glossed over Stella's relationship with Adelmo. Mike joined us with our drinks, and I picked up the story where I'd gone to see Ben. When I got to the part where I sprayed Ben with the Mace, Mom's lips curled in a brief smile, and Mike nodded his approval.

I didn't want to tell her about the kidnapping but knew if I left it out, the rest wouldn't make sense. So, I downplayed the danger and skipped the part where Prez chased me with his gun drawn.

A sick sensation came over me when I reached my encounter with Ben in that room filled with the stench of terror and decay. Admitting

I advocated for mercy when I asked Adelmo to turn my ex over to the authorities would disappoint her. I included it, anyway, hoping my role in taking Prez out would satisfy her. Granted, it wasn't intentional, but it should still count.

When I concluded with the lightning bolt that destroyed the trailer with Ben in it, the room went silent.

"Somebody say something," I begged. "I'm sorry, Mom. I should have been strong enough to tell Adelmo to pull the trigger, but—"

"Stop, Grace, please stop!" My mother held up a trembling hand. "I'm the one who's sorry. When I first got the word about Stella, I lost it. And that thing with Justin, uh, well, that was crazy. Thank God, Mike understands me well enough to know I would never do something like that if I were in my right mind."

I sputtered on a sip of lemon drop. She must not have told him about Uncle Roy. Or she didn't think I remembered that night. Either way, now wasn't a good time to bring up her past proclivity for murder.

"Mike knew from the beginning that lovely young man didn't plan to kill Ben. He was only going along to protect you and to work with the police to get to the truth. But I should never have let you go." Tears trickled down my mother's cheek. Mike rushed to sit by her, his arm around her shoulders. The gesture made me think of Justin.

"It's okay, Mom. Really, I'm fine. Everything turned out just fine." Only it hadn't. I couldn't shake the nagging feeling I'd had since our flight departed. A brain glitch telling me I had left something important behind—something that explained Stella's transformation.

"Please, honey. You're not fine. A sensitive person like you can't go through what you did, and it not affect you. Your sister was a different story. That's why when she and Ben ran off, I wasn't too upset."

My fury and pain at her calm, resigned approach to my loss of the man I loved had consumed me. I assumed it was because of her unspoken preference for my sister, that she thought if Stella wanted him, why shouldn't she have him?

"I don't understand."

"I know. And I should have said something. I should have spoken out as soon as you brought that monster home. I could tell he was trouble. But Gran and I agreed telling you how we felt would only make you more determined to have him." She wiped at her eyes and patted me on the knee. "You've always been a bit of a hard head."

I'd been hearing a lot along those lines lately.

"But I thought you wanted me to marry him, that he was the best thing that could have happened to me."

"Well, I didn't. I knew he was a man who'd take someone like you and crush your spirit. He would beat you down and make you feel you weren't enough. So, when he and Stella ran off, this massive relief came over me. Your sister could give as good as she got. I almost felt sorry for the asshole when he married her. I was a horrible mother because I kept thinking at least it wasn't Grace. And, God help me, I still am." Her voice broke, and she leaned forward, holding her head in her hands.

Mike patted her back, reassuring her everything was all right. She jerked away from him.

"No, it's not all right!"

Scarlett trembled and pressed her body into me.

"As soon as I got the news, one thought kept running through my mind: *It could have been Grace. It could have been Grace.* I would have given anything to have traded places with your sister. I'd give my life for either of you. But when I heard Stella was dead, my only comfort was it could have been Grace, and, thank you, Lord, it wasn't." She sank into the sofa.

I reminded myself to breathe as I processed my mother's words. I had no strong memories of life before my sister, but I imagined I was the sun and Mom revolved around me. Once there were two of us, I was happy to move aside and let my sister take center stage. She was infinitely more suited for the spotlight. I assumed being the favorite child was part of the package for someone as special as Stella and accepted the role of second sister without realizing no one had offered it to me.

Watching my grief-stricken mother struggling with the additional burden of guilt for what she considered her role in Stella's fate, I saw how fragile she was. I joined her on the sofa and held her. For that brief time, I was the parent, and she was the child.

"It's okay," I said, rocking her. "You didn't love Stella less. You loved her differently. She would understand." And the words weren't just true for my mother. They were true for me.

I thought of Mom's relationship with her sister and wondered if she had felt like the lesser of the two. Regardless, she didn't falter when it came to defending Aunt Rita, where I argued against punishing Ben. But, if I were honest with myself, while I refused to give Adelmo my permission to kill Ben, his death didn't bother me at all. It didn't matter to me how he died, as long as he was gone. Maybe I was more my mother's daughter than I wanted to admit.

CHAPTER 36

My mother's confession exhausted her, and Mike half-carried her to her room. He and I agreed I would return tomorrow to discuss the details of Stella's memorial service.

"Your mother loves you more than you can imagine, Grace. And she loved Stella, too," he said as Scarlett and I were leaving.

I assured him I was aware, and I was telling the truth.

On the drive home, I concluded that my adoration of Stella hadn't been fair to either of us. The pedestal I put her on created a barrier— one that, as an adult, she resented. I saw her the way I wanted her to be, not as the lovely but flawed creature she was. And it was those flaws that made her who she was. Because I refused to see them, I never saw the real Stella.

For me, her loss was an open wound. Sometimes it only throbbed, other times it shot bolts of pure agony through my entire being. The knowledge I had missed out on having a genuine relationship with her, that I didn't get to celebrate the new and improved version of my sister, was like losing a limb. Phantom pain for something that wasn't there and, in my case, never had been.

But it was the torment of never understanding the catalyst for her transformation that plagued me the most. Without that, I would continue to obsess over what I might have done to save her. That missing piece of information prevented me from accepting her death. It left both our relationship and my soul incomplete.

By the time I got home, I had fallen into a frenzy of sadness and guilt.

Miss Scarlett, however, was having none of it. It was impossible to focus on my misery when my four-legged companion was frantic with delight.

I shut the garage door before releasing her. She ran wildly around the vehicle three times. Leaping and barking, she followed me until I opened the patio doors and let her bound into the backyard. I watched from inside as she sniffed and peed and rolled in the stiff, frozen grass. Finally, she returned and jumped up to lick my face.

"It is good to be home, isn't it?"

It was almost midnight, and I couldn't remember the last time I ate. I whipped up a can of tomato soup for me and a bowl of kibble for her. My phone rang shortly after we finished.

"Hey. I hope I didn't wake you. I wasn't expecting you to answer. I was planning to leave a message." It was Justin.

"I wasn't sleeping. Scarlett and I were enjoying a late dinner." I gave him a summary of my visit with Mom. I spared him the details about our mutual epiphany, concerning the different ways people love one another.

He explained he had work to catch up on the next day but wanted to come by tomorrow evening if that was okay. It was way more than okay, but I played it cool and said seeing him would be nice.

I'm not sure who was happier to be back in our bed, me or Scarlett. Before turning off the lights, I stared at the ceiling, considering how to approach the subject of Uncle Roy with my mother. Thoughts of whether Eva would ever call and worries about Adelmo crossed my mind, but I was too spent to concentrate on them. I fell asleep and didn't wake until after nine.

After rolling out of bed, I unpacked my suitcase and checked in with a few clients. I answered a message from Cara Frazier and set up a meeting to help her with some promotional material. Around one o'clock, Lesroy dropped by with sandwiches from our favorite deli. He insisted it was because he missed me so much, but the way he and Scarlett fawned over each other, I was certain it was the dog he came to see.

We talked about Stella, and I shared my misgivings about leaving Ecuador with so many unanswered questions. I asked him if the two of them ever discussed the night his daddy disappeared.

"What made you think of that?" He hid behind his giant corned beef on rye.

I told him that while the lightning itself failed to score a direct hit, it jostled puzzling memories. I was careful not to say too much. Since Stella remembered the details of our uncle's disappearance before they returned to me, I suspected she had brought up the subject to Lesroy. But if I was wrong, I didn't want to be the one who delivered the news my mother killed his father.

"Finally." He set down his sandwich and took a swig of soda. "We always wondered why you didn't remember. I said we should get it over with and tell you, but she worried it might do something to your delicate psyche."

"So, she told you about it?"

"About how Gran and Aunt Marilyn pushed Daddy's truck into the lake with him in it? No, Grace, Stella didn't tell me." He wiped his mouth with a napkin. "Mother did."

I sat speechless, trying to piece it all together. Rita's break-down, her avoidance of our family — it made sense now. Lesroy said she grew suspicious after a few months with no word from his father. She noticed them acting strange whenever she brought up the subject of her missing husband but never suspected they had done anything drastic. Until our grandmother slipped up and mentioned something about my uncle's pickup being a worthless piece of shit just like Roy and how neither would be missed.

As soon as the words left Gran's mouth, Rita's bullshit detector went off. She kept on and on at them. But the women didn't break, not until the cops fished the truck, with her missing husband in it, out of the lake. That was when she confronted them, and they copped to the crime.

Instead of going to the police, Rita flipped out. Screaming and sobbing, she shared the story with her young son. If she expected him to be angry or vengeful or even sad, she'd been disappointed.

"I told her she shouldn't be mad at Gran and Aunt Marilyn. They'd been taking care of us the best way they could." He took another bite of sandwich. "And we never talked about it again."

"Holy shit, Lesroy! I can't believe you didn't tell me."

"Thought you knew." He shrugged. "Stella did. But when we figured out you didn't remember, we let it go. You know, Grace, if your mother hadn't helped Gran get rid of my daddy, he would most likely have killed us both."

He gave Scarlett the last bite of his sandwich.

"But, hey, I didn't come by to dredge up old memories. Mike asked me if we would help plan the memorial. Are you up for it?"

I wasn't, but I agreed to go anyway.

When we arrived, Mom and Mike were already hard at work selecting scripture and hymns and floral arrangements. The service would be in the church my mother began attending shortly after the death of my grandmother. I assumed her newfound religion assuaged her grief over losing Gran. Now it seemed more likely she was getting a little nervous about hellfire waiting for her since she violated one of the biggies: Thou shalt not kill.

Mom assigned me and Lesroy the task of writing my sister's obituary. Reducing Stella's life to her death notice was more depressing than I imagined. The list of survivors was pitifully short. It was as if she left no real legacy at all. When I voiced this gloomy sentiment to him, he shook his head.

"You're wrong, Grace. We're all the legacy anybody would need. I mean, it's not like we're finished creating our stories, and Stella's always going to be a part of them because she's a part of us."

We reviewed the plans for the memorial service we scheduled for the day after tomorrow. I pretended to be interested in the details, but I couldn't get it out of my head how amused Stella would have been at our choices.

About an hour later, after debating whether to have the organist play "Amazing Grace" —I was violently opposed, but lost the argument—Lesroy and I gathered up our coats and the extra frozen casseroles, and he drove me home

Justin called to say he would come by after seven with dinner. I said there was no need for him to bring anything, that I would whip something up. Then I checked the freezer for one of the church-lady meals. Since my mother hadn't bothered to label them, I took out what looked like chicken with cheese sauce and stuck it in the oven

Scarlett barked and twirled in circles at the sound of the doorbell. "Don't make a fool of yourself, you little hussy." I held her by the collar and opened the door. She slipped from my grasp and nuzzled Justin's crotch in canine ecstasy.

He laughed and knelt on one knee. "I'm glad to see you, too. But let's take things slow." Scarlet ignored him and covered his face with slobbery kisses.

"Enough!" I commanded and was shocked when she stopped her affectionate assault and moved away from the door.

"Something smells great," he announced on the way to the kitchen. He took off his coat and draped it over a chair. "What are you cooking?"

"You'll just have to wait and see," I answered, hoping it wasn't tofu and soy curds prepared by Mom's vegan friend.

Luckily, it turned out to be chicken divan. Justin raved about what a good cook I was throughout dinner. I would have kept up the ruse, but later, when we were sitting on the sofa, he questioned me about whether I used cumin or curry, and I confessed I couldn't tell the difference.

"You mean you lied to me, Grace Burnette?" he asked, as he rubbed my neck. He pulled me closer, his breath warm on my skin. "That's very disappointing. What should happen to girls who lie?"

"I'm not sure," I whispered.

"Well, there are many ways you can make it up to me." He led me to the bedroom.

In Montañita, sex with Justin was hot because it was unexpected and new. We were both in an unfamiliar place with relative strangers. Here it was different. The need was still urgent, but now we could take our time, explore each other's bodies, tease and touch as long as we could stand it. And when we did surrender, it was with the understanding we were only beginning.

· · · · ·

Mom called early to ask if I could double-check the arrangements. When I got there, Rita's car was parked in the driveway.

To me, my aunt had always been ditsy and irresponsible. As a child I hadn't understood the helplessness she must have felt living in constant fear of both pain and humiliation. Her timing as a victim of spousal abuse was terrible. Well before people officially recognized battered women as a syndrome, it was a time when it was still okay to ask what the woman had done to deserve her harsh treatment.

I could tell even Gran and Mom blamed Rita. Their attitude—both spoken and unspoken—was that it was one thing if she didn't have the self-respect to leave her miserable husband. It was quite another if she didn't protect her son.

Today the world was more compassionate, but I hadn't been. I blamed her for letting my uncle belittle and bully my sweet cousin. To me, all the wailing and crying over Roy's death showed how weak she was.

Now I understood a lot more about my aunt. She was the softer sister. Unlike Mom, she couldn't find it in her to kick her husband to the curb even though she would be better off without him. Rita didn't have enough strength to raise a child on her own. And when she discovered the two most important women in her life stepped up for her, she couldn't handle it.

Mom opened the door before I rang the bell. She looked somewhat better. Her hair was clean, and her make-up was mostly in the right places. More important, she looked less vacant. She greeted me with a fierce hug and led me to the den where Rita sat drinking coffee. I eased into the recliner across from them.

"How are you doing, sweetie?" Rita set her cup down. "And don't say 'fine' like you always do. I want the real scoop."

Another flood of emotion came over me. I looked away, unsuccessfully trying to swallow it down.

"It's all right, honey. You don't have to talk," Rita said as my mother sat down beside her.

The two of them sitting there so close to one another filled me with an additional source of anguish. I ached at their sisterly complacency. Stella and I would never grow older together, never hurt or comfort one another the way only sisters can. I couldn't suppress the urgent need to hear their story. For whatever reason, I hoped it might provide a blueprint for my healing process.

"There is something I want to talk about." I began.

Mom shifted in her seat, and Rita stared at her lap.

I took the direct approach. "I remember what happened the night Uncle Roy disappeared."

"Right. We wondered when it would come back to you."

I couldn't say what I expected from my aunt, but it wasn't this calm acceptance.

She set down her cup and continued. "A few months before your sister ran off, she came to see me. She put some things together about Roy *going missing*." Rita gave Mom a look. "She was positive about the events of that night. But when she mentioned it to you, you seemed clueless." She took a sip of coffee.

Mom picked up the story. "That's when we realized you girls had been on the porch."

My aunt waved a hand, and my mother stopped talking. "I told Stella she should talk to her mother about what happened, but she insisted she didn't need to. That she was aware of everything that went on. And she was. She figured it out a long time ago. She said she understood why her mother and Gran killed her uncle. What she wanted to know was if I had forgiven them."

I did the math and calculated my sister must have been planning her exit with Ben when she visited Rita.

"Marilyn, why don't you get us some of those sugar cookies your church lady friends dropped off?"

"You want cookies now?" Mom asked, but she scurried to the kitchen without waiting for an answer.

"So, were you able to forgive them?"

"I'll be honest. At first, I hated them, but not for the obvious reasons. They took matters into their own hands because they thought

I was too weak to act for myself. They expected I would take that miserable son of a bitch back, even after he hurt my baby boy."

Mom returned with a plate of pastries and put it in front of my aunt. She selected one and took a dainty bite.

"Umm," she murmured. "Church ladies make the best cookies in the world. It's almost enough to get me back into religion. Almost." She grinned and gulped her coffee. "As soon as I got my boy out of the hospital, I went straight to a divorce lawyer. I didn't tell your mother or Gran because I knew they'd roll their eyes at me. But I was dead serious. Of course, it turned out Roy was plain old dead, so I never got the satisfaction of serving him with papers."

"You mean you weren't upset with them about, well, you know." I was still squeamish about the whole murder concept.

"Sure, I was. It's more than a little unsettling when you find out your sister and mother killed your husband. God help me, I still loved the man, but I hated him, too. And I loved your cousin more than life. I guess you could say I got knocked off-kilter."

It said a lot about my aunt she remembered her stint in the mental institution as being "off-kilter."

"But when I got back on track, I understood what they did and why they did it. I was even a little grateful. Divorcing Roy wouldn't have gotten him out of our lives. Most likely, I would have had to kill him myself." The frown lines on her forehead deepened as she scowled at Mom and added, "But he was mine to take care of."

"Still, you forgave them?"

"Oh, yes. I forgave them a long time ago, and I told Stella that. I explained no matter what happens between you and family, there's always forgiveness. And I told her that was especially true with sisters because, well, it's not like sometimes you're sisters and sometimes you're not. And you always forgive each other. Don't get me wrong. I'm not making up excuses for what Stella did. It was low down, and she knew it. Your baby sister lacked in the character department but having you in her life mattered to her. So, you see, Grace, she didn't die without knowing you'd forgive her."

I let my tears fall freely, and so did the sisters. They came to me, one on each side of the worn leather recliner. Together, the three of us cried for the depth of our loss and the power of our forgiveness.

We froze in that tableau of grief and hope and stayed that way until Mike came into the room.

"Oh, my, God, girls! Let me get you something. More coffee or tissues or—oh, my God!"

The sight of my mother's big, strong soldier running his hands through his buzz cut before he threw them up in the air, ended our communal sobbing. Mom walked to where he stood and put her arms around him. Rita and I looked at each other and began laughing.

We let Mike fix us lunch and take care of us for the rest of the afternoon. My aunt gave her approval of the memorial plans, remarking once, out of my mother's earshot, what a hoot Stella would have gotten out of all that singing and sanctimony.

I used Scarlett as an excuse to leave before dinner. On the drive home I considered how strange it was to know someone your entire life and continue to uncover secrets and surprises that make you reconstruct your view, not only of the person you loved but of your entire world.

Scarlett greeted me with the same enthusiasm she showed when I first returned, and I wondered if she'd forgotten her original mistress. Or was she more practical than I gave her credit for and decided she might as well love the one she was with? Either way, I was equally happy to see her.

Justin called to say he had to work but would meet me at the church before the memorial. I was exhausted, so the Doberman and I retired early, sleeping soundly until morning.

"I am not looking forward to today, Scarlett." At the sound of her name, the dog gazed at me intently. "Of course, no one enjoys a funeral, do they?" She hopped onto the bed and snuggled close, obviously happy she wasn't expected to attend.

I chose the same black suit I wore at Gran's service. When I opened my jewelry box to take out the diamond earrings Mom gave me for graduation from college, I saw the gold locket. I hadn't put it on since Stella and Ben's elopement. Today it was the perfect choice. The necklace glowed softly against the dark fabric of my dress. A random bubble of memory struggled to pop to the surface, something I forgot and needed to remember. But it refused to show itself.

Lesroy's car was already at Mom's. Vincent opened the door, looking dapper in suit and tie. He gave me a one-armed hug and a kiss on the cheek.

"Heads up," he said, "it's bat-shit crazy in there."

"When isn't it?"

"Good point. Sometimes I wonder what I've gotten myself into, but Lesroy's worth it," Vincent replied, then added. "Rita's passing out Xanax like Halloween candy; I suggest you grab one. And help me keep an eye on Lesroy, please. He's already downed two."

At Gran's funeral, the drug of choice was Valium. I barely remember being there.

Vincent and I joined the rest of our group in the kitchen. Rita pressed a pill in my palm as soon as she saw me. Mom was sipping a clear drink with lime—and probably a kick—in it. Lesroy stared out the window with a dazed look on his face. And poor Mike was trying to corral everyone to get coats.

I dry-swallowed Xanax and helped Vincent get my cousin into his jacket while Mike led the sisters to his car. Vincent assisted me into the back seat, and we were off. The church was only a few miles away, but Lesroy was dozing before we pulled into the lot. Vincent had to go around to the passenger side to shake him awake and pull him out of the car. I was trying to get out of the back without flashing passersby when Justin appeared. He took my arm and hoisted me to my feet, where I yanked my dress down and smoothed my hair.

He held me tight before asking how everyone was doing.

"Except for Mike, we're all high as kites," I confessed. "I'm not sure Lesroy's even fully conscious."

"Oh boy." He sighed and steered me into the building.

The minister was younger than I expected, not much older than me, I guessed. I imagined he hadn't conducted too many funeral services and would have bet he hadn't done any with a group like us. Thanks to the miracles of modern pharmaceuticals, we were all amiable when he sat us down to explain how we would proceed down the aisle to take our seats on the first two rows.

It wasn't until he lined us up to enter the church that things got a little dicey. Mom and Mike were supposed to go first, but she had a slight problem with balance and required extra support. So, she requested Lesroy take her other arm. Justin and I were to follow. Rita grumbled about wanting to walk with her son before taking Vincent's arm and bringing up the rear.

Pictures of Stella were scattered on one end of a table by the pulpit. Birthdays, graduation, Christmases—it was a tableau of her life. The gold and bronze urn with her ashes dominated the other end.

The minister had never met Stella and didn't seem too familiar with my mother. He gave it his best shot, though, speaking about the joys of living a Godly life as a sister and a daughter and the comfort of knowing we would all be together again someday. And everyone was invited to the fellowship hall for a reception.

Justin stood beside me in the receiving line where people filed by expressing condolences. Cara was there, and I vaguely recalled seeing several college and a few high school friends. The comfort their appearance brought caught me off guard. Even Alisha Beaumont gave me a warm feeling despite her inability to wrinkle her forehead when she cried. Stella would have appreciated her friend's Botoxing up for the occasion.

The memorial was harder than I expected. After the shock of losing my sister and the horror of her actual death, I hadn't thought something as tame as a farewell tribute could be so devastating. Maybe it was because it marked the official end of Stella's time on earth. Or maybe it was because our family seemed so small without her.

CHAPTER 37

The night of the funeral and many nights after, I woke in the middle of the night sobbing. Justin stayed with me. Whenever he had to leave, it was with the unspoken understanding he would soon return.

A few weeks after the service on one of our off-nights, I received a box from Ecuador. The return address was a general post office number. Inside were baggies filled with jewelry on top of folded clothes. There was a note taped to a baggy.

Dear Señorita Grace,

I am sorry we did not get another chance to talk, but one day I will explain.

I could not meet with you before you left. When your sister came to stay with my family, there was not time for her to pack much. She collected only a few valuables and pieces of clothing. I am enclosing them for you. I, too, loved your sister, and I share the pain of your loss.

Eva

When it came to expensive jewelry, I didn't have a clue. But Stella did. The pile of rings, earrings, bracelets, and necklaces on the bed most likely came to an impressive total. But the gold locket from Gran wasn't among them. Had Stella stopped wearing it and tossed it aside in a drawer? Or lost it? Then I remembered Alisha's album.

I stacked it on top of the one from Gran and shoved them both under the bed before leaving for Ecuador. I spotted the pink edge of the book, pulled it out, and blew off the dust bunnies.

Flipping to the page of party photos, I stopped at the one of Ben and Adelmo standing with my sister between them. It transported me to another world. It was a happy time, one where Stella glowed next to her lover, even though her husband also stood beside her. And then I saw it: the locket. She was wearing it the night of the party. I thumbed through the pages, and in all but the shots of Stella in a bathing suit, she was wearing the locket. My sister hadn't stopped wearing hers, so where was it now?

The most likely explanation was she had it on the night of her murder. She and Prez struggled, and he ripped it off while strangling her. But wouldn't such a violent effort have scratched her delicate neck? Justin had given me copies of the horrible pictures taken by the seaside. Now I needed to examine them. My hands shook as I removed them from my desk drawer. Scarlett stood beside me, whining.

"Me, too, sweet girl. But I've got to look."

The close-up was as gruesome as I remembered. Purple outlines of Prez's fingers looped around her throat. But those were the only marks on her slender neck. This didn't prove she hadn't been wearing the locket, but it increased the possibility the locket might still be out there somewhere. It made no sense, but finding it had become important to me.

· · · · ·

Although we made it home in time for the holidays, no one felt like celebrating. Even though Stella hadn't spent the past three Christmases at home, the knowledge she would never be there again was agonizing. Another reminder of how different our world was without her.

Our grandmother always gave me, Stella, and Lesroy matching pajamas on Christmas Eve. When Stella wasn't home for the holiday, Gran mailed the pjs to her. After Gran's death, my mother kept up the tradition.

This year Mom broke down a few days before Christmas, confessing she tried to pick out matching pajamas, but just couldn't do it. I assured her it was okay, but it wasn't.

When we gathered at her house for Christmas Eve dinner, there were four packages under the tree marked "Open Xmas Eve" and labeled: Grace, Justin, Lesroy, and Vincent. They were flannel pajamas Mike had picked out.

After the winter holidays, Lesroy's graphics business took off, which meant more work for me. I discovered Justin didn't just work for a security firm; he owned it. He, too, had more than he could manage.

With our busy schedules, we agreed it was silly for us to live apart. So, we moved in together, neither of us acknowledging the significance of the decision. We might have downplayed the direction our relationship was taking, but Lesroy most certainly did not. Thrilled that I had found Mr. Right, he admonished me not to screw it up.

The prospect I would not end up a withered old maid excited Mom and Rita, too. To my amazement, however, they played it cool around Justin, most likely out of fear they would spook him.

Winter melted into spring, and Justin planted a tea-rose bush in our backyard for Stella. He screened in the back patio, creating the perfect space for Scarlett to watch squirrels and catch the afternoon sun.

He kept in touch with Harry, who hadn't heard from Eva. Even Eduardo had gone MIA. Harry had, however, been in contact with the lawyers in charge of probating Ben's and Stella's wills. The situation was complicated, but he promised he'd stay on it.

Mild, breezy spring days evolved into steamy, hot summer weather well before the middle of May. Scarlett spent her afternoons lounging on the sofa near the air vent. Justin and I spent our evenings in bed with the ceiling fan whirling on high.

No day passed without a reminder of Stella. The sight of a slender, blonde woman ahead of me in a crowd. The return of bluebirds to the house we watched Mom and Gran put in the backyard. A song with the power to buoy me up or break me down or both.

She continued to float through my dreams. Sometimes it was the peaceful Stella, smiling with the sun on her face. Other times, it was my sister lying broken on the beach. Once, she came to me open-handed, the missing locket in her palm. Adelmo showed up occasionally but never in the same dream as Stella. Even in the realm of my subconscious, they were forever separated. Whether I woke whimpering or stifling a scream, Justin was there to hold me.

On the last day of May, my phone rang at a little after nine in the morning. For a few seconds, I couldn't place the familiar voice, soft and sibilant.

"I hope I am not disturbing you. This is Luis Cordoza, Harry's friend from Guayaquil. I am in Atlanta on business and hoped we might get together. I wish to share some important information about your sister."

"Information?" What could he have to share? Unless he had news about Adelmo, and I wasn't sure I was ready to learn the fate of the man who had loved Stella enough to kill for her.

"The kind best delivered in person. I am staying at the Ritz Carlton, but I'm only in town through tomorrow evening. Could you drop by around lunchtime today? I am sorry for the late notice, but I assure you, your time will be well spent. And I would ask that you come alone, please."

I had planned on rewriting a radio spot for a client, but he didn't need it until next week. Anything else could wait. I agreed to go to his hotel room at noon. I was uneasy about the coming-alone clause but remembered him as a gentle, nonthreatening man. Regardless, Justin was away on business, and Lesroy was tied up in meetings all day. There was no way I would take my mother. So alone was it.

"Scarlett, what do you think Señor Luis Cordoza's important information is?"

The dog regarded me intently before turning away to lick herself. I took the hint and got ready without asking for any more canine opinions.

Unsure of morning traffic, I left early and reached the hotel with thirty minutes to spare. A smiling young man wearing a long-sleeved shirt and vest in the now-sweltering heat parked my car. I carouseled into the reception area through revolving doors, where a burst of frigid air hit me.

With time on my hands, I strolled to the restroom and stood at the mirror. I didn't look all that different from the woman in my engagement picture. No one had coaxed my hair into unnatural curls, but it was the same light brown. My cheekbones were as hollow, but it was from grief instead of my starvation-wedding diet. My eyes were still the same silvery gray as Gran's, but they were tinted with a shadow of sorrow. Regardless of the similarities, I wasn't the same person. In the photo, I was someone's sister. Now I wasn't.

On the elevator ride to Luis's floor, I tried to recall my last conversation with him. It was when he told me Ben had Stella's body cremated.

I recognized him as soon as he opened the door. His hair was shorter, and he wasn't wearing his wire-rimmed glasses, but his large dark eyes held the same kind expression.

"Señorita Burnette, welcome." I stepped onto plush, cream-colored carpet. Spotless sliding glass doors revealed a balcony where the city sprawled below like a canvas painted especially for the inhabitants of this room. The bedroom door was closed, but I noticed the door to the adjoining suite was ajar.

"Wow."

"I agree, wow. Normally, my accommodations are not so lavish. But my government hopes to impress some of your local businessmen and lure them to our country. Enough about business. Please, have a seat."

A tray with tea, coffee, and tiny little sandwiches sat on the table in front of the sofa. Luis told me to help myself and took the chair across from me.

"Señorita Burnette," he began.

"It's Grace."

"Grace, it is good to see you under less tragic circumstances. How are you and your family coping with your terrible loss?"

Some people shy away from questions about your state of mind after losing a loved one. They might ask how you're doing, but it's obvious they don't want to hear you have trouble sleeping or your mother keeps losing weight or you have unexpected bouts of sobbing. They expect you to stick to the pleasantries and move the conversation along. Luis Cordoza wasn't one of those people. When he asked, I could see that he cared about what I had to say.

I spent the next several minutes admitting it was hard and not getting easier and that Christmas was a nightmare.

"I wish I could make your loss less painful. But no one can do such a thing. When we love someone, we are always at risk for suffering. But perhaps what I have to share will ease your sadness." He stopped to ask if I would like coffee or tea. I wanted neither but asked for tea. Tendrils of steam drifted from the cup as he poured.

"First, Grace. I must confess I was not forthcoming with you when you visited me in my office. I did not intend to mislead you, but I was not at liberty to reveal certain details to you. The situation has changed, and I can explain more about your sister during her stay in Ibarra with Eva."

The situation had changed for me, but I wasn't sure how it had for him.

"I also have the letters stolen from your room. Unfortunately, the laptop was damaged beyond repair."

"Stella's letters!" I had given up any hope of recovering my sister's last communication with me.

"Yes. It was one of Adelmo's men who took them for reasons you will soon understand. And I have a letter Stella was unable to send." He waved his hand. "But I am getting ahead of myself. When you came to my office, I wanted to tell you what might await you in Montañita, but I had promised to remain silent. I was aware of your sister's relationship with Adelmo and that he loved her too much to hurt her. But I also knew you would never take the word of a man you had only just met. And Adelmo had sworn me to secrecy."

"Is he a friend of yours? Have you had any word from him since he disappeared?"

"He and I grew up together and were once as close as brothers although I was only the son of a servant in the Balsuto household. Sadly, I have heard nothing from him."

"I thought his family ran some big crime ring in Ecuador."

"You Americans want everything to fit into neat little packages. It is true Adelmo's family committed many crimes, but they were also kind and generous to the people who worked for them. His father paid for my education and sent me to the same school as his son. Adelmo, however, didn't care so much for formal education." He smiled and shook his head. "He was more a student of life."

I thought of the man sitting in the garden speaking of his love for Stella. Luis was right. I did want everything wrapped in neat little packages.

"He wanted to be an artist. His father would have none of that, and I had to watch my friend become less himself and more the person his family demanded. Until he met your sister. She brought about a revival of spirit in Adelmo. He told me she made him want to be a better man."

He continued his account of their great love, explaining how Adelmo wanted to leave the country with her and start a new life. For him, settling in the States was impossible, but for your sister, it was a dream he could help her achieve.

And then there was Ben. Adelmo's business dealings with him had been illegal, and Stella's husband was a very greedy man. Adelmo might have been able to buy him off to ensure a quick divorce, but that wouldn't have solved the problem of where he and Stella could begin a new life together. Plus, there were additional complications. He hesitated at this point in the story.

"What complications?" I urged. But he ignored me.

"He came to me for advice last August. He made it clear Stella would be miserable if she could not return to her family, and he could not live with himself if she was in pain. Also, because of his line of work, he had many enemies. He had avoided serious relationships in the past for fear these violent men would hurt anyone he loved. That was another reason to keep his love for your sister a secret."

When Adelmo contacted him and asked him to help find a place for Stella to hide, Luis was surprised. Eva agreed to stay with Stella, and he set up the trip to Ibarra.

"I don't understand. Except for learning you and Adelmo were friends, our conversation sheds no new light on anything. If she went away to stay safe, why did she go back to her house? And what about the airline ticket? Was she trying to escape from Adelmo, too?"

"I believe it would be best if you read your sister's letter before I answer any more of your questions. Stella left it at the home of Eva's sister with instructions to mail it. But it was misplaced in the confusion over getting your sister out of the country. Eva didn't find it until after Stella died. She didn't feel right about opening it, so she gave it to me."

"What is so complicated about a letter from my sister?"

"That is for you to decide. I will leave you alone with it now." He stood, handed me the letter, and left the room.

Dear Grace,

It seems I've gotten myself in a "pickle," as Gran used to say. If you've read my letters, you know I've been seeing a wonderful man. His name is Adelmo Balsuto. You're probably thinking he's another one of my mistakes, but this time I found my one and only true love, like Gran. As usual, though, my timing sucks. I asked Ben for a divorce and – surprise, surprise – he's being a total ass-hat. He doesn't love me, probably never did, but he hates to lose. Things got so bad I had to get away for a while. So that's problem number one.

Problem number two is Adelmo won't marry me. The reasons are complicated, but trust me when I say they're pretty damn good. He insists I go home without him. Says he will come when he can, but we both know it won't happen.

So, Grace, I'm really coming home this time. If you haven't forgiven me, I'm not giving up. I think when you see me all the bad stuff between us will disappear, and you can help me start a new life.

Before I leave Montañita for good, I have to make one last trip to Ben's for my locket. Eva doesn't want me to go, but remember what we used to say about those lockets? No way am I leaving it behind. Ben won't be there, so I should be able to get in and out without him even knowing I was there.

I can't wait to see you and for you to see how different I really am.

Love you forever.

Your Favorite Sister

So, she had died because of the locket. We had taken the necklaces as symbols of the strength of our family bond. Gran said we could pass them down to our daughters if we were lucky enough to have them. Instead of good fortune, hers had gotten Stella killed.

I gazed at the Atlanta skyline, shimmering in the afternoon heat, and tried to make sense of Stella's letter.

Luis cleared his throat as he reentered the room. "Are you all right?"

"How can I be when it seems my sister died for a piece of jewelry?"

"Eva told me why it was so important to Stella. But I will let her explain."

He went to the adjoining suite and tapped lightly on the door, then opened it. Eva stood on the other side. "I would like to introduce you to my mother, Eva Cordoza."

"Grace," she held out both arms and moved to embrace me. I allowed her to make contact but was too stunned to do anything other than stand immobile.

"Come, sit with me." She led me back to the small sofa.

"You are too thin, just like our Stella," she said. "I was sorry to send you away with so many remaining questions. I wish I could have answered them, but there were so many difficulties with the truth. I will begin closer to the beginning. Perhaps some tea, my son?"

He poured tea for his mother and eased into one of the matching chairs. "I was Adelmo's nanny, I think you call it. He and Luis were babies together. We lived in the Balsuto home. When he grew up, he brought me to Montañita to manage his household. But I soon learned he had not left his family business behind, so I resigned from his employment and began my own cleaning service. Señor Wilcott was one of my clients. That is when I met your sister. She was so sad and lonely. She begged me to work full time for her, and I agreed."

Eva added sugar and cream to her tea. I fidgeted next to her, and she put her hand on my knee.

"I was working at the party where she and Adelmo crossed paths. I warned her not to get involved with him. But it was useless. They were careful not to be seen together, but Montañita is a small town, and rumors began circulating. Señor Wilcott was too indebted to Adelmo to make much of a fuss. Besides, he was drunk most of the time. But Adelmo was terrified people would see the depth of his feelings for Stella. You must understand, the Balsuto family is both feared and respected, and there are many who wish them harm. He knew all too well the dangers of being part of his family. When he was twelve years old, a rival family kidnapped and killed his younger sister."

Eva paused, looked at her son, then continued.

"He encouraged her to leave her troubled marriage, to return to her home, and forget about him. And I think she was ready to do as he wished. But a few weeks before last Easter, she became ill, only she was not sick. She was with child."

"Pregnant? Are you saying she was expecting a baby?" That explained her letters about coming home around that time.

She nodded. But the idea of Stella with a baby was incomprehensible to me.

"She was very frightened. She did not think her husband could be the father, but it was not impossible. And if the child was Adelmo's, he could never acknowledge it. She made me promise not to tell anyone, and I kept that promise."

She succeeded in getting Stella to a doctor who told her she was six weeks pregnant. Ecuador not only prohibits abortion but also punishes women who get illegal procedures with up to two years in prison. If she decided not to keep the baby, she would need to return to the United States. Somewhere in the middle of her dilemma, my sister realized she wanted the child.

She and Eva came up with a plan to convince Ben he was the father. Once the baby arrived, Stella would take the infant back to the States and file for divorce. She hoped Adelmo would be a part of her life but was realistic about the situation. And she wanted what was best for their little one. So, she broached the subject of fatherhood with Ben.

"That's when that pig of a husband of hers laughed in her face. He told her he had no intention of having children. To be sure, he'd had the vasectomy." Eva pronounced each syllable with great care and contempt. "He had this done before he and Stella married. Almost a year before they eloped."

A year before they eloped, Ben and I were engaged. We had discussed children and agreed we both wanted them. I wondered if he'd already had his tubes clipped when we talked about filling a house with babies. Nausea hit me and I feared I might be sick, but I took a deep breath and encouraged Eva to resume her story.

At least now she was certain who the father was, but the women were not in agreement about the next step. Eva wanted my sister to go to Adelmo for help, but she didn't want to burden him with the information. She was afraid it would only worry him, so she stayed silent about the baby until she could find a time to escape Ben and come home.

But Adelmo was no fool. He realized she was pregnant and demanded she reveal the child's father. When she told him the truth, happiness overcame him.

"I cannot remember a time when I have seen him like that. It was as if she had given him the chance to throw off his past and start a new life." Eva smiled, then sighed. "But there was so much that he could never leave it all behind."

So, he helped Stella plan her escape. But he became increasingly unpredictable when they were together. He told her he could not let her leave until he met his child. He spoke with Luis and came up with the idea to hide Stella in Ibarra. Once the baby was born, he would get them both out of the country.

Unfortunately, she experienced serious complications and went into labor almost seven weeks early. They made it to a hospital in Quito, where she delivered a little girl weighing less than three pounds.

Luis explained she had put Ben's name on the birth certificate to protect the child from the danger of being a Balsuto. Adelmo met Stella's daughter and promised he would join my sister in America. She believed he would. The plan was to get her and the baby out of the country and when they were safe, she would keep up the pretense Ben was the father. This would allow him to save face as long as he would agree to a quick divorce and give her sole custody.

Before leaving the hospital in Quito, she met with Luis to draw up a will, making me the baby's guardian. My sister's death complicated matters. If Ben found out about the baby, he could claim her as his for spite. Torn between letting us in on their secret and keeping the child himself, he took the letters to find out how much Stella had told me. He needed to meet me to make sure my anger toward her wouldn't have a negative impact on his tiny daughter.

After our meeting, he told Eva he wanted me to take the baby home, but first he would have to deal with Ben. So, that day at the trailer, Adelmo had never intended to let him go. It wasn't a simple matter of wanting revenge. Ben's death ensured safety and security for Adelmo's daughter.

Luis had been working with the government to process Stella's will and bring the child to her rightful guardian. He feared I would come to Ecuador in a frenzy if I'd known what was going on. Having me there would have only increased the bureaucratic red tape, so he kept me in the dark.

Eva had also agreed it would be better if I knew nothing until they settled the matter. Just when the plans were finalized, the child came down with a fever high enough to send her to the hospital.

"Please, Eva," I begged. "Are you telling me my sister's baby didn't make it?"

Eva put her arms around my shoulders and held me close. I braced myself.

"Luis, could you help me, please," she said, still holding me tightly.

I heard him open the door to the adjoining suite and speak in Spanish. I turned and saw he was carrying a baby with dark brown curls, a heart-shaped face, and wide silver-gray eyes. A thick gold chain holding Stella's locket fell almost to her waist.

"Grace," he said. "Meet your niece, Señorita Emma Grace."

EPILOGUE

"Emma Grace, you did not just give Miss Scarlett a cheese doodle, did you?"

My three-year-old daughter and the dog ignored me and continued to share the bag of salty treats. I picked up the protesting toddler and swabbed a wet wipe over her face, smearing it with orange residue. Scarlett followed my every swipe.

From that day, over two years ago, when I brought my niece home, Scarlett had been Emma's dog. She still loved me, but when the baby was in the room, she refused to leave her side. And my dog's shift in loyalty was only one of the many changes that came with Emma.

After Eva put Stella's child in my arms, Luis and I struggled for over half an hour to get the car seat positioned and Emma Grace strapped in. Driving away from the hotel, I wondered what in the world my sister had been thinking to leave someone like me, a woman barely capable of handling her own life, in charge of another human being. Most mothers have at least nine months to consider how parenthood will change their lives. I hadn't known my new daughter existed until a few minutes before Eva appeared with her.

A few blocks from the hotel, I gasped for air and was sure I was having my first panic attack. I pulled into a grocery store parking lot and turned to the baby.

"I guess it's me and you, kid."

Emma Grace regarded me with solemn eyes.

"Well, not just you and me," I said, as much to reassure myself as to comfort my niece. "You've got a new grandmother and a step-grandfather, and…" I wasn't sure how to classify Justin but felt certain he was on the team. "And you've got this great-looking guy to help take care of you, plus you've got an uncle—okay, he's a little on the crazy size, but he's the best friend anyone could ever have. Whatever, you've got your very own Lesroy."

"See? You've got this." My sister's voice was strong and clear, as if she were sitting beside me.

"Looks like he isn't the only insane one in the family," I said to my new daughter. But the sound of my sister's triumphant words comforted me, and I couldn't wait to call Mom. I explained I had Stella's baby and asked her to please meet me at my house because I had no idea what I was doing. I hung up before she could respond.

By the time I arrived, she and Mike were waiting in the driveway. Both had tears in their eyes as we unloaded the baby and all her accouterments. Emma Grace regarded her new grandparents with her trademark wide-eyed stare, remaining calm and unimpressed. Lesroy burst through the door. "Oh, my, God! She is the most beautiful little girl in the entire world," he said, dancing with excitement. Emma Grace allowed him to carry her around but never cracked a smile, not even when he swooped her over his head.

The only one who could get a giggle out of the child was Justin. He was in a meeting when I left him a convoluted message and was home in less than thirty minutes. At the sound of his voice, the baby turned toward him and broke into a snaggle-toothed grin. When he blew on her tummy, she dissolved into fits of laughter.

In the weeks and days that followed, my terror at becoming a mother eased into a state of hyper-vigilance, like that of most new mothers. Some days the sunlight played across Emma's face, transforming her into a replica of my sister, paralyzing me with longing. Other times a shadow of her father appeared, and while it frightened me at first, I came to realize it was not the visage of the

Adelmo I saw at the trailer, the one filled with an incapacitating blood lust. It was the gentle man I sat with on the garden bench, my sister's devoted lover and friend, one from whom I had nothing to fear.

.   .   .   .   .

"Please be still, Emma Grace." One cheek was free of cheesy goo, but the other was covered in orange snail trails. And my daughter was approaching her limit. She stiffened her body, and her lower lip trembled with the onset of toddler fury. Sensing the approaching storm, Scarlett took over, sending Emma into fits of giggling, as she licked away the last trace of doodles.

My husband called from the backyard where he and Lesroy were drinking beer and waiting for twilight. When I opened the door, child and dog tumbled out to join them.

Emma ran toward the men but stopped and turned her face to the sky, where a squadron of tiny blinking lights descended on her. She raised her arms, and fireflies settled on the tips of her fingers.

"Wait for me," Lesroy shouted, grabbing the jar by his chair.

He cupped his hands over my daughter's and transferred the flashing insects into the container. Emma Grace pressed her solemn little face to the glass. Their fairy flashes sparkled in her eyes. She pushed away the lid and danced as they flittered around her before flying into the night sky.

Justin wrapped an arm around my shoulders as we stared at our miracle child. Like all children, she was an incredible combination of all the wonderful and tragic events that came before her. But Emma Grace was more than that to us, and we had Stella to thank. This child was my sister's gift, the gift of hope.

ACKNOWLEDGMENTS

I would like to express love and appreciation to my incredible husband. Without his constant encouragement, I wouldn't have had the courage to pursue my dream. I'm also grateful to my daughter Kate, whose insightful comments as a reader and editor helped me be a better writer. Special thanks go to my daughter Laura, who provided inspiration for the book's message about family and to my son, Nick Pinkerton, who continues to teach me about the power of love and forgiveness.

I am grateful for the advice and guidance I received from members of the Roswell Critique Group. Much gratitude goes to Tom Leidy. Without him, I would never have had the confidence to join the group. Great appreciation goes to Kim Conrey for her sweetness and empathy, to April Dilbeck for her sharp insights and wicked humor, and to Gaby Anderson for her positive comments and gentle suggestions. These women improved my writing and my spirits.

I'm thankful to the men in the group for giving me tips on how the male animal thinks: Marty Aftewicz, who showed me how baseball can be a metaphor for life; Fred Whitson, who schooled me in all things military; Bill Barbour for his positivity; Chuck Storla, my corporate advisor; Mike Shaw, punctuation pundit extraordinaire; and Walter Lamb, my travel guru.

Most sincere gratitude goes to George Weinstein, executive director of the *Atlanta Writers Club*. Without his knowledge and generosity, I wouldn't have understood how to "make it better."

I am thankful to novelists Joshilyn Jackson and Jenny Milchman for their encouraging critiques of my writing. Their kindness and expertise were overwhelming.

I would like to recognize the wonderful women of my book club. These friends have been there for me through good books and bad. They have provided unbelievable support and encouragement along the way: Sharon Bartels, Jolly Douglas, Ann Ligon, Peggy Pitman, and Jan Wilson.

I want to express my gratitude to Cheo Bohachek and Janet Turner for celebrating with me and to Larry Lynch and Greg Earnest for introducing me to the joys of travel.

Finally, I want to thank the best sisters a sisterless girl could have, my dear friends Pat Schernekau and Janice Ledford Scott.

ABOUT THE AUTHOR

Katherine Nichols lives in Marietta, Georgia with her husband and two rescue dogs. She is the proud mother of two lovely daughters. In addition to her passion for writing, she enjoys reading, hiking, and traveling. She is a member of the Atlanta Writers Club and Sisters in Crime and has been published in *ALAN reviews*, *Equill Atlanta Writers Club* magazine, and *Shout Them from the Mountaintops: Georgia Poems and Stories*.

NOTE FROM THE AUTHOR

Word-of-mouth is crucial for any author to succeed. If you enjoyed *The Sometime Sister*, please leave a review online — anywhere you are able. Even if it's just a sentence or two. It would make all the difference and would be very much appreciated.

Thanks!
Katherine Nichols

Thank you so much for reading one of our **Women's Fiction** novels.
If you enjoyed the experience, please check out our
recommendation for your next great read!

City in a Forest by Ginger Pinholster

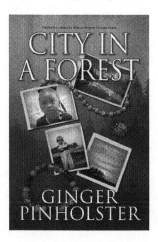

Finalist for a *Santa Fe Writers Project Literary Award*

"Ginger Pinholster, a master of significant detail, weaves her
struggling characters' pasts, present, and futures into a
breathtaking, beautiful novel in *City in a Forest*.
–IndieReader Approved

View other Black Rose Writing titles at

Made in the USA
Columbia, SC
27 June 2021